Letting Go

THE LOVE ON CAMPUS SERIES

THE LOVE ON CAMPUS SERIES

JESSICA RUDDICK

Entangled Publishing, LLC
644 Shrewsbury Commons Ave
STE 181
Shrewsbury, PA 17361
rights@entangledpublishing.com

Embrace is an imprint of Entangled Publishing, LLC.

Edited by Alycia Tornetta
Cover design by Bree Archer
Cover photo from simonmcconico/Getty Images

Manufactured in the United States of America

First Edition May 2015

embrace

To all my boys, for treating me like a princess and letting me rule like a queen

Chapter One

"Guess what, Cori?" Amber squealed. "We're paired with Beta Chi!"

I cringed at the decibel of her voice and continued making my bed. The sheets were hot pink and the comforter was zebra print. I generally opted for more neutral and less obnoxious colors and patterns, but when Amber had insisted we have matching bedding in our room at the Alpha Delta house, I let her pick. When it came down to it, I didn't care that much.

"Great," I said, not because I thought so, but because I knew she expected me to say something. I tried to remember which fraternity Beta Chi was. While there were only a dozen sororities on campus, there were three times as many fraternities. I couldn't keep track of them.

"I know, right? Homecoming this year is going to be awesome." She walked around the room and nudged aside a pile of stuff with her foot. I fought back a sigh. Even though I'd only arrived this afternoon, my half of the room was already nearly put together, but Amber hadn't unpacked the first thing, and she'd gotten here several hours before me.

One of our sisters stuck her head in our room. "The social chair from Beta Chi just called. The first party is tonight." She carried on down the hall spreading the news to the other girls.

Amber hauled her suitcase up onto her unmade bed and unzipped it. "What a great start to the year."

She rummaged through her suitcase, pulling clothes out, inspecting them, and then throwing them on the floor. In less than a minute, it looked like her suitcase had vomited all over her side of the room.

I wrinkled my nose. "You could just unpack, you know."

"Huh?" Amber looked over her shoulder at me and then looked down at her mess. "Is this bothering you, Miss Neat Freak?"

"A little."

"Don't worry. I'll clean it up later." She held up a red strapless dress, shaking the wrinkles out of it. "What do you think of this?"

"I like it." It would look good on her. Amber was built like a short Barbie doll. She was barely five feet tall, but she had curves in all the right places and blond hair and blue eyes.

She walked over the clothes strewn on the floor to stand in front of the full-length mirror. She pressed the dress to the front of her body and frowned. "I don't know."

"Stop fishing for compliments. You know you'll look hot in it."

Amber tossed the dress onto her bed, with a grin that told me she'd gotten the response she wanted. "What's your schedule like this semester?"

"Not too bad. I have to take biology though."

She made a gagging noise. "I have an eight a.m. that I need to change. We all know that's a disaster waiting to happen. I can barely make it to my nines on time."

"Make sure you do that," I said. "I don't want an alarm going off in here at oh-dark-thirty any more than you do. In fact, I'll switch it for you. What class is it?"

I sat down at my desk and opened my laptop. I was greeted by a photo from my graduation that served as my wallpaper. My high school boyfriend, Tyler, had his arms wrapped around me. His face looked like he'd just sucked on a lemon, while my nose was scrunched up and my eyes were closed. He definitely won that round of our ongoing ugly photo competition. I touched the image of his face with my finger.

"English 102," Amber said, and I snapped to attention, jerking my finger away from the screen.

"Didn't you already take that?"

"I dropped it last spring, remember?"

I pulled up the schedule and scanned the course offerings. "There's a four o'clock, but nothing else."

She considered. "That's still sucky, but it's better than the eight."

She gave me her password and I added her into the class. I continued checking the course list to see if I should change any of my classes. I didn't know why I did it. Force of habit. I spent half the summer tinkering around with my schedule, so it was pretty much perfect.

Behind me, Amber was on all fours digging through a huge duffel bag. "Where is that damn jewelry pouch?"

"Just unpack." I pulled up my email. Most of it was junk except for a letter from the financial aid office. I quickly scanned it—something about financial aid paperwork. That was my parents' department, so I forwarded it to them.

"Later," she said. "I want to shower before the party. You'd better figure out what you're going to wear. I don't want to be late."

"I'm not going," I said automatically.

Amber sighed. "Already?"

"I'm going to start taking notes on the bio reading," I said, sticking my chin out. "I heard the professor is a nightmare."

"That's bullshit and you know it."

I straightened my back and pulled my bio textbook off the shelf above my desk. I looked over at her as I opened the book in front of me.

"Come on, Cori. Don't be lame."

"Good grades aren't lame," I protested. "They're going to get me into law school."

Amber snorted. "You could get good grades in your sleep. I think you did last semester, actually. Didn't you sleep in Intro to Psychology, like, half the time?"

I huffed. "A chimp could get an A in that class. And I only fell asleep once. *Once.*"

"Hey! I got a B. So what am I? A chimp?"

I rolled my eyes. "You know what I mean." I'd actually said a chimp *could* get an A in that class. Since she didn't get an A, I didn't know what that made her. Not a chimp. It kind of made me a chimp. Huh. Maybe I needed to rethink that.

Amber came over and wedged herself between me and the desk, sitting in my lap. "Cori."

"Amber," I said back.

"Cori," she said again, wrapping her arms around me.

I sighed. "I can't see my textbook."

"That's kind of the point."

I tried to avoid her gaze, but she gripped my cheeks in her hands and turned my face to hers.

I jerked away.

"Come to the party with me," Amber pleaded. "You can study later. Classes haven't even started yet!"

"That's the point. I want to get a head start."

"One word for you: *lame.*"

After Amber disappeared into the bathroom, I pulled

out a new pack of index cards and unwrapped them, placing them on my desk next to my textbook. I was halfway through the first chapter—which was a *long* chapter—by the time the bathroom door flung open and steam billowed out, followed by Amber wrapped in a hot pink towel. She had a matching towel wrapped on her head, turban style.

"Did you change your mind yet?" she asked hopefully.

I shook my head. It was too soon. It'd been four months since my world had gone to hell, and I was still on the road back. Socializing with my textbooks was about all I could manage. For now. I wanted to get back to normal, really I did, but I wasn't there yet. Soon.

Amber prattled on about how great this year was going to be now that we were living in the house and were no longer freshmen. I nodded and murmured at the appropriate times.

"Some of the girls are going out to eat before we head over to the Beta house. Do you want to do that at least?"

I shook my head. "I ate earlier."

She stepped into a pair of silver platform stilettos. "I hate leaving you home alone on our first night back."

I looked down and picked at my cuticle. "It's fine. There will be lots of parties."

She waited a moment, and I could practically hear the wheels turning in her head as she tried to come up with a compelling reason that would convince me to go. Finally she said in a defeated tone, "Text me if you change your mind."

The house was eerily quiet after the last hour of the girls' primping and preening. I returned to chapter one in my biology text, reading the paragraph where I'd left off. Then I read it again. And again.

I couldn't tell you what the first word was.

Damn it.

I tapped my pen against my book. So what if I didn't want to go to a stupid party? There was nothing wrong with staying in. I was fine. Better than fine. Good even.

I grabbed an index card and wrote the title of the section in purple ink and the first subheading in green ink. That was more like it. I gritted my teeth and read the paragraph again.

Two minutes later I was back to tapping my pen. Ugh. Biology was the pits. Thank God this was the last science class I had to take.

I shoved my textbook aside and pulled the laptop closer to play the latest time-sucking game that some computer geek was making millions on. I could feel my brain cells rotting.

Maybe I should go to the party. It might be good for me. Perhaps a party would jump-start my return to the world. When was the last time I went out?

The fact that I was asking that question told me the answer. It still didn't inspire me to strap on my party shoes. And making my grades a priority wasn't a bad thing, either. Discipline was sorely underrated.

My cell phone rang.

"Hi, Mom." I automatically turned the volume down and propped the phone on my shoulder so I could continue to obliterate my brain cells.

"Hi, honey!" My mom's voice was loud and clear.

"Hi, Corinne, it's Dad, too." His voice was harder to hear, but I would rather strain to hear him than be blasted by my mother's excessive exuberance.

"Are you all settled in?"

"Yup."

"What about Amber?"

I snorted. "What do you think?"

My dad chuckled. "Some things never change." He had a point there. Amber and I had been friends since we were little girls. My Barbies were always lined up neatly in my pink plastic Barbie Dreamhouse with their clothes organized in a shoebox according to color. Amber's Barbies were lucky if they retained all of their limbs.

"Yeah," I agreed. I clicked the mouse furiously in an attempt to beat the current level, silently cursing the computer geek who unleashed this game to torment me.

"Is everything else going well?" my mom asked brightly.

"Yes." I tried to keep the annoyance out of my voice. I just saw them yesterday. Not a whole lot had changed.

"How's the car running? No strange noises or anything?" my dad asked.

"Good. No noises."

"I was worried the, ah, catalytic converter might be rattling, but you say you didn't hear anything?"

I pulled the phone away from my face and stared at it for a moment, as if it could tell me why my parents were suddenly acting so weird. For one thing, my dad had inspected that car from headlight to tailpipe not once, but twice. There was no way he would've let me drive it if there was so much as a bug carcass splattered on the windshield.

"It's fine, Dad. I should probably go. I have a million things to do." Not exactly a lie. This stupid game had to have a million levels, although it would probably take me a million attempts to get to level two at this rate. I huffed as the telltale music came on, signaling that I'd failed the level yet again.

My dad cleared his throat. "There's a reason we're calling, Corinne." Then he paused.

"Okay," I prompted.

My mother sniffled loudly.

That caught my attention. My mom *never* cried. You know the law of physics that everything that goes up must come down? Not true with my mom's moods. She was always, annoyingly, up.

"Mom, what's wrong?"

"We just got off the phone with Mrs. Pullman."

My hand stilled on the mouse. "Is she okay?"

"She's fine…" Her voice trailed off.

"What is it?" More silence. "Mom, just tell me."

"Oh, honey," she blurted out. "She told us Tyler's car accident wasn't an accident."

I gripped the phone, my knuckles whitening.

My mom took a shaky breath. "It was suicide."

Chapter Two

I placed a hand on either side of the sink and stared at the paleness of my face in the mirror.

Suicide…suicide…suicide…suicide…

The word kept replaying over and over in my head, taunting me.

My heart hammered in my chest.

It couldn't be true. There had to be some mistake. The cops made a mistake, or maybe my mom hadn't understood Mrs. Pullman correctly.

The "suicide" chant abruptly changed. To something worse. To the last conversation I'd had with Tyler. To the last conversation he'd had before he died.

I squeezed my eyes shut and started doing breathing exercises I'd learned in my singing days. Excellent for stretching the diaphragm, even better for calming nerves.

Clutching my stomach, I swayed as waves of nausea hit me. *How could he do it?* I peered in the mirror, not recognizing the wild look in my hazel eyes. And it scared the shit out of me.

"Get it together, Corinne," I whispered to my reflection.

I splashed cold water on my face and looked in the mirror again. The wild look was fading. My shoulders slumped, and I took a deep breath.

"Cori?" Amber called from outside the door. "I forgot my wallet. Have you seen it? I can't find it anywhere."

"Haven't seen it," I called through the door in a shaky voice.

"Oh, wait. Here it is." She knocked on the bathroom door. "This is your last chance. You want to go?"

I stared at my reflection, at my eyes that still had a slight wild look in them. I closed my eyes and took a deep breath. I couldn't stay here alone.

What the hell.

"I'm in."

. . .

Amber had me ready in twenty minutes flat. I sat numbly while she did my makeup and chattered on. I wanted to wear jeans, but at Amber's horrified stare, I compromised and wore a jean skirt and a navy blue halter top. Wedge sandals topped off the look. There was no time to do anything with my hair, so my long copper locks were hanging loose and straight.

At the last second, I'd slipped on a silver necklace with a music note pendant that had once been a fixture around my neck. I'd only recently started going without it, but the feeling of the smooth metal on my throat was both familiar and comforting. I breathed a little easier.

I rode with Amber and a couple other girls. The Beta Chi house was on the outskirts of town in the middle of nowhere. The driveway was a long gravel road that led up to a sprawling yard. In the darkness, I could make out a basketball hoop on the blacktop and a volleyball court out back where, despite the August heat, they already had a bonfire going.

A blond-haired guy sauntered to our car as we were getting out of it. "Ladies, welcome." He smiled a game-show-host smile. "I'm Brad, the social chair. Make yourselves at home. Anything you need, I am at your service." He bowed and waved his hand with a flourish.

"Anything?" Amber asked suggestively. One of the girls, Kayla, poked her. Amber just grinned, slapping her finger away.

"Beer's on tap in the party room. Enjoy," he said and then to Amber, "See you later?"

"Maybe." She gave him a coy smile.

"I'll take that as a yes." He raised his eyebrows suggestively and trotted off.

"Holy crap, Amber," Kayla said. "Forward, much?"

"What?" Amber asked, her tone belying innocence. "I'm here to have a good time. And Brad looks like a good time."

We headed to the party room. Here's something I learned about frat houses last year as a freshman. They looked nothing like the ones on TV. Most were dirty, smelly, and in disrepair. I mean, honestly, what did you expect when you put two dozen twenty-something guys in a house? This particular frat house was actually a converted barn. You know that old saying, *do you live in a barn?* The answer was yes. They literally lived in a barn.

The party room was a huge room on the far side of the house that had concrete floors with a drain in the center. It smelled faintly of paint, and what was that other smell? Rose? Freesia? An odd smell for a fraternity house. I found the source of the scent in the outlets—scented plug-ins. Man, they were pulling out all the stops.

Three of the four walls were a clean cream color, which I attributed to the paint smell. The fourth wall was covered top to bottom in writing. A square DJ booth was in the center of the room and large speakers were bolted in each corner near the ceiling. Folding metal chairs were scattered about and a beer pong table was set up.

I wouldn't go barefoot in here, but I was pleasantly surprised with how clean it was. Of course, the semester hadn't started yet. In another week or two the fresh paint smell would probably fade, the plug-ins would dry up, and the walls and floor would be covered with a sticky coat of grime.

No one was manning the keg, so we helped ourselves, using the red cups that were stacked next to it. I took a sip and was pleasantly surprised yet again. They'd gotten quality beer instead of the cheap crap that was normally served at frat parties.

Amber and the other girls went outside to the bonfire, but I opted to stay inside. Even though I'd agreed to come to this party of my own free will, I still wasn't feeling overly social. But I didn't trust myself to be alone—the crazy look in my eyes earlier had scared me.

After Tyler died, my parents had forced me into therapy. I hated it. So much talking—*how did I feel about this? How did I feel about that?* Talking about my feelings wasn't going to bring Tyler back, so what was the point?

After about the third session, I'd figured out that they were worried I'd be so overwhelmed with grief I'd hurt myself or something. So I'd given in at the sessions and talked and cried and then talked some more. It was enough to convince my therapist that I wasn't a danger to myself.

I could have told them that, saved my parents some money.

But an hour ago, I couldn't have been so sure. Tyler and I had been so alike. If he committed suicide, then was I capable of it, too? Were my parents right in their fears? Was I really capable of hurting myself?

Had Tyler glanced in the rearview mirror before he did it? Had he seen a maniacal look in his eyes like the one that had been in mine earlier?

No, I'm not doing this.

I wanted—no, needed—to forget. I couldn't deal with this right now. Every time Tyler's image entered my mind, I— *No.* The whole point of coming out tonight was to *not* do this. I needed a distraction.

I wandered over to the wall with all the writing. The earliest signature I could find dated back to 1994—*Bunny was here*—and the latest one was 2006—*For a good time call 555-9284.* 1994 was probably when Beta Chi moved into the house, and 2006 was probably when the wall became too full for any more signatures. At one point, one of the Beta Chi brothers must have been quite the artist. In addition to all the signatures, there were several drawings of comic book style women with twelve inch waists and forty inch busts. Gravity being what it was and all, that was just impossible. A woman of those proportions would topple over or at least have serious back problems. But hey, at least they were clothed.

The door at the back of the party room led to a narrow hallway. There was a sign that said BETA CHI MEMBERS AND AUTHORIZED GUESTS ONLY and a padlock on it that was currently hanging unlocked on the hasp. Brad had told me to make myself at home, and I was here by invitation, which I assumed made me an authorized guest, so I crossed the threshold. Bedrooms lined both sides of the hall. Some doors of the more trusting brothers were open while the more practical brothers had closed theirs. A few of the rooms were occupied and I got a cursory wave as I passed by.

I walked up a flight of stairs and found myself in another hallway identical to the one below. More bedrooms, more cursory waves. Composite pictures lined the hallway and I chuckled at the ones from the 1980s. Powder blue bow ties, mustaches, and mullets. The Beta Chi boys were at the height of fashion. Swoon.

My phone vibrated in my pocket. It was Amber. *Where are you? Things are getting started in the party room.*

Tucking my phone away, I went back the way I'd come. Everyone had returned to the party room and it looked like a middle school dance—girls on one side, boys on the other. The only two who were interacting were Brad and Megan, the social chairs, who were standing in the center of the room. Amber motioned me over.

"What's going on?" I asked.

"They're doing some kind of ice breaker or something." Amber shrugged. "Megan wouldn't tell us, but she was excited about it."

"Ladies, welcome to Beta Chi," Brad said with a dashing smile. "If I haven't met you yet, I apologize. I'm Brad, the social chair. Megan and I have put together a little thing we like to call Neckties, Zip Ties, and Mai Tais."

"So in that basket"—Megan pointed to a laundry basket sitting on the beer pong table— "are neckties belonging to the brothers of Beta Chi. Each Alpha will pick one."

"Now here's the fun part," Brad chimed in. "You'll be zip tied to the owner of the tie for the remainder of the evening." He picked up a paper bag that had been sitting at his feet and pulled out a handful of plastic zip ties.

At about that point, my mouth fell open. Around me, my sisters buzzed with excitement. *Excitement.* They actually wanted to be tied up to a stranger for the night.

"Once you get all tied up, help yourself to a Mai Tai over there." Megan pointed to a makeshift bar that had been set up next to the keg.

I raised my eyebrows and looked at Amber, who was laughing. "This is going to be good," she said, then leaned in to whisper, "When we were outside Brad told me he loves orange plaid. *So* random, right?" She laughed again.

This was not my idea of a good time. Luckily, there were twice the number of girls, which was typical. Fraternities were always much smaller than sororities, and Beta Chi was no exception. So all I had to do was stand in the back until they ran out of ties.

It wasn't hiding. It was more like strategic positioning.

"Can I pick first?" Amber called over the hum of voices.

Brad smiled. "Of course."

I took a step back, but Amber had other plans. She grabbed my hand and pulled me along with her before I could wrest free from her grasp.

Crap, crap, crap. So much for hanging in the back.

Amber dug around in the basket and finally came up with one of the ugliest ties I had ever seen—orange plaid with just about every shade of orange under the sun, a veritable rainbow of pumpkins and goldfish and carrots.

She smiled coyly at Brad, who chuckled.

"It's my lucky day," he said.

Amber walked over to him—although walked is probably too meager a word for what her hips were doing. *Sashayed* was definitely a better description.

Brad made a show of pulling out a zip tie and wrapping it around their wrists. Then Megan helped fasten it.

"Cori, you're next. Pick your tie!" called Amber—the pint-sized traitor. Some of my sisters cheered.

All eyes were on me. There was no escape.

I looked into the basket of ties. There were stylish ones, ugly ones, and downright bizarre ones. One had a Santa Claus with a fuzzy yarn beard riding Rudolph, whose nose was a red lightbulb. Another one was tie dyed hot pink. There were both *Star Wars* and *Star Trek* themed ties.

I wasn't ready to be zip tied to the recipients of any of those. I didn't want to be zip tied to anyone, really, but that ship had sailed. I played it safe and chose a solid royal blue tie with a diamond texture. The owner of it had to at least be somewhat normal.

I pulled it out and turned to face Brad and Megan.

"Hold it up," she instructed.

I did as I was told and tensed, bracing myself.

Chapter Three

At first, no one came forward. The only thing worse than being zip tied to a stranger was *not* getting zip tied to one while all eyes were on me. I felt like the kid who got picked last for teams on the playground. Did no one want to claim the blue tie dangling from my fingers?

With my luck, I'd probably get paired with one of their freshman pledges.

"That's mine." The voice was deep and came from the back of the room. My lungs gratefully expelled the breath I'd been holding.

The Betas parted to make way for the owner of the tie. I bit my lip and crossed my arms over my chest, looking down. That meant that I saw his lower half first—faded jeans that hugged his thighs and rode low on his hips.

How come it's perfectly acceptable for guys to wear jeans, but when I wanted to, I got vetoed? Of course, when you made them look as melt-in-your-mouth yummy as this guy did, you could probably get away with wearing them anywhere.

"I'm Luke."

At his words, I looked up and was startled by the blueness of his eyes. In the world of Crayola, they would be labeled Cornflower. In girl world, they were dreamy. In my world, they were a welcome distraction. I could lose myself in those eyes. Would that be such a bad thing, just for an evening?

"Hello. I'm Corinne. Cori, actually," I said, holding out my hand, then feeling stupid at my formality. We were about to be zip tied together, for Christ's sake, and I was introducing myself like we were at a church picnic.

I blamed the jeans. I couldn't think straight.

He shook my hand though, not seeming to notice the absurdity of my actions. "Nice to meet you, Cori."

Still holding my hand, he led me over to where Brad was waiting with a zip tie. We held our wrists out—my left, his right—and Brad zipped us up then flashed a huge grin. "Have fun, kids."

I handed Luke his blue tie, and he shoved it in his back pocket.

It was awkward trying to walk in relative tandem while maintaining minimum contact, especially when he was several inches taller than me. I was wearing wedge sandals, so he had to be over the six-foot mark. We took a few steps out of the way to watch the rest of the tie picking.

I had assumed the Beta guys would be all over this zip tie thing—we Alphas were an attractive group, and let's face it, what guy wouldn't want a hot girl literally tied to him?

Apparently this one.

Out of the corner of my eye, I watched him as he shifted uncomfortably and ran his free hand over his hair, which was dark brown and cut short, super short, like a buzz cut. I didn't normally go for the military look on guys, but it worked for him. He could carry it off with his strong jaw.

He caught me looking at him before I could look away, and it was my turn to squirm. *Damn.*

"Do you want a Mai Tai?" he asked.

"Um, sure," I said. That was the whole point of the party, right? Part of the whole tie/tai thing?

Unfortunately, we were not in sync yet with our walking, which meant I turned left while he turned right, wrenching both our wrists. I crashed into his chest and he wrapped his arm around me to steady me. I thanked God I had talked Amber out of those stilettos and insisted on my wedge sandals. Otherwise, I'd be eating pavement right now or would have broken an ankle or something.

As it was, I ended up with my nose in Luke's collarbone. It kind of hurt, actually. My free hand had landed on his chest, and as soon as I regained my balance, I jumped away, causing the plastic of the zip tie to dig into my skin.

"Sorry," I muttered, inching over to give my wrist some slack.

"No, it's okay," he said. "I, uh, zigged and you zagged."

I looked up at him. "I really need that Mai Tai now."

His smile started at his eyes before traveling down to his mouth. "Of course." He gestured for me to walk first, so I started toward the bar and he followed my lead.

Luckily the social chairs had thoughtfully prepared the drinks in advance, so we didn't have to attempt any drink prepping and pouring. I took one and drained half of it. After watching another sister get paired, I downed the second half and picked up another cup.

It was going to be a long night.

Luke leaned down to whisper in my ear. "Look, don't take this the wrong way or anything, but can we get out of here?"

I raised my eyebrows.

"They're going to run out of ties soon, and I wouldn't put it past Brad to zip us guys up to another girl." He looked pointedly at his free wrist.

"Gotcha." He didn't need to tell me twice. We shuffled through a door in the party room that opened to a narrow set of stairs. It was a tough squeeze with his broad shoulders, and we nearly fell out of the doorway at the top of the stairs.

I burst out laughing. The Mai Tai was beginning to take effect, and now that I had a little buzz going, I could see the humor in the situation.

Luke chuckled. "This is freaking ridiculous. Hang a left into that room."

I did as he instructed and found myself in a room that seemed to be a den of some sort. It was decorated with Beta Chi paraphernalia, including paddles and their framed charter. A huge window lined one wall, and when I stood on my tiptoes, I could see that it overlooked the party room.

"Wait just a sec," Luke said, using his left hand to dig in his right pocket. His brow furrowed. "This is a lot harder than you'd think."

I giggled, until he brought his hand out of his pocket, holding a pocket knife.

I stilled. "What's that for?"

He grimaced. "I can see I'm not making a great impression, but it's about to get better." He slipped the knife under the zip tie and pulled up until it split and fell harmlessly to the floor.

I rubbed my wrist. "Isn't that against the rules?"

"What they don't know won't hurt them." He pulled a handful of zip ties out of his pocket. "If you'd rather—"

I held my hands up and shook my head. "No, that's okay."

He grinned. "That's what I thought. I'll be right back."

While he was gone, I looked down into the party room. The laundry basket was down to one last tie, and true to Luke's prediction, Brad asked for volunteers to be tied up to additional girls. A few came forward, while some of the other girls merely shrugged and tied themselves up to one another.

A few guys were hovering in the corner without any attachments. Huh.

When Luke came back into the room holding a beer, I asked him, "What's the deal with those guys? Why aren't they tied to anyone?"

He walked over to stand beside me. "Oh, those guys. Potential pledges. Can't officially include them in any events until they commit."

"Freshmen?" I didn't need an answer to that, though. I could tell by their eager stares that this was their first foray into college coed life.

"Yeah." He took a swig of his beer and looked down at them. "I'm the pledge master, so hopefully they'll be cool. Honestly, I just hope they don't make asses out of themselves tonight."

"That's pretty much a certainty."

"Unfortunately." He paused. "I was one of those rare freshmen. I can say with certainty that I never made an ass of myself, especially in front of a hot girl."

"Are you sure about that?" I countered, my eyebrows raised. And yeah, I'd noticed that he called me *hot*.

His smile was more of a smirk. "Oh, yeah."

"I don't know... That 'can we get out of here?' thing sounded like a lame pick-up line."

"If I wanted to give you a lame pick-up line, I'd say, 'hey girl, are you tired?'"

"'Cause you've been running through my mind all night," I finished.

The corners of his mouth quirked up. "That's a nice shirt—"

"But it'd look better on my floor in the morning."

"Do you believe in love at first sight—"

"Or should I walk by again?" I nodded at him with a smug look on my face.

"Damn." He chuckled. "You really have heard them all."

"Sadly, yes."

He leaned on the window next to me. The music was thumping below.

I turned toward him. "Tell me you've never actually used any of those lines."

He grimaced. "Guilty." He gestured to the cocky freshman who was down in the party room hitting on one of my sisters. "That was me two years ago."

"And look at you now," I teased. "You've come such a long way."

"I like to think so."

We watched as the freshman, whom I'd dubbed Cocky Boy, was rejected by not one, but two of my sisters who were tied together. We couldn't hear what was being said, but I could imagine. He'd picked probably the worst two girls to try to pick up. Ashley and Kayla were seniors who chewed up guys and spit them out when they were done. Then stomped on them for good measure.

"The difference between me and him is that my lame pick-up lines actually worked."

I laughed, a nice belly laugh. "Oh, come on. No, they didn't."

"They did," Luke said earnestly, trying to keep his expression serious and failing. "Once. She was pretty drunk though. She thought I was hilarious."

"But you weren't trying to be funny, were you?"

"I plead the fifth on that one." He pointed at my cup. "You're empty. You want to go downstairs for a refill?"

I looked down at the forgotten red plastic cup in my hand, then tilted my head. "Is that your way of asking to tie yourself up to me again?"

"Shit." He glanced down at the party room. "Everyone's still tied, so I guess we'd better." He pulled out a zip tie, then stared at it for a second before stuffing it back in his pocket. "You know what? Fuck that. Game over."

Luke led us downstairs. I could tell by the way his brothers nodded to him deferentially that he must be a *Big Deal* in his fraternity. No one said a thing to him about us being untethered. He got me a Mai Tai and pulled himself a beer from the keg while I waited near the signature wall. I read more of the signatures while keeping an eye on him and my cup. He seemed like a nice guy, but you could never be too cautious. I was ready to cut loose, but I wasn't stupid.

He handed me my drink. "I put us on the list for beer pong."

Beer pong wasn't normally my thing, but tonight I was up for anything, even a game in which the sole purpose was to get drunk.

Especially a game like that. The more I could get out of my own head, the better.

"Are you any good?" he asked.

"Does it matter?"

He pointed to a trophy sitting up on a ledge. "You see that trophy over there?"

I squinted. It was about a foot and a half tall and sitting on a board that had been nailed to the wall. I peered closer.

"Is that a guy bowling on top of it? And a pink Post-It note where the name goes?"

He waved his hand dismissively. "Those details aren't important. That trophy is for the Beta Chi monthly beer pong championships and it's had my name on it for the past nine months."

"Three of those months were summer months. They don't count."

"Smart-ass," he said, but he smiled when he said it. "The point is I've got a reputation to uphold. So, I'll ask again—are you any good?"

I held my hand up and shook it, the universal sign for *so-so*. I was halfway into my third drink. I didn't have enough experience with beer pong to determine if being drunker made me a better player. I guess I was going to find out.

Our opponents were two guys named Derek and Hunter. Luke easily sank his first shot. He smirked and winked at me. "Think you can keep up, Cori?"

I gave him my best *you're crazy* look and took the ball he offered me. I held my hand up and flicked my wrist. It hit the edge of a cup and bounced off.

Luke gave me an approving nod. "Not bad for your first shot."

Derek took his first shot and sank it. Luke reached for the cup and downed it. Hunter missed the next shot.

Luke tossed the ball and it sailed right into the cup without even touching the sides. He handed me the ball and stood behind me.

"You have to arch your wrist," he said, putting his hand over mine and demonstrating the motion.

I smiled at him over my shoulder and imitated him. "Like this?"

"Yeah." He moved his hands from my arms and rested them on my hips, watching over my shoulder. I could feel the front of his thigh against my ass.

As if that wasn't distracting.

I picked up my drink, took a long sip for confidence, and then took my shot. By some miracle it went in. Luke made the next one. My turn again. This time he didn't stand behind me, and I missed.

I spun around, palms up, with a pout on my face.

He pointed at the trophy in mock anger and shook his head.

The other team made the next shot and Luke reached for the cup again. I stopped him.

"You took the last one." I grabbed it and put it up to my lips.

"You sure?" he asked. "I don't mind. It's got to be warm and gross by now. Besides, beer and liquor don't mix." He nodded to my Mai Tai cup, which was once again empty. I frowned. When did that happen?

"Come on," he said, prying the cup out of my hands. "You'll give yourself the hangover from hell if you do this."

He was right about that. Learned that the hard way my freshman year. I might be tipsy, but I wasn't foolish, so I let him have the beer.

I pointed to my cup. "I'm going to get another one. You want something?" Luke shook his head, and I wandered over to the bar. The prepared Mai Tais were gone, but there was an array of liquor and mixers.

While I was mixing myself a Fuzzy Navel, Amber appeared by my side.

"What's going on?" she asked.

"You're looking at it."

"You having fun?" She didn't let me answer before she was asking another question. "Where's your other half?"

"Huh?" I asked, then realized she must mean Luke. I nodded to the beer pong table. "Over there."

"I'm so glad you came. And guess what? Megan asked me to be the assistant social chair. Isn't that fantastic?"

Brad appeared and slung an arm over Amber's shoulders. "Hey, beautiful."

She smiled and put her hand on her hip. "Hey, yourself."

He nodded to me with a lazy grin. "She's beautiful, isn't she?"

Amber beamed. I considered it a rhetorical question and didn't respond.

"I need a pong partner. You up for it?" Brad asked. "I'll even drink your cups."

"Sure," she said, stretching the one syllable word into three syllables.

"Hey, Cori!" Luke had his hands cupped around his mouth to be heard over the music. He motioned for me to come back.

I gave my drink one final stir, grabbed my cup, and returned to the table. Several more of our cups were missing. "What happened here?"

Luke shook his head, a downtrodden expression on his face. "It's been bad since you left."

"Defense! Get your head in the game."

Luke laughed. "It's your turn, and remember"—he pointed to the trophy—"my honor is in the balance here."

I nodded solemnly and crossed my right arm in front of my chest to stretch it out.

"You remember the motion?"

"You might need to show me again."

Wait, was I *flirting* with him? I must be drunker than I thought.

He stood behind me like before and guided my hand in a practice shot. And just like before, he rested his hands on my hips and watched over my shoulder to monitor my throw.

I made it.

"Go, Cori!" Amber cheered. Brad still had his arm around her. His blond hair, blue eyes, and tan made them look like Malibu Ken and Barbie.

I giggled.

"What's so funny?" Luke asked.

I burst out laughing, leaning over and wrapping my arms around my middle.

"Nothing," I managed to say between laughs.

Luke handed me the ball somewhat reluctantly. "It's your shot."

I tried to put my game face on, but giggles kept escaping.

"I think she's gonna choke, man," Brad commented. "There goes your title."

"No! No!" I shrieked amid fits of laughter. "I got this."

Except I didn't. That annoying Barbie song was in my head now. Every time I looked over at Brad and Amber, I started laughing uncontrollably.

I took my shot, but it went way wide and didn't even land on the table. Derek sank our second to last cup and then Hunter finished us off.

Luke hung his head. He grabbed the last cup and bumped it with mine. "Cheers."

"Where's the bathroom?" I asked.

Luke did better than tell me where it was. He escorted me to it.

When I was finished using the toilet, I looked in the mirror. My eyes were glassy, and I had a stupid grin on my face. I laughed. It felt good not to be lame.

When I exited the bathroom, I found Luke leaning against the wall, waiting for me. And looking delicious.

I stopped in my tracks. "You waited for me?"

He grinned. "Sure. You want to go out to the bonfire?"

I looked down at my hands. They were empty. "I seem to have lost my drink."

"We'll swing by the party room on the way out and get you one."

He held his arm out, letting me go first. I stumbled a little in the hallway and his hands were immediately on my hips to steady me. "Whoa, you all right?"

I nodded, then realized he couldn't see that since he was behind me. "Fine."

In the party room, he poured himself a cup of beer and mixed me a rum and Coke. By that time, it was slim pickings at the bar.

I followed him outside, prancing behind him. *Prancing.*

Tighten up, Corinne. Prancing is ridiculous. Plus, I was liable to break a leg prancing in these shoes.

Thank God he couldn't see me. But I couldn't stop myself. Prance, prance, prance, prance. I giggled.

He glanced over his shoulder at me. "Are you okay back there?"

I pasted a serious look on my face. "Never better," I said solemnly. Then I ruined it by giggling.

Luke commandeered some camp chairs for us. "Has everyone met Cori?"

A few of my sisters sat in a group on the other side of the bonfire. I gave them a little wave. Some of the guys introduced themselves, but I forgot their names as soon as they said them. It was hard to concentrate on things like that when Luke was sitting beside me.

He was *hot*. And I didn't think that was the beer goggles talking, except that it wouldn't be beer goggles, because I hadn't had any beer thanks to Luke's thoughtfulness. They were Mai Tai goggles and the view through them was great from where I was sitting.

The campfire lit up Luke's profile. His features were perfectly proportional. You know how some people only looked good from the front and others looked good from the side? Luke looked good from all sides.

I didn't normally go for guys with buzz cuts. I liked guys with a wave of hair. But with Luke, I was so tempted to run my hand over his hair to see if it felt fuzzy.

Just as I was reaching out my hand toward his head, one of the guys—Joe, John, Josh?—started strumming on his guitar.

Fuzzy hair was forgotten.

He played a few experimental chords and made some tuning adjustments.

"Okay," he said. "I know y'all know this one." Then he

sang the first line, "A long, long, time ago."

"I can still remember how that music used to make me smile," I sang.

Next to me, Luke groaned. "Josh, you need some new material."

I shushed him. "I like this song. Keep going, Josh."

He strummed the next few chords and by the middle of the song, everyone, even Luke, was singing.

When the song was over, Luke nudged me. "You're pretty good."

I smiled. "Thanks."

"Any requests?" Josh put his pick in his mouth and adjusted the strings once more.

"Um, 'Landslide'?" I said tentatively.

Josh experimented for a few minutes with the chords. "Okay, I think I got it."

He strummed the guitar and the familiar music washed over me. I closed my eyes and sang. No one joined in this time.

I sang like a diva in concert, letting loose in a way I hadn't been able to in a long time. I hadn't sung in front of people since my high school graduation when I sang the national anthem, which I had tenaciously rehearsed for months. I never sang in public unless I was thoroughly prepared, but my inhibitions had flown the coop several hours ago.

When the song ended, someone behind me said, "Holy shit."

I turned to see Vanessa, the Alpha Delta president. She marched over to me. "Why didn't you tell anyone you could sing like that?"

I was stunned. "Why would I?"

She poked me on the shoulder. "You're performing in the Greek talent show."

"Wha—?"

But she had already left.

What…the…hell. I should have kept my mouth shut. My singing days were behind me, part of my life that no longer existed, part of my life that died when Tyler did. I wasn't that girl anymore.

I stared at the fire, watching as the twigs, sticks, and logs glowed then turned to ash. One second they were shining bright, then the next they were nothing. I wondered if the intensity of the glow had anything to do with how quickly it burned itself out.

Here I was getting all existential at a freaking frat party. What was wrong with me? Why couldn't I turn this shit off?

I ran my hands over my face. Then someone from the party room yelled, "Line dance!"

I groaned. In the nineties, the Alpha Delta sisters created a line dance to an old Shania Twain song. Now whenever the sisters drank, one of them inevitably yelled "line dance" and then we were all, like, *required* to go do the dance. It was kind of a tradition. A lame one. One that should have been left in the past.

I hoisted myself out of my chair with a grumble.

Luke looked at me with a question in his eyes. "Line dance?"

"You don't want to know."

The light from the fire reflected in his eyes, making them seem like they were dancing. "Oh yeah, I think I do."

He followed me into the party room. I joined one of the lines in the back, hoping to blend in with the crowd.

The song started and I performed the dance almost mechanically. I could do it with my eyes closed. It was one of the first things we had to learn as new sisters.

When the song ended, I tried to skulk away. Luke found me and caught my hand before I could escape. "That was enlightening," he said with a grin.

"Well, you know," I said, flipping my hair over my shoulder with more confidence than I felt after those shenanigans. "We are in a barn."

"True," he acknowledged. The DJ resumed the regular dance music.

Luke scanned the room. "I need to check on those freshmen and make sure they're not passed out somewhere. Are you good?"

I nodded. Luke was sweet to keep track of me, but he wasn't my babysitter. I could socialize on my own.

Maybe.

I headed to the bar to see if there was anything decent left. Amber found me and grabbed my arm.

"I like him," she said in whispered excitement.

"Who?" I asked, looking around.

"Brad," she hissed. "What do you think?"

I held up a bottle of Coke, shaking it. Empty. "I don't really know him. Where is he?"

She stood up on her toes to peer around the room. "I don't know. I lost him with that whole line dance thing. Talk about bad timing. Oh, well. You want to dance?"

"Shots first?"

Amber gave me the eye, the one that meant *are you freaking nuts?* "Seriously? You hate shots."

I shrugged. "All the mixers are gone."

Amber scrunched her face up for a minute, then sighed. "All right. Let's do this."

I poured some rum into two red cups and we mashed them together in a cheers.

"To a great year," Amber said. "To new memories."

I nodded, not wanting to add anything, not wanting to think too deeply on it. I didn't want to think about new memories while I was still trying to forget the old ones.

After we drank, I set down my red cup. I was leaving a

trail of them in my wake. *Sorry, Earth. My bad. I'll be green tomorrow.*

Amber and I danced to songs I didn't even recognize. Geez, I was out of touch. Maybe she was right. Maybe I did need to get out more.

Right on cue, Amber said, "I'm *so* glad you came out tonight. This is just like old times."

Not exactly. There was one very important detail that was different. I squeezed my eyes shut and forced that thought out of my brain. I wouldn't think about that, about him, tonight. The whole point of tonight was to forget, if only for a few hours.

"Hey," Amber said, concern in her eyes. "Are you okay?"

I had stopped dancing and didn't even realize it. "I'm just thirsty," I said, walking off the dance floor. I poured myself another shot.

Amber was headed toward me when Brad intercepted her. She grinned at me when he wasn't looking and mouthed *so cute*. I smiled back at her.

Wait, was the room supposed to be spinning?

I abandoned my shot—and another red cup—and stumbled over to a wall, taking my chances by leaning against it. Now that I was stable, the room wasn't spinning, but it wasn't exactly staying still either.

I didn't care. I watched everyone else dance and play beer pong. The DJ was playing a game of flip cup on the DJ booth. One of my sisters, Dana, was fighting with a guy on the other side of the room. I couldn't hear what they were saying, but it looked pretty heated. I wondered how they could have that much to fight about after only a few hours, then I remembered someone saying that Dana's boyfriend was a Beta Chi. That was probably how we got matched up with them. She might be regretting that decision. We'd have events with the Beta Chis all year.

Luke finally returned. His smooth confidence intrigued me, and I watched as he chatted with some of his brothers and flirted with some of the girls.

Not that I was jealous. I'd just met him. I had no claim on him. That zip tie had been cut hours ago. It's not like he hadn't already devoted the whole night to me. I could let the other girls have a turn with his attention, right?

Luke spotted me from across the room and made his way over.

He leaned a hip on the wall and crossed his arms. "Those damn freshmen."

"What'd they do?"

"Just one of them actually." He shook his head. "He was passed out upstairs."

"I can guess which one." Cocky Boy.

Luke confirmed it. "Good pledges are so hard to find." I'd heard that before. With all of the fraternities on campus, there was stiff competition.

I looked up at him. The room was starting to spin again, but he wasn't. He was stable.

I reached up with my right hand and put it on the back of his head, rubbing his hair slightly. Yup, it was fuzzy.

He chuckled, but he didn't remove my hand. "What are you doing?"

"I wanted to see if your hair felt fuzzy."

"And does it?"

"Yes," I whispered.

He leaned down closer. "I didn't hear you."

"Yes," I said again. His face was so close to mine. I stared at his lips for a second. They were full and a nice pink color. I bit my own lip.

He was saying something, but I wasn't listening. His teeth were white and straight. I watched his lips move as he talked.

Then I stood on my toes and pulled his head down to

meet mine.

I kissed him. His lips were as soft as they looked. It only took him a second to recover from his surprise, and then he put his hand on the small of my back, steadying me and pulling me closer.

I parted my lips to deepen the kiss.

He tasted like beer. I probably tasted like a mixture of Mai Tais and Fuzzy Navels.

"Cori!"

I broke free of the kiss with some reluctance to find Amber standing next to me. "It's our turn to take the DD."

Luke removed his hand from my back so I could step away from him. Was it my imagination, or was he reluctant to let me go?

"Come on," Amber said, grabbing my arm and dragging me away before I could even say good-bye.

Right before she pulled me out the exit, I glanced back to see Luke still standing where I'd left him, watching me.

Chapter Four

I groaned and rolled over. Then rolled over the other way. Why was I so uncomfortable? I peeled one eyelid open and saw my jean skirt had migrated up my body and was scrunched around my waist.

Oh, yeah. That.

When Amber and I got home last night, I hadn't bothered changing. I'd flossed and brushed my teeth, but only because I was a fanatic about dental hygiene. Then I'd flopped facedown on my bed and fell asleep immediately. My hot pink pillow was now covered with black mascara smudges. Ugh. I didn't even want to think about what my face looked like. It probably matched the zebra comforter.

I heaved myself out of bed and stumbled toward the bathroom, stubbing my toe on one of Amber's boxes. I cursed out loud and hopped around holding my foot. She didn't even stir. There were no sheets on her bed, and she was wrapped up in her comforter like a burrito.

I avoided the mirror in the bathroom and stripped down, stepping into the shower. The hot water felt heavenly and I let it run over me, basking in it for a good five minutes before I began the process of washing my tangled mess of hair.

Feeling human again, I slipped into my robe and padded back into the bedroom. Amber's eyes were open, but she was still in burrito mode.

"Good morning," she said groggily. She wriggled into a sitting position, keeping the comforter secure. "Did you have a good time last night?"

Did I? I had to think about that. "Yeah," I said slowly, "I think I did."

"It looked like it," Amber said. "I had to pry you off Luke to get you to leave."

My hands flew to my lips.

Fuck.

I'd conveniently forgotten all about that. What did I do?

I must have had a look of panic on my face, because Amber said, "It's okay. I'm not judging you. I'm just a little surprised, that's all." She grinned. "Shocked, to be honest."

The memory of last night came rushing back. Luke leaning against the wall, looking down at me with his ice blue eyes and a teasing expression. Me wrapping my arm around his neck and pulling him closer, kissing him. His response—pulling me against him so the lengths of our bodies were touching.

I covered my face with my hands. "Oh God, oh God, oh God."

Amber got out of bed, dragging the comforter with her. She wrapped her arms around me. "What is it?"

"How could I?"

Amber stood back. "How could you not? I mean, you just met the guy, but Luke is *hot.*"

My cheeks burned with the memory. "I acted like a hussy."

Amber burst out laughing. "*Hussy*? Seriously, who uses

that word anymore? And you weren't a hussy. You were just having a good time. Loosen up."

I chewed on my cuticle. Last night was not like me. I *did not* throw myself at random guys and make out with them.

Amber abruptly brought one of her hands up to her mouth. "Oh my God. I just tasted my own morning breath. Not good. Have I been blowing you away?"

I laughed in spite of myself. "A little."

Amber backed away so fast she stumbled and nearly fell. "I'm just going to—" She pointed to the bathroom and ran into it, slamming the door behind her.

Impulsive. That's what I'd been last night. Not out of control, just impulsive. Somehow that made it seem better. Being impulsive was like being spontaneous. And being spontaneous was supposed to be a good thing, right? Right.

It was normal. *I* was normal.

I yanked the sheets up on my bed, lining them up perfectly with the edge on the mattress before carefully draping my comforter on top, back in its rightful place. I fluffed my pillows and laid them on top, mascara stain side down. That would have to do until I had time to do laundry.

I felt better already.

I placed my shoes from last night back on the shoe rack in the closet and looked around to see if anything else was out of place. Nope. Everything was in order. On my side of the room, anyway.

With a preemptive cringe, I dared a look at Amber's side. She'd promised to be better this year. Naively, I'd believed her. I loved the girl, but her living habits made her a less-than-ideal roommate.

The running water of the shower sounded from the bathroom. If I knew her, it was going to be a while, so I might as well make use of my time.

I hefted her first suitcase onto her bed and unzipped

it. Clothes exploded out of it. They weren't even folded. Appalling.

I sat cross-legged on her bed in my underwear and started smoothing out the wrinkles in the clothes, folding them, and placing them in neat stacks according to type of clothing and color.

Ah, soothing.

While I folded, my mind wandered to the conversation I'd had with my parents last night, which had ended shortly after they'd dropped that bombshell on me.

Suicide.

Unwelcome grief swelled within me, grief that had subsided, but was now running at high tide again. It was familiar, but oh-so-different at the same time.

Suicide.

I'd pictured Tyler's last moments in my head many times, imagining the worst, but hoping for the best. Hoping it'd been painless, that he hadn't felt anything, that he hadn't known what was about to happen.

Suicide changed that vision.

My parents had explained that the police were reluctant to label car accidents as suicide because it was hard to prove, which is why it had taken them so long to classify his case as suicide. It had been four months.

Four months of insomnia, four months of no appetite, four months of living in a fog. The only thing that had held me together was the summer course load I was taking. Between the online classes and two courses at the local community college, it was a full load and then some. It kept my mind off things I would rather not think about.

My breath caught in my throat as I remembered our last conversation, those angry words we said to each other five minutes before his car wrapped itself around that tree like a vine, his last five minutes of consciousness in this world.

He'd been brain dead by the time he got to the hospital. If the brain was dead, what use was the rest of the body? It was just a shell, a physical entity we could say good-bye to. But he had already left this world.

By choice.

A choice I'd influenced.

If we hadn't fought, would he—

No. Shut it down. Turn it off.

I wouldn't think about that.

My hands shook as I folded yet another tank top. Noting the uneven lines, I shook it out to refold it.

Focus. Left side in, right side in, smooth out, bottom up, flip over, and place in stack.

If I focused on the little things, the big ones faded into the background.

• • •

Biology was as bad as I expected. The professor looked like Napoleon Dynamite. The only thing missing was the moon boots, but I wouldn't put that past him. It got pretty cold here in the winter. Moon boots could make an appearance later in the semester.

My next class was Intro to Women's Studies. I was a few minutes early, so I took a seat at the front of the classroom and slouched down to wait. I opened the textbook and started flipping through it as if I hadn't already seen it. Or taken notes.

Someone slid into the seat behind me and tapped me on the shoulder. "Why are you sitting in the front?"

I turned to see a familiar-looking guy grinning at me. The party. He was the guy with the guitar. Josh.

"All the cool kids sit in the back," he said.

Inwardly, I cringed. I hadn't considered that any Beta

Chis would be in my classes. *Awkward*. I tried to remember if Josh was around when I accosted Luke. How would I know, though? I was too busy sucking face.

"My secret's out," I said. "I'm a nerd."

Josh shook his finger at me. "You know, I could tell that about you."

"Really?" I frowned.

Josh laughed and shook his head. "No. I'm just messing with you."

"Oh," I said, feeling foolish. There was only a minute or two left before class began and the room was filling up. "Looks like you're stuck being a nerd for today." I nodded toward the back of the class. All the seats were occupied.

"No!" Josh exclaimed in mock outrage. "You're a bad influence on me."

I smirked. "Welcome to Nerdsville."

The professor glided into the classroom in a billow of scarves. They were everywhere—tied in her curly, frizzy hair, cinched around the waist of her long floral dress, and wrapped around her neck.

"Students," she said in a whimsical tone, "today you begin your journey to full appreciation and understanding of the divine being that is woman. I am Dr. Eugenia Nantis." She said her name with a flourish.

When she moved to the other side of the room to pass out her syllabus, I looked over my shoulder at Josh. He had his hand up to his mouth, doing his best not to laugh. *Stop*, I mouthed to him.

He cleared his throat and donned an appropriately serious expression right as the professor got to our row.

"Ah," she said, looking at Josh. "A proud gentleman in our midst."

Josh nodded solemnly. When the professor turned away, his face turned red and he started shaking with silent laughter.

Okay, it *was* funny, but he needed to cut it out. If he pissed off the professor on the first day and she associated him with me, it could potentially hurt my grade, thus damaging my GPA. That's another thing I learned last year as a freshman in college. In real life, sucking up mattered. I was not above sucking up if the situation dictated it, but I preferred to find a happy medium between sucking up and not pissing off the professor.

"As part of the class, you will be expected to volunteer at least ten hours in some capacity at the women's center. Do not, I repeat, do not wait until the last moment to satisfy this requirement. Exceptions to the deadline will not be made." A scathing look backed up her statement. "The major event this fall is the annual Take Back the Night rally. On your syllabus you will find contact information for Ms. Hannah Bright, the rally organizer. Although I don't require you to participate in this particular event, it is highly recommended." She looked around the room slowly, making eye contact with each student. *To get an A, go to the rally.* Check, message received loud and clear.

I raised my hand. "When is the rally, professor?"

"Excellent question, Miss...?"

"Corinne Elliott."

She rattled off the date, and I wrote it in my planner.

At the end of class, she strode out, scarves swelling behind her just like when she'd come in. Apparently she liked to make an entrance *and* an exit.

Josh grinned. "This class is going to be *fun.*"

"Don't take this the wrong way, but why are you in this class?" I didn't know him well and didn't want to insult him, but if his behavior was any indication, he didn't take the class seriously.

"I like women," he said with a roguish smile. There were only one or two other guys in the class besides him. I knew what that meant.

I looked at him skeptically. "I don't think hitting on girls in here will win you any points with the professor."

"It might get me a date, though." He shrugged. "Plus I heard this class was easy."

"I don't know," I said, looking at the syllabus. "There's a lot of reading here." Our textbook was relatively thin, but she'd listed several supplementary online articles for each week.

He stood and stretched. "Nah. I never do the reading anyway."

I blinked, the idea unfathomable to me. Zipping my backpack, I stood. "I guess I'll see you Wednesday. I'll be the nerd in the front row."

I stepped around him toward the door. My next class was several buildings over, so I needed to get a move on or I would be late. I *hated* being late to class.

"Cori, wait up," he called, jogging to catch up to me in the hallway. "We're having a party tonight."

"Another one?" I was surprised. Our mixer was just two days ago.

"Not a formal party or anything, just a small first day of school celebration, if you will. You should come and flex the golden pipes again."

I shook my head. "My party days are over."

He stopped dead in his tracks. "Say what?"

"Saturday was a one night thing," I said, turning around to face him and walking backwards for a few steps. "I need to concentrate on classes."

That and I wasn't ready to return to the scene of my crime yet. I'd have to eventually since the Alphas were paired with the Betas, but the longer I could put off seeing Luke, the better.

Awkward encounters weren't my thing.

"Man, you weren't joking about being a nerd, were you?"

You might be a nerd, but you're my nerd. Tyler's voice sounded in my mind. My lower lip threatened to tremble, but I sucked it in, sucked it up.

I wasn't doing this. Not now, not here. My focus was on school. I'd process all that other stuff...later.

"Nope. One hundred percent nerd." I smiled tightly, spun around, and kept walking.

"If you change your mind," he called after me, "you know where to find me."

I stuck my hand up in a wave and turned the corner.

And ran smack into Luke.

Chapter Five

"Whoa," Luke said, using his hands to steady me.

My body was plastered against his, similar to two nights ago. He smelled clean and fresh, like he had the other night, only without the hint of campfire. His scent permeated my senses, and my belly tightened. I blushed at my body's reaction to his proximity, avoiding looking up at him.

What are the odds in a campus with twenty-five thousand students that I would not only see the one person I didn't want to see, but also literally run right into him?

Apparently, better than one might think.

I jumped back a step, out of his reach and away from physical contact. The more distance between us, the better.

"You all right?" he asked, concern in his blue eyes. "Sorry for running into you like that."

"Fine," I said. "And I'm sorry. I should have been paying more attention." I didn't even bother to ask if he was okay. I'd bounced right off him like a tennis ball on a brick wall. There was no chance I'd done any damage to him.

He smiled, drawing my attention to his mouth and those

perfect teeth.

Damn, he had a nice smile. And nice full lips.

Nope, not going there. I averted my eyes.

"I gotta go," I said quickly. "I don't want to be late on the first day."

He stepped aside so I could pass by, but he made no move to continue on his way. I nodded stiffly and stepped past him, very much wanting to break into a run.

"I'll see you later, Cori," he said, and I could feel him watching me. I stuck my hand above my head in a wave, which was quickly becoming my Beta Chi salute. I didn't dare turn around though.

As much as I wanted to blame my behavior two nights ago on the booze, it was more than that. We'd had a definite connection, booze aside. Would I have acted on it had the drinks not been flowing? The answer was a firm *no*, but that didn't negate the fact that the connection existed.

I could tell he had felt it, too. Seeing him again, even for those few brief moments, confirmed that.

I'll see you later. It didn't sound like the casual *I'll see you later* meaning *bye*. It had sounded more like a promise.

Okay, now I was making it seem creepy, which it wasn't. It was probably just a general *I'll see you later because my fraternity and your sorority are paired up.* Or was it? Did he *want* to see me later?

I needed to stop. I had been out of the dating game for so long I didn't know what these signals meant. Not that I was back in the dating game. I was far from it. All I knew was my pulse was racing and it wasn't from the brisk walk to make it to my next class.

This was exactly why I was going into full-on hermit mode, effective immediately.

• • •

Vanessa charged into my room and laid a neon yellow flier on my desk. "Greek talent show. You'd better make us look good." Then she turned on her heel and walked out.

I picked up the flier with my thumb and index finger and held it at arm's length.

Amber laughed. "Your expression is priceless."

I shot her a dirty look. "I don't want to do this."

"Good luck telling Madame President no. What Vanessa wants, Vanessa gets. How do you think she got to be president?" Amber tapped her chin. "You know, I don't know that anyone really likes her so much as they're scared of her."

I sighed and took a closer look at the paper. It wasn't a competition, which was a small blessing. Instead it charged admission, and the proceeds went to the local animal shelter. It was also a way for fraternities and sororities to get their names out before recruitment. Amber had dragged me to it last fall when she was trying to convince me to join a sorority.

"I haven't performed since—"

"High school," Amber said, not looking away from her laptop, where she was creating playlists for her iPod. "It's about time you got back into it."

I shook my head. "I've given it up."

"Like I said before, you're on your own telling that to Vanessa."

I curled my lip, but she was right. When I weighed my options, I decided that performing in the talent show would be a lot less painful than living down the hall from a pissed off Vanessa all year. Plus it would help dogs and cats. What kind of person would I be if I refused to help raise money for needy animals?

"What should I sing?"

"How about this?" Amber did a few quick dance moves as some vintage Britney Spears boomed out of her speakers.

I pretended to consider it for a minute. "Tempting, but no."

Amber turned down the music. "I'll tell you what you can't do. None of that opera crap."

"Hey! It's not crap."

"No, it's not. It was perfect for your pageants, but this isn't a pageant, Miss Chesapeake."

I didn't bother to correct her, to tell her that my reign as Miss Teen Chesapeake was over. And I didn't bother to explain, yet again, that the pageants were just for scholarship money. I hadn't even really liked them—I just happened to be good at them.

I stuck my tongue out at her. "Broadway, then?"

Amber pushed her chair away from her desk and spun around. "Do something modern that people will recognize."

"That's exactly what I *don't* want to do. I don't want to be compared to the original artist."

"Why not? You're just as good as most of them."

I snorted. "When is this thing anyway?" I searched the flier for a date, my fingers tightening on the paper when I found it. "Holy crap. It's Friday."

"Huh," Amber said, unconcerned.

"As in *this* Friday," I repeated for emphasis.

"Yeah, I got that."

"Could you at least freak out a little on my behalf?"

Amber held up a finger and cleared her throat. Then she exclaimed, "Oh no!" and assumed a stricken expression.

I pursed my lips. "Very funny."

She didn't get it. I had been good at the pageants because I was *prepared*. Natural ability could only get you so far. The rest was up to preparation.

"No, what's funny is you freaking out."

"This doesn't leave me enough time to refresh myself and rehearse a song I already know, much less learn a new song. I'm going with 'Popular.'"

"No."

"Why not? *Wicked* is very popular." If not for the seriousness of the situation, I would have laughed at my own pun. "People will recognize it."

"Do you really want to be the only one singing a Broadway song? Just pick a popular non-Broadway, non-opera song and sing it. It's as simple as that."

"Fine." I slapped the flier down on her desk.

She chortled. "Now you're really being funny, but if you insist." She cleared her throat and opened her mouth. If anyone was outside in the hallway, they would have sworn a cat was being strangled in here. I should have known better. This wasn't the first time my eardrums had been tortured by the vocal stylings of my dear best friend.

How could such a horrific sound come from this petite Barbie doll–esque girl?

"Stop," I begged, "just stop."

She grinned. "You asked for it. The sad part is I was actually trying."

"You've got to be tone deaf."

"Probably," she agreed matter-of-factly. "It runs in my family."

I sighed and picked up the flier.

I scrolled through the music on my computer and tried to remember what people did last year. If I recalled correctly, one fraternity had a magic act, so not everyone took this show seriously, or at least the guys didn't. The girls all seemed to.

I played the beginnings of a couple different songs and hummed along to them. Nothing seemed right. I drummed my fingers on my desk.

If only I could find the right song, then I'd be okay with this. I ran my fingers on the music note pendant on my necklace.

I hadn't performed since Tyler died. I'd never performed without him in the audience.

My breath caught as that realization hit me.

"Stop stressing," Amber said without turning around from her laptop. "I can feel your stress from here."

I made a face at her behind her back, but her comment snapped me out of it. I shut my laptop. I didn't have time to worry about this right now anyway. I needed to remember what was important—my grades. They didn't let just anyone into law school. And since I didn't get any reading done for biology this weekend, I was behind.

Well, not really. But for me, if I wasn't ahead, then I was behind.

I grabbed my textbook, index cards, and colored pens and shoved them into my backpack. I had to get out of this room.

The Greek housing was located on the edge of campus, and it was still hot outside, so I caught the shuttle to the library. I loved the library, especially at the beginning of the semester when there were few students. It was calm and smelled of old books, the perfect environment for studying.

I found my favorite study carrel from last year, which was ironically amongst the science stacks. Few students came back here, unlike the literature and history sections of the library.

I spread everything out on the table and opened my textbook to chapter two titled *The Study of Life*. Ugh. Stick a fork in my eye. No, scratch that. Just rip my eyeballs out with barbed wire.

It took about an hour to outline chapter two, and I decided to keep the momentum going and start on chapter three as well, even though it wasn't assigned until next week. First, though, I needed to find a snack. I had one of those growling stomachs that sounded like a small volcano was erupting. It was downright embarrassing. And right now, it was in full eruption mode.

The second floor vending machine was completely picked over. The only things left were Skittles and not-so-fresh-looking honey buns. No, thank you. I figured my stuff would be safe enough for me to venture to the first floor in search of another vending machine. I had yet to see another student since I sequestered myself in the study carrel.

The first floor vending machine was right by the front doors and looked like it had recently been restocked. I couldn't decide between a bag of chips or peanut butter crackers, so I stood there staring at them, my hand poised above the coin slot with the final quarter.

Someone tapped me on the shoulder and I jumped, dropping my quarter, which rolled under the machine. I spun around.

Luke stood there with his hands up, palms facing me. "Sorry. I didn't mean to scare you." He rubbed his neck, gazing down at me sheepishly and looking freaking adorable. "That's twice in one day I've had to apologize to you. Damn."

"No, I'm sorry," I said. Hadn't I already had this conversation once today? "I'm a little jumpy."

Awkward. My tongue had been in his mouth just two nights ago, but I barely knew him. I didn't even know his last name. I thought it started with an *E*, and the only reason I knew that was because I had seen it on the pink Post-It on the trophy in the party room.

Should I bring it up? Say, oh, I don't know—*hey remember when we were literally connected at the wrist? And then we were attached other ways? Yeah, about that...*

"Josh told me you two have a class together."

Oh, good. A safe subject. I could talk about academics all day long.

"Yeah, Intro to Women's Studies."

Luke laughed, a warm sound that made my gut tighten. Even his laugh was sexy. "Oh, that'll be good. I should sign up for the class just to see Josh make a fool of himself."

No, you shouldn't. Then I would have to drop it. Seeing

him on a regular basis would seriously threaten my sanity.

I nodded, figuring my best defense was not participating in a long conversation that would encourage him to stick around. The library was frigid, but I was suddenly sweating. Sweating as in I'd-better-keep-my-arms-down kind of sweating. I resisted the urge to do a little sniff check.

I couldn't help but stare at his mouth, his mouth that had done wonderful things with my mouth. My gaze drifted to his strong arms that had been wrapped around me. I continued looking lower, and I abruptly snapped my neck up once I realized where my gaze was headed.

Seriously, Corinne? Checking out his stuff in the middle of the library? Hussy!

My attention was drawn to his hair. His damn fuzzy hair, the texture of which had seemed so fascinating in my drunken state. His damn soft, fuzzy, nice-to-run-my-fingers-over hair.

I shook my head a little, trying to physically shake those kinds of thoughts from my head.

"Did you get what you wanted?" he asked.

My eyes widened. What did he think I wanted? My eyes had just consumed his body like a starving woman consumed potato chips, so I could only imagine what he might be referring to. To be honest, no, I hadn't gotten what I wanted. He was facing me, so I wasn't able to check out his ass.

Shit. Where did that come from?

He gestured to the vending machine behind me. Oh, yeah. Food. Of course. Most people didn't hang out in front of vending machines unless they wanted something, like food.

"No, I, um, dropped my quarter." I reached up to the return coins button.

"Wait." He put his hand into his pocket and pulled out a quarter. "Here."

I shook my head. "I can't take your money."

He looked down at the coin and then back at me. "It's a

quarter. Besides, it's my fault you lost yours."

Everything inside me was screaming not to take it. Stupid, I know. It was as if accepting the money meant something that it didn't. It was just a measly quarter.

I held out my hand and he placed the quarter in it, his fingers brushing my palm. The physical contact made my palm tingle, making me wonder what other parts of my body would tingle at his touch. I stepped closer to the vending machine, wanting to put some distance between us before my traitorous thoughts got the better of me again.

I turned my back to him, hoping he couldn't see how flustered I was. I put the money in the machine and randomly selected something, which turned out to be a bag of pretzels. At least it wasn't an old crusty honey bun.

I gave him a tight smile. "Thanks for the quarter."

"Cori," he said as I was walking away.

Damn. So close to escaping. I turned around slowly.

"Is this"—he gestured between the two of us—"weird because of what happened Saturday night?"

My cheeks burned. I guess he saw past my guise of normalcy. "No, of course not." *Yes, it's totally weird. Is it weird that I'm feeling that urge to run my fingers over your hair right now?*

"You just seem kind of, I don't know, unnerved or something."

I shrugged and put my hands out, palms up as if to say *I don't know what you're talking about.*

But I knew what he was talking about. He was talking about the way he made my hair stand on end, the way tingles were forming in my belly, and the way I could practically feel the softness of his lips. The way he looked at me with an intensity that made my knees go weak, knees that had been firmly locked in place for so long.

Something about him got to me.

He took a step closer to me, narrowing the distance that

I so desperately needed. "It was just a kiss."

Technically, it was several kisses. Or maybe since we never broke apart from the initial kiss, it was considered one kiss? Either way, it was several minutes of lips and tongues and heat.

"I know," I said. Except I didn't know. I didn't usually kiss random guys I'd just met. I was out of my element.

"Good." He flashed his killer smile. I noticed now that his teeth weren't quite as perfect as I originally thought. In the blinding light of the library, I could see his left canine was slightly crooked. "So I'll definitely see you at the next Beta Chi and Alpha Delta event?"

"Maybe."

"Let me put it this way." He leaned on the snack machine, looking at me. "I hope to see you at the next event."

"Um, okay," I stammered, refusing to look at him. Lord only knew what I would agree to if I didn't extricate myself from this situation. "Bye."

I turned on my heel and walked—not ran, though I wanted to—back to the stairwell to return to the safety of my second floor study carrel.

Once there, I groaned and banged my head against the desktop. It took several minutes for my heart to stop racing. I just had one thing to say about that.

What the hell?

I didn't even know this guy. He was practically a stranger. And besides that, I wasn't ready. It wasn't right, not when Tyler... When I...

Luke was just a momentary distraction, and that moment was over.

So why were my hands shaking so badly I could barely open my bag of pretzels? I needed to get a grip, and fast, because I was hanging on by a thread, and Luke could very well cut it.

Chapter Six

"Come look at this," Amber said.

I peered over her shoulder at her laptop, where she had Brad's Facebook page open.

"What are you doing? Stalking him?"

She made a face. "*He* friended *me*. There's nothing wrong with being interested in my new *friend*."

I snorted. "Good comeback."

"Thank you, but yes, I am stalking. After some of the guys I dated last year..." She cringed.

She had dated some doozies. I'd gotten a play-by-play after each of her dates. There was the guy who sent his food back to the kitchen at a restaurant because the vegetables and the meat were touching. Another guy we'd dubbed the Catman lived alone in his apartment with seven cats. She'd dated one guy for about a month, and she'd really liked him, but then his sister came to visit and he'd kissed her on the mouth both when he greeted her and when he'd said bye to her. After witnessing that, Amber couldn't bring herself to kiss him.

So I could understand why she was doing some recon on a potential boyfriend.

"His relationship status is single, so that's a relief." She'd also dated a guy who'd been cheating on his girlfriend to go out with her.

I'm telling you—Amber attracted all the winners.

"Go to his pictures," I directed. The first one that popped up made me burst out laughing. He must have been in middle school, and he had to have been the biggest geek ever. He was sitting with a tuba. His T-shirt was tucked into his jeans, and he wore thick glasses and had a mouthful of braces.

"Stop laughing," Amber chided, but then she started giggling, too. "This is so wrong. We shouldn't be laughing at him."

"Okay, okay," I said, regaining my composure. "See what other pictures he has posted."

Amber clicked on the other pictures. "Aw, look how cute he is in a tux." The picture was probably taken at his high school prom.

"His date's pretty," I commented.

Amber gave me a look that said *why are you saying nice things about his old girlfriends?* Oops. Girl code violation.

"He has good taste," I placated. "That's probably why he likes you."

She tilted her head. "Good point. There's Luke." She elbowed me and I pushed her arm away.

I turned away from the screen. I'd managed to go a full twenty-four hours without seeing him, and I didn't want to somehow jinx it by looking at pictures of him online.

"When are you going to spill?" she asked. "What's the deal with you and Luke?"

"There's no *deal*."

"Then why are you being all weird about him?"

I gave her a look. Why did everyone—meaning Amber

and Luke—think I was being weird? I wasn't being weird. And anyway, I wasn't discussing it with her because there was nothing to discuss. It was a one-time thing, the result of too many Mai Tais and definitely one too many zip ties.

She sighed and clicked on the next picture. "Look, there's Vanessa." She leaned forward and looked into the background of the photo. "Is that…?"

"Make it full screen." I peered at it.

Neither of us said anything for a second. Then we slowly turned to look at each other.

"Oh, shit," I said.

Whoever took the picture had caught Luke and me kissing in the background. It wasn't noticeable at first, but once you knew it was there, it was pretty obvious. Obvious that I was the aggressor in the picture.

My arms were wrapped around Luke's neck, pulling him closer to me. My body was pressed against his and his arms were around me. I was stuck on him like a suction cup.

My belly tingled as I remembered the feel of his lips on mine, his tongue tangled with mine. I swallowed.

The tingling turned into a brick of guilt as I stared at the evidence of my indiscretion. How could I have lost control like that? It was wrong.

"No, no, no," I whispered. "This is bad."

"I don't know." Amber tilted her head to get a look at the picture from another angle. "You can only see half your face, but it's actually a pretty good picture of you."

"That's not what I meant."

She grinned. "I know, but you're so fun to mess with."

"This isn't funny." I pinched the bridge of my nose, trying to stay the impending flow of tears.

Amber put her hand on my arm. "Cori, what is it?"

"I'm not tagged in it, am I?"

She checked. "No."

"Thank God."

"What's going on? Talk to me."

I ran my fingers over the smooth metal of my silver necklace. "What if someone from back home sees it?"

Understanding shone in Amber's eyes. "It's been four months. It's okay to move on, you know?"

I did know that. I had known it. I'd even begun to feel more normal, to the point where Tyler wasn't my first thought when I woke each morning. And I'd been determined to make a fresh start this year.

But now after finding out he'd killed himself—

I choked back a sob, wrapping my arms around my body.

She came to me and hugged me. "I know you don't like to talk about this, because, well, he died and all, but weren't you two having problems anyway?"

We had been, which is why our last conversation hadn't been the most pleasant. We'd screamed at each other, said some hateful things. Now would have been the perfect time to tell Amber about the suicide.

To tell her about the conversation that might have driven him to crash his car into that tree.

If I said it out loud, it might make it true. As long as the thought remained locked away in my head, it was just that—a thought.

I didn't kill him.

Did I?

Amber's eyes were full of compassion and sympathy. If I told her, would that change? Would she look at me differently knowing I drove Tyler to his death?

I couldn't. I just couldn't say the words. Another sob tried to escape, but I held it in.

Lock it away. If I let it out now, I would lose what little control I had left.

I pulled away and wiped the tears out of my eyes with my

fingertips. I took a deep breath and pasted a shaky smile on my face. "You're right. I'm overreacting."

She smiled. "It's about time you admitted that. When are you going to admit I'm always right?"

I closed my eyes, and when I opened them, Tyler was securely tucked away in the furthest corner of my mind.

I looked at Amber skeptically. "Aren't we stalking a guy on Facebook because of your bad judgment when it comes to guys?"

She stuck her tongue out at me.

• • •

I crossed campus early the next morning, excited to get to my first class of the day, criminology. I opened the door to the auditorium-style classroom fifteen minutes early and flipped on the lights. Perfect. First pick of seats.

I put my stuff down and went in search of a soda machine. I'd lain in bed tossing and turning after my late night Facebook stalking session with Amber, so I was running on about four hours' sleep.

The only diet soda that was in the first machine I came to was decaffeinated. What was the point of that?

I checked my watch. I still had time and my backpack was keeping my carefully selected seat safe, so I continued in my search of diet caffeine. I splurged and got myself a Pop-Tart as well. In my haste to get to class early, I'd skipped breakfast.

I settled into my seat in the front row. Students were slowly starting to trickle in, but only a few others were sitting in the front half of the room. I just didn't understand that, especially in a class like criminology. I mean, come on, this stuff was interesting, even for non-nerds.

I pulled out my notebook and colored pens and laid them out in front of me. Then I popped the top on my soda and took a sip.

"Hey," someone said and touched my shoulder.

I choked and starting coughing, sending the soda up my nose. It burned something fierce. I looked up to see who had touched my shoulder.

"Sorry," Luke said, grinning down at me. "You weren't lying when you said you were jumpy." He slipped into the seat next to me. "Are you okay?"

I nodded, not trusting myself to talk. I never noticed how close together the seats were, but I was certainly aware of it now. He was mere inches away from me, and the seats were bolted to the floor, which meant I couldn't do anything about it unless I wanted to be super obvious and switch seats. I scooted my notebook over, careful to leave enough space between us so that I wouldn't accidently brush his arm. He pulled out a binder and a pen.

I stared straight ahead. Damn. I was so looking forward to this class, and now I was full of nerves.

Nerves and something else in the pit of my stomach I didn't want to admit to. Why did he have to smell so freaking good?

I could feel Luke's eyes on me. After about a minute, I couldn't take it anymore, so I turned to him. "What?"

"You're being weird," was all he said.

"No, I'm not."

"Yes, you are."

"Am not."

"Are too."

"Am— Are we really doing this?"

He poked my arm with his pen. "You started it."

"No, I didn't."

He raised his eyebrows.

I sulked. "Okay. You made your point."

"My point is *don't*. Be weird, I mean."

"Okay," I said.

"Good."

"Fine." I grinned in spite of myself.

Okay, so maybe I was being weird, just a little. Luke seemed like a nice enough guy. There was no reason we couldn't be friendly acquaintances. The kiss didn't have to mean anything, even if it was delicious. I was being immature. Guys and girls could be just friends.

If only my hormones had gotten that memo.

The professor walked in then. She wasn't actually a professor, but a doctoral student. She insisted we call her by her first name, Tanya. She told us she'd been a detective until she'd gotten shot for the third time and decided a change of career was in order. Her lecture was both informative and entertaining, peppered with personal stories from her cases. It was awesome. I was so enthralled with what she was saying I forgot to take notes a time or two. Praise from me didn't get any higher than that. Luckily, all of the materials would be posted online.

Plus, I admitted to myself begrudgingly, I could always ask Luke for what I missed. I could already tell he was a much better student than Josh by the way he actually took notes the entire class. And he didn't heckle me about sitting in the front row.

"Where would you have sat if I wasn't in this class?" I asked.

"What made you think I sat here to be next to you?"

I blushed.

He laughed. "Don't worry. I sat next to you on purpose. I'd probably sit in the second or third row, though. Why?"

"No reason." Not front row, but close to it.

He gave me a strange look as he zipped up his backpack. "I thought we agreed you weren't going to be weird anymore."

"If you think this is weird, you've seen nothing yet."

He stood up, grinning. "Looking forward to it."

Oh, boy.

. . .

As I was walking across campus, my phone chimed, indicating an incoming email. Another notice from the financial aid office. I read over it—they were still missing documentation for my financial aid.

I handled almost everything in my life, but this was one thing I had no control over since the financial aid office required paperwork about my parents' income. *Ugh*. My parents were slipping. Couldn't they take care of just this one thing?

I stepped off the walking path to call my mom.

"Did you get that email I sent you?" I said when she answered.

"Email?"

"Yeah, the one about the financial aid?"

"Um...let me think. Which one was it again?"

I ground my teeth. "The only one I sent you."

"Oh, yes. That one. I got it."

I tried to keep the annoyance out of my voice. "Did you take care of it yet? I just got another one."

The line went silent.

"Mom?"

"About that, honey. Well, you see, the darnedest thing happened..."

Uh-oh. I sat on a bench. "Spit it out, Mom."

"You're not eligible for those grants anymore."

I closed my eyes, dreading the answer to the question I was calmly about to ask. "Why, Mom? Why?"

"We missed the FAFSA deadline."

The air left my lungs, and I was glad I was sitting down. I

put my head in my hands.

"Mom, how could you? I reminded you. I wrote it on the calendar. In red marker. And I circled it."

"I just…forgot. These things happen."

I clutched the phone tighter and breathed deeply.

This shouldn't come as a surprise. These things were always *happening* to my parents. My parents had never been good with anything money related. My mom could keep any houseplant alive no matter how complicated the maintenance, but she couldn't balance her checkbook. Our dog never missed a grooming appointment, but one year she forgot to file their taxes. How does that happen? I just didn't get it.

Stupid, I chided myself. I should have stayed on top of her. But when she said she'd handle it, I'd foolishly believed her. Stupidity on my part. But I couldn't go back now.

A queasy feeling settled in my stomach. "What am I supposed to do now?"

"Don't worry about this semester. Your father and I can handle this semester." I sensed a *but* coming on. Sure enough, she continued. "But you have to figure something out for next semester."

"How could you let this happen?"

She avoided the question. "You could get student loans or go to community college for a while. It's cheaper. Or get a part-time job."

I kept my voice neutral, masking the anger that threatened to spill over. "When were you going to tell me about this?" The FAFSA was due last spring, six months ago. *Half a year ago.* And I'd lived at home all summer. She didn't even think to tell me about it?

"It didn't seem like the right time, you know, with the news about Tyler."

A lump formed in my throat at the mention of his name.

I swallowed it down.

"You could have told me this summer. Or when you first missed the deadline. I can't believe this. What am I supposed to do now?"

"I told you, honey. Student loans. Or you could come home."

I fought the urge to slam my phone into the pavement. Instead, I politely said good-bye and disconnected.

After all, if I didn't have money to pay for tuition, then I certainly didn't have money to buy myself a new phone.

All of the scholarships I'd won had been applied to last year's tuition. I had some money that I'd carefully stashed away in high school that was enough to cover my car insurance and give me a small allowance every month. Luckily, a sorority scholarship paid for my dues and room and board in the house since my GPA raised the sorority's average.

I'd meticulously calculated so that I'd have enough to get by until at least next year. I didn't factor in having to pay tuition.

I bristled at my mother's *solutions* to this dilemma. I didn't have time for a job with my course load. And I didn't bust my ass all last year earning a 4.0 GPA just to move home and transfer to community college. GPAs didn't transfer.

Anger bubbled in my gut. I'd been offered full scholarships to two other schools, but I'd declined them in favor of attending this school, my dream school. I was beginning to reconsider the wisdom of my decision.

But it wasn't my actions that fucked everything up. I had my shit in order.

My fingers tightened on the straps of my backpack as I fought the urge to scream.

I might be angry with my mom, but I was furious with myself. I always promised myself I'd never be as irresponsible with money as they were, accumulating debt I couldn't handle. I'd seen the stress caused by foreclosure notices and debt collection phone calls. No, thank you. I'd be damned if I was going to finish school with tens of thousands of student loan debt.

I was just going to have to come up with tens of thousands of dollars in scholarship money on my own before next semester.

My shoulders slumped. Fuck.

I'd think about it later. For now, I had to get to class.

Chapter Seven

My feet were so sweaty they slipped down in my peep-toe heels, making it hard to walk. The result was the beginnings of blisters from hell. I'd forgotten how much these damn shoes hurt.

"Shit." I rubbed my sweaty palms on my dress.

Amber gave me a sidelong glance. "You don't look so good."

I stopped walking and put a hand to my stomach, trying to stop it from twisting. "I don't feel so good."

It was Friday night, and we were on our way to the student center for the Greek talent show. I was not prepared. I'd only chosen my song two nights ago, which left me little time to rehearse. My accompaniment was an mp3 karaoke download, which was not up to my usual standards, but it was the best I could do on short notice.

She looked at me quizzically. "Has this happened before?"

She'd never seen me directly before a pageant, and my stage fright wasn't something I advertised, even to my bestie.

I didn't like to acknowledge my weaknesses. It gave them power.

I nodded. "It usually passes by the time I get backstage, but it's been a while. And I'm...I'm just not prepared. How did I let myself get sucked into this?" There was nothing in this for me, absolutely nothing. My stomach heaved and I choked back the vomit. I picked the wrong damn time to be a people-pleaser.

Amber pulled me over to a bench, and we sat. I used the tissue she handed me to wipe the moisture off my palms.

"Do we have time?" I rotated the tissue in my hand, systematically shredding it. "I don't want to be late."

"You're as white as a sheet. We'll make time."

I counted to ten and did breathing exercises to calm myself down. Inhale, move my hands up toward my face in a gliding motion. Exhale, hands down and out. Inhale, exhale.

I looked to my phone as a reflex to my budding hysteria. No new messages. With a jolt, I realized there would be no text message, no message of encouragement.

Tyler was gone. And even if he weren't, our relationship had been so damaged, I doubted he'd be there to support me for this anyway.

Instinctively, I reached up for the silver necklace at my throat. Panic rose up in me again. "I can't do it."

"Yes, you can," Amber said. "I came prepared." She opened her purse and pulled out a tiny bottle of rum.

"What is that?" I hissed. I shoved her hand back into her purse, looking to make sure no one had seen. We were underage. What was she thinking waving that around? I peeked in her purse to find a stash of little bottles. My jaw dropped a little.

She rolled her eyes. "Relax. I'm not going to force you to drink it. It was supposed to be for a pre-game for me and some of the girls, but you need it more."

I licked my lips. "Thanks, but no."

Amber cocked her head. "Wasn't it your drunken campfire singing that got you in this mess in the first place?"

"Don't remind me." I knew it was my own dumb fault I was in this position, but a repeat of my drunken performance didn't seem like a good solution.

"Here." Amber put the bottles in my purse. "Just in case."

I gave her a wary look, but I didn't object.

When we got to the auditorium, I was directed backstage with the rest of the performers. Amber gave me a kiss on the cheek.

"I'd wish you luck, but you don't need it."

I nodded, too unnerved to speak, and she left.

Despite my fears about being late, I was actually one of the first performers backstage. The backstage manager told me I was number twenty out of twenty-three performers. I did the math in my head. Five minutes per act times nineteen performers in front of me meant I had an hour and a half to kill before it was my turn. I would prefer to just get it over with, but something told me the stressed-out stage manager who was barking orders into a headset wouldn't care what I preferred.

I paced backstage until it became too crowded. Some of the other fraternities had full bands representing them and other sororities had groups of girls in matching dance outfits. How could I compete with that? They had entire acts planned out while I would just be holding a microphone.

I peeked out into the audience. My vision blurred at the sight of the nearly full auditorium. There had to be thousands of people out there.

Somehow I didn't think the old technique for overcoming stage fright would work. There were way too many people to imagine them in their underwear. Not that it ever really worked anyway. Nothing beat proper preparation, but it was too late for that.

"Don't you know better than to look out there?"

I jumped away from the curtain. It was Josh, and he had his guitar with him. A relieved smile spread across my face. I almost hugged him.

"I do," I said sheepishly, "but I couldn't help it."

The lights blinked, indicating that we only had five minutes until showtime. I followed Josh backstage and out a door to a waiting area in the hall.

"I didn't know you were performing tonight," I said.

"Neither did I," he said with a lazy grin. "Apparently they signed me up and forgot to tell me."

A look of horror crossed my face. "What are you going to play?"

He shrugged. "Don't know. I'll figure it out when I get out there."

The very thought of that made me twitchy. He just leaned against the wall like he hadn't a care in the world, like he wasn't about to go onstage in front of thousands of people. I wished I could channel a little of his calmness, his nonchalance.

A girl dressed in black with a clipboard and a headset announced, "Beta Chi, you're up next."

"Sweet," Josh said. "I guess I'm second."

I went backstage with him to show my support, not that he seemed to need it. He was perfectly at ease. I was more nervous for him than he was.

They called his name and he walked onstage holding his guitar. When he got to the center, he grinned and held his guitar up in one hand while motioning with the other hand for the audience to cheer.

Which they did.

If I tried that, crickets would probably start chirping.

"What do y'all want to hear?" he said into the microphone.

Immediately someone in the audience yelled "Freebird!" I rolled my eyes. There was one in every crowd. Then there was a cacophony of shouted requests.

Grinning, Josh rocked back on his heels and looked around the audience. He put his hand up to his ear. "What was that?"

The audience shouted their requests again. "I heard Dave Matthews from the lovely lady in the front. What's your name, sweetheart? Kimberly?" He winked at her. Actually winked. "I'll see you after the show."

He sat on the stool behind the microphone and adjusted the strings on the guitar. He played a few simple chords before starting his song.

He was awesome. From his casual and carefree demeanor, you'd think he was sitting by the bonfire again instead of in front of thousands of people. He called out for the audience to sing along with him, and they complied. With no preparation whatsoever, Josh managed to lead a sing-along for an audience full of people. Unbelievable. At the end of his song, he left the stage and went into the cheering audience rather than returning backstage.

The next group was a sorority with a choreographed hip-hop dance routine. They wore tiny black shorts and blue sequined tops that showed both cleavage and belly buttons. Their performance was amazing—very high energy—and the audience responded with their own enthusiasm.

It dawned on me like a flashlight in my eyes. I'd picked the wrong song. All the breath left my body and my already tenuous grip on my confidence slipped.

I'd chosen a ballad by Adele because I liked it, but more importantly, I already knew it. On short notice, I didn't have much time to learn something new. Also, it showed off my range. I was used to being judged, so I naturally chose a song that would showcase my vocal talent.

But that wasn't what this show was all about. This show was about wowing the audience with a fun performance, not demonstrating technical skill. After watching Josh and the last dance routine, the audience was sure to fall asleep watching me sing a ballad. Even my *outfit* was wrong. It was the quintessential little black dress, strapless and fitted, hitting mid-thigh. Yeah, it was tight and showed a little leg, but it wasn't anything that the audience would get excited about, not like the dancers' ensembles.

I rushed out to the waiting room and found a bathroom, locking myself in a stall. I clutched my stomach, expecting to puke at any moment. I leaned my forehead against the cool metal of the wall, using sheer will to keep down the contents of my belly.

It was too late to change my song and I certainly couldn't ditch the show. I'd committed to it, and I always followed through on my commitments. Plus, Vanessa would probably scalp me in my sleep if I made Alpha Delta look bad with a no-show.

I pulled my phone out, thinking I'd play a game or something to distract myself, and my gaze was drawn to the messages icon.

No new messages.

My finger hovered over the text button. I could scroll back through my old messages and since my phone was almost two years old, Tyler's would still be there. Maybe just a peek to calm my nerves.

My hands shook and I paused.

This wasn't a good idea.

Before I thought too much about it, I reached into my purse and pulled out a bottle. I drank the whole thing in one shot, coughing as it burned my throat. I waited ten minutes, and when I didn't feel anything, I downed a second one.

I returned to the backstage area to start warming up. Still

an hour to wait.

Beside me, a guy was warming up with an accordion. Was he for real? I giggled.

"What are you playing?" I asked him.

"A cover of 'Take on Me,'" he said. "You know, A Ha."

"I *love* that song!" I said, and I wasn't just being nice—I actually did. "Can I get a preview?"

He grinned. "Sure."

He played the opening riff and sure enough, it was "Take on Me."

"I can hear it. You're really playing 'Take on Me' on the accordion. That's awesome. Wait, wait, I know this part." I sang along to the chorus and then fuddled my way through the rest of the words.

I clapped when he was done. He gave a little bow. "I hope everyone else likes it as much as you do."

I nodded knowingly. "They will. I mean, come on. Who wouldn't like eighties music on an accordion?"

The girl in black called him to go backstage. Before he left, I asked him what number he was. Sixteen.

Twenty minutes to go.

I went back to the bathroom to touch up my makeup one last time. As I was searching through my purse for my lipstick—lipstick is essential onstage or else your lips blend in with your face—I found another bottle. I looked at it for a second and then shrugged. No sense leaving one. As they say, one is the loneliest number. I giggled at my own joke. Then down the hatch it went.

After another coat of powder, I went backstage. There was only one person left before me.

I started yawning, the last vocal warm-up I always did before going onstage. The only thing was this time it made me tired. That was new.

The guys in front of me did a pseudo strip routine, which

was cut short by the curtain. I guess the powers that be didn't want to see their full monty. To be honest, I didn't either. There was a little too much body hair happening.

My name was announced, and I felt the blood drain from my face and land in my feet, making them feel like blocks of concrete. I closed my eyes and forced my feet to move, one step at a time, until I was out onstage behind the closed curtain.

"Representing the ladies of Alpha Delta, Cori Elliott."

The curtain rose, and the lights weren't as bright as some I've been in. I could actually see the audience, not as a faceless blob, but as individuals. I searched the faces for a familiar one, hoping it would make me feel more at ease. I could see people's mouths moving in chatter, but I could only hear the *thud, thud, thud* of my own heart.

In the fourth row I found Amber sitting next to Brad.

And Luke.

Even in the darkness, I could see his blue eyes perfectly, watching me.

The opening chords of my song filled the auditorium, and I placed my hand on the microphone, pulling it down slightly to make it the right height.

"Go Cori! Woo hoo!" Amber definitely didn't have a singing voice, but from years of cheering, she certainly knew how to project.

"Yeah, girl!" Even though I couldn't see him, that one had to be Josh.

A grin played at the edges of my lips. I barely swallowed the laugh with enough time to take my breath for the first line. I placed my hand on my stomach so I could feel the inhale of air.

It was going to be okay. *I* was going to be okay.

Because I had this.

Chapter Eight

"Raise 'em up!" Brad said, passing around shooter glasses filled with lime green liquid.

Amber, Luke, Josh, Kimberly—yes, *that* Kimberly from the talent show—and I each took a shooter and raised it up.

"To Cori!" Amber declared.

"To me," I seconded, then downed the shooter. Sour apple, yummy.

We'd gone downtown after the talent show, which was a short walk from the student center. *Thirsties* was busy tonight, but the guys had managed to snag a table in the back corner of the bar, the one corner that couldn't be seen by either the bartender or the bouncer, so those of us who were underage could indulge in relative safety.

"Because of you two," Luke said, "the animals at the shelter are going to live to see another day."

In the midst of my freak-out, I'd forgotten all about the fact that the proceeds of the show were going to help needy animals. But because of that, Josh and I were the "guests of honor" and no one would let either of us pay for anything.

Good thing given my recent financial woes, but that was a worry for another time. For now? It was time for a good time.

I'd survived the talent show, and the relief was immense. So was the pride, actually. I'd kicked butt, despite my freak-out.

"I miss my cats," Kimberly said. She was a freshman and from the little bit she'd said, I gathered that she hadn't been away from home much.

"I've never liked cats," Luke admitted. "At home, we have this cat that is the devil incarnate. She's old, like fourteen or something, and she still tries to attack me whenever she sees me. I mean, what the fuck? Until I left for college, she saw me every day of her life."

"Dogs are better," I said.

"Dogs rule!" Amber agreed.

"I don't know," Josh said, his arm around Kimberly. He smiled at her. "Cats are pretty cool."

I rolled my eyes. Josh would agree that up was down if it got him one step closer to Kimberly's panties.

"If I were a dog what kind of dog would I be?" I asked.

"Ooh, good one," Amber said. She cocked her head and studied me. "What are those big ones with red hair? Not golden retrievers. Wait, Irish setters. That's it. You'd be an Irish setter."

I frowned. "Really?"

She shrugged. "They have red hair."

"Luke's definitely a black lab," Brad said.

I turned to look at Luke. He cocked an eyebrow while I studied him. Eye candy—that's what he was. His features were perfectly proportioned for his face, his jawline strong. His skin tone was naturally tan, contrasting with his eyes, those sinfully beautiful eyes. They were like an Alaskan glacier.

I leaned forward to get a better look. "Nah. They don't

have blue eyes, and Luke's eyes are *very* blue."

Those blue eyes locked on mine, stayed there while he tilted his head back to take a swig from his bottle. My gaze shifted briefly to his neck before snapping back up to his eyes.

"What about me?" Amber asked, and I tore my gaze away from Luke.

"Shitzu," I said without hesitation. "They're petite and pretty."

"Aw, thanks." Amber beamed.

"They're also little divas," I said.

Amber made a face and threw a crumpled straw wrapper at me.

"And Josh is a hound dog," I announced. "For obvious reasons." I smirked. Josh did not. Kimberly just looked confused. Poor girl.

"Hey, there's a pool table," I said, pointing.

"Do you play?" Luke asked.

I didn't, not really, but I wouldn't mind him teaching me.

"I can hold my own."

"So that means no." He laughed.

"Hey!" I protested, lightly punching him on the shoulder. It was solid. I resisted the urge to inspect it further.

He shrugged. "That's what you said about beer pong and look where that got me."

"Aw," I said, sticking out my lower lip. "Has your ego been bruised?"

"Actually, yes," he said indignantly. "The guys have been giving me shit all week."

"You'll have to pair up with someone else, then."

"Nah," he said with a wicked grin. "My partner was hot."

I smiled sweetly and batted my eyes. "At least you've got your priorities straight."

Amber looked at me with raised brows, best friend code for *what the hell?*

What the hell was right.

Luke was dangerous for me—and by dangerous, I meant tempting. I liked him.

But I was in no position to get involved with anyone. So I did what any logical person would do—avoid, avoid, avoid.

During the day, I avoided him because in the light of day, things were stark, clear, black and white. But at night and in the party atmosphere, things were hazy, edges were blurred. It no longer seemed so criminal to have a little fun. Besides, there was safety in numbers. As long as we were hanging out in a group, a little flirting was harmless, right?

At least that's what I was telling myself.

We left the bar in search of food. Josh suggested Waffle Hut, which was about a mile away. None of us were in any condition to drive, so we decided to hoof it over there.

We paired off on the walk. Luke had me switch places with him so that he was on the side near the road. He didn't say why he was doing it, but he didn't need to. That's just the kind of guy he was—thoughtful, the kind of guy who put my safety first without making a big deal about it. The kind of guy who I could fall for if I just let go.

Suddenly, even though we were still walking as a group, I felt very much alone with Luke, very much in danger of falling.

"How was your first week?" he asked. Whew, a safe topic. I breathed a little easier.

"Good, I guess. Napoleon Dynamite is one of my professors."

"Oh, yeah, Dr. Dunnall? I had him freshman year. He's a trip."

"I'm dying to know," I said, clutching his arm, "does he have moon boots?"

He nodded. "Oh, yeah. Just wait until the first time it snows."

I giggled.

"He's actually pretty cool, though. He knows about the Napoleon Dynamite thing and plays it up on purpose."

"My Intro to Women's Studies professor is Professor Trelawney."

"Better Trelawney than Snape."

"Aw, come on. Snape got a bad rap. He was a good guy in the end."

Luke shook his head. "He treated Harry like shit."

"At least he could teach. I mean, Hermione failed Trelawney's class. If Hermione can't pass, then you know she's a bad teacher."

Luke considered. "True. Josh tried to talk me into adding that class yesterday."

"He's just trying to pick up girls."

"I know. And no offense, but I have no interest in women's studies."

"Why do people always say 'no offense' when they know damn well what they're about to say is offensive?" I stumbled on a curb, and Luke reached out to steady me.

"Damn heels," I muttered. "I'm okay." Even still, Luke kept his arm around my waist, just in case. Good thing, because I stumbled again a few feet later, making me feel like such an idiot. The street lights were dim and the sidewalks uneven, not the best terrain for stilettos.

He looked at me quizzically. "You sure you're okay?"

I nodded. "Fine." But I wasn't so sure. I hadn't eaten dinner before the show because of my nerves, and now my hands were shaking—a definite sign of a drop in blood sugar. Those shooters I'd had couldn't have helped, either. Thank goodness we were almost to Waffle Hut. A tall stack of pancakes smothered in syrup sounded delectable about now.

I shivered. There was a chill in the air despite it being August. I leaned in to Luke. His eyes might be ice blue, but that was the only cold thing about him. Heat radiated from his body, and I instantly felt warmer.

Closing my eyes, I inhaled. He smelled so good. I didn't know what kind of cologne he wore, but I liked it. When I turned my head to get a better whiff, my nose was level with his throat.

I rubbed my nose on his throat a little. Smooth as a baby's bottom. Not that I'd ever had my nose on a baby's bottom for comparison, but that was the saying.

Luke chuckled, and his throat vibrated against my nose. "What are you doing?"

I stilled. That was an excellent question. What the hell was I doing? Had I really just gotten caught sniffing Luke? Definitely not my smoothest moment.

Fuck it.

I wasn't going to stress over it. I'd more than met my stress quota with the talent show.

"You smell good," I said. Might as well admit to it.

He laughed again. "Thanks."

"Has anyone ever told you that before?"

"Not recently."

"But sometime?"

He smiled sheepishly. "Yeah. Maybe once or twice."

"Are you a hound dog?" I asked. Suddenly I wanted to know in the worst way. I wished I'd friended him on Facebook so I could spy on him, maybe catch a look at some old prom photos, like we had with Brad.

"I don't take classes just to pick up girls," he replied. "That should count for something, right?"

It did, but honestly? I hadn't ever realized that was something guys actually did.

We looked ahead at Josh, who was wrapped around Kimberly. "Isn't she a freshman?" I asked.

"I think so. Josh is a decent guy, though. I wouldn't want

him dating my sister or anything, but he won't take advantage of her, if you know what I mean."

I definitely knew what he meant. Josh seemed like a nice guy, not setting off my asshole radar, so it was good to know I'd judged him correctly.

"Do you have a sister?"

Luke nodded. "Two. One older and one younger."

"I have a brother. He's a senior in high school. He thinks he's the shit, but here's a secret." I leaned forward, and Luke leaned in as well. "He's not." I laughed.

We got to Waffle Hut and luckily they were able to seat us right away. Luke ordered the triple stack pancakes with eggs and a double side of bacon. I ordered a double stack with fruit and sausage.

Luke raised his eyebrows as I handed the waitress my menu. "What?" I asked. "I'm hungry."

Kimberly ordered oatmeal and toast. "I'm a vegetarian," she said in explanation.

Josh did a double take. He'd ordered steak and eggs. It might be the end of the line for Kimberly.

"I can't decide if I want bacon or sausage," Amber said, biting her lip.

"Bacon," Luke said at the same time Brad and I said, "sausage."

The waitress sighed impatiently and snapped her gum, pen poised above her tablet.

Amber looked back and forth between Luke and Brad and me. "Sausage," she finally said.

"Links or patties?" the waitress asked, and Amber got a pained look on her face.

"Links," I said, taking the menu out of her hands and handing it to the waitress.

When the waitress walked away, Luke shook his head. "You're leading this girl astray. Both of you."

I snorted.

"Sausage is juicy and succulent. Bacon is just burned fat," Brad said.

Amber mouthed *succulent?* to me, and we both giggled.

"I think you mean crisp and crunchy." Luke's tone was haughty. "Sausage is just a breakfast hot dog."

"Pancakes are eaten with a fork," I chimed in, "so the side dish should also be eaten with a fork. You don't eat bacon with a fork."

"What kind of logic is that?" Luke laughed.

"Think about it," I said. "Hamburger and fries—both are eaten with your fingers. Pizza and breadsticks—both are eaten with your fingers. Steak and baked potato—both are eaten with a fork. Thus, bacon is *not* the proper side for pancakes."

Brad, Josh, Luke, and Kimberly stared at me with incredulous looks on their faces.

I hunched my shoulders and fiddled with my silverware. "What?"

"She's pre-law," Amber said by way of explanation.

Everyone nodded, as if that explained everything. I rolled my eyes. My major had nothing to do with logical thinking.

"She makes a solid argument, bro," Josh said.

"Eating animals is wrong," Kimberly said. We all ignored her.

"She didn't talk about the taste though," Luke said, not willing to give in so easily, which actually earned him my respect, even though he was oh-so-wrong in this case. "I'll give her the point about the fork thing, but bacon tastes better. And with food, isn't that what's important?"

"What's your major?" I wanted to know. "Is it marketing?"

"Business."

I crossed my arms, nodding. "That makes sense."

"Why?"

"Because you're not using logic in your reasoning. You're just trying to sell us on something. That's business thinking."

"Damn, girl," Josh said. "I think the shooters made you smarter. My brain can't handle this kind of talk after a few drinks."

"This *is* her being dumb," Amber said, then added, "she was valedictorian."

Luke looked at me, obviously impressed. I blushed. I was saved by the arrival of our food.

It's not that I wasn't proud of my accomplishments, but I didn't like to advertise them either. No one liked a braggart. Besides, high school was over, which meant the slate had been wiped clean. It was time for new accomplishments.

Luke offered me a piece of his bacon. "Truce?"

I leaned forward and took a bite. "Mmm. Crisp and crunchy." I smiled as I chewed.

"You mock me, but you know you like it. Just admit it."

I swallowed and simply continued smiling at him. I did see something I liked, and it wasn't the bacon.

After our meal, Brad called the Beta Chi DD, and we sat outside the restaurant to wait.

Amber pulled me aside. "Brad wants us to go back to the house with them."

Now that I had eaten, I was starting to think more clearly. "I don't know."

The night had been fun, but going back to the house? I had my reservations.

"Please," Amber said. "I don't want to go alone, but I *do* want to go." She glanced over at Brad. "I really like him."

I sighed. My gut told me that they were good guys, but we'd only known them a week. Brad did seem to like her, and for once, she might have attracted a non-loser. I didn't want to be the reason she missed out.

"Okay, I'll go."

The DD's car was a compact, so it took some creativity to fit all of us in. Brad and Josh sat in the backseat with Amber and Kimberly on their laps. That left the front seat for me and Luke.

I looked at him nervously. He climbed in the front seat and patted his lap, grinning at me. I clambered in after him and tried to do it as gracefully as possible. With the tight quarters of the car, I was lucky I didn't flash my goods.

There was nowhere to comfortably put my arm, so I wrapped it around his shoulders. That brought me in close contact with his throat again. When I tilted my head down, I could smell his cologne. And bacon.

I wouldn't ever think of bacon the same way again.

Luke wrapped his arms around me. My dress had hiked up when I sat, and his hand rested on my bare thigh. I tensed. If Luke noticed, he didn't let on.

"Where to?" the DD asked.

"Lawrence Hall," Kimberly said, earning a collective sigh of relief from the rest of us.

When we got there, she jumped out and ran into her building without even saying good-bye.

"Strike out," Brad said.

"Nah," Josh said, good-natured. "She doesn't eat meat. It wasn't meant to be."

"I think you're just disappointed she won't be eating your—" Brad didn't get to finish his thought because Amber smacked him.

On our last drive out to the Beta house, I hadn't noticed how bumpy the road was. Now that I was sitting on Luke, I was aware of every bump, twist, and turn in the road that jostled my body into his, making our physical contact that much more intimate.

Except it wasn't. Not really. Luke didn't take advantage of the situation at all. He was a perfect gentleman.

"I hope I'm not too heavy."

Luke chuckled. "Are you kidding? I could bench press you."

I didn't even want to think about the logistics of that. Where would his hands go?

The DD dropped us off at the Beta house and sped off to pick up more brothers. Josh headed to the party room to join in some beer pong, and Brad, Amber, Luke, and I headed up to Brad's room.

Brad opened his mini-fridge and handed Luke a beer. "Ladies, what's your poison?" He gestured to a shelf above the fridge that had at least a dozen bottles of liquor on it.

"What can you make?" Amber asked.

Brad listed a dozen cocktails, and Amber decided on an Amaretto Sour. I had the same just to keep things simple.

Amber and I settled onto the couch while Brad mixed the drinks. Luke pulled over the rolling chair from the desk. Amber nonchalantly looked around the room, but I could tell she was inspecting it. His desk had a haphazard stack of papers and books on it, but his movies and video games were neatly organized on a shelf next to his TV. There were no dirty clothes in sight, but there were several pairs of shoes lying around. For a guy, he was pretty neat. He was much neater than Amber was. I was still waiting for her to finish unpacking.

I picked up a pack of Uno cards from the end table. Amber snatched them. "I haven't played this in years."

Brad handed us our drinks and took a seat next to Amber on the couch. "You want to play?"

Amber nodded and started dealing the cards.

"Here's the rules," Brad explained. "You drink for every card you have to draw. If you throw down a wild, everyone else has to drink."

"Sounds fun," Amber said, placing her cards facedown

on the coffee table. She took a sip of her drink.

"Pace yourself, my dear," Brad warned. "I'm a beast at Uno."

Luke laughed. "It's a game of luck."

Brad chuffed. "There's definite strategy involved. Only the most skilled Uno players know the optimal time to play the wild cards and the reverse cards to maximum advantage."

"Yeah, right," Luke said. "You're just skilled at looking at everyone else's cards."

The look on Brad's face was one of indignation. "Are you implying that I'm a cheater?"

"No." Luke took a swig of his beer. "I'm warning the girls to guard their cards."

"I don't cheat," Brad protested. "I'm just really good at reading people."

"Okay." Luke leaned forward in the chair, resting his elbows on his knees. "How many blue cards do I have?"

Brad rested back in his chair, shaking his head dismissively. "It doesn't work that way."

I laid my first card down. "I'm starting."

We played a few rounds, and I had to draw nine cards. Two wilds were played. My cup quickly became empty.

It was fun.

About halfway through the game, Luke nudged me with his knee and nodded at Brad, who was suspiciously craning his neck and leaning close to Amber.

Luke leaned close to me to whisper, "Do you want to call him out or should I?"

I looked over at Brad again. "I don't know. He might not be cheating. I think he might be checking out her chest."

Luke leaned to the other side to get a fresh angle on the situation. "Close call."

He picked up a pen and flung it at Brad, hitting him square in the forehead.

Brad rubbed his forehead, smearing the bit of blue ink from the pen. "Not cool, man."

"Eyes on your own cards," Luke said pointedly.

"I wasn't looking at her cards."

"Then what were you looking at?" I asked.

Brad wore a serious expression. "I'm a gentleman. I don't know what you're talking about."

"Uno." Amber grinned.

I looked down at the bevy of cards fanned out in my hand. Damn.

Amber happily laid her last card down in the next round, despite our attempts to thwart her win.

I put my cards on the table and excused myself to go to the bathroom. When I came back, Luke was leaning on the wall outside Brad's door, which was partially closed.

"What's wrong?" I asked.

"I left for a second and when I came back, there was this." He nodded at the crack in the door.

I peeked in and saw Amber and Brad sitting close together on the couch talking. His hand was on the inside of her knee. Their faces were inches apart, and they were laughing at some private joke. I looked away when they started kissing, feeling like a Peeping Tom.

"I didn't want to interrupt," Luke said.

"Yeah, I guess not," I said. Now what?

"Come on." Luke grabbed my hand and pulled me down the hall. "Let's give the lovebirds their privacy. My room's this way."

Swallowing, I stumbled behind him.

His room was at the end of the hall. It was similar to Brad's, with a double bed, a couch, and a desk. Like most college guys' rooms, there was also a big-ass flat screen. Unlike most college guys' rooms, it was as neat as mine. His textbooks were neatly lined up on his desk next to a black metal desk lamp. No shoes were in sight, and the closet door was closed. The bed was neatly made with a navy blue comforter. There was even a matching throw pillow. I wondered whose touch that was.

Luke grabbed the remote from the top of the television. "You want to watch something?"

Luke was a gentleman. Despite what our friends were up to down the hall and despite our kiss from that first party, he had made no assumptions, attempted to take no liberties.

It definitely did not go unnoticed.

"Sure," I said, and Luke tossed me the remote. I settled on the couch and pushed the on button.

"Hungry?"

I patted my stomach. "Nope. Still full of pancakes. I could use some water though."

Luke handed me a bottle of water and sat on the couch next to me. He kept a fair amount of distance between us. I mean, he was definitely sitting next to me, but our legs weren't touching or anything. I felt a mix of relief and disappointment. *Snap out of it, Corinne.* It was better this way. Less complicated.

It was what I wanted. Right?

I clutched the remote, not answering my own question. "What do you want to watch?"

He shrugged. "Whatever you want is fine."

I flipped through the channels, acutely aware of Luke's presence next to me. He stretched out, putting his arm along the back of the couch. I stiffened for a moment, thinking he was pulling the oldest trick in the book, but he kept his arm on the couch and didn't try to put it around me.

My cheeks burned. Just because I threw myself at him last weekend doesn't mean he was going to reciprocate. The memory of those moments flooded my mind. His hand on the small of my back, holding me against his lean body. The feel of his hair under my fingertips. The warmth of his lips on mine. My belly tingled.

I looked at Luke out of the corner of my eye, petrified he could read my thoughts. His posture was relaxed and he seemed content just to hang out. Unlike mine, his mind obviously wasn't in the gutter.

And why wasn't it?

"Stop being weird," he said without looking at me.

I crossed my arms. "I'm not being weird," I said through my teeth. *Damn. I was totally being weird.*

"Your honor is safe with me. It's me who should be worried."

I gasped, and my entire body blushed.

He laughed. "I'm just messing with you. I'm not worried." He waited a beat, then grinned. "You can jump me anytime you want."

I punched him on his shoulder, harder than I meant to. It hurt my knuckles a little.

"Ouch." He rubbed his shoulder. "We're friends, right?"

I considered. We'd sat next to each other twice in criminology and now we'd hung out two weekends in a row. I guess that did make us friends. I nodded.

"Then let's just leave it at that, okay? We can have fun together."

I nodded again and turned my attention back to the TV, my posture stiff. He was being so cool about everything. I, on the other hand, was closing in on being neurotic. My behavior last weekend was completely out of character for me, and I was still having a hard time coming to terms with it. Luke didn't seem to think anything of it. Apparently my plastering myself to him in front of his fraternity and my sorority was no big deal.

Then again, guys like him were probably used to girls throwing themselves at him. With his baby blue eyes and well-toned body, he was eye candy—the kind of candy that didn't leave you with a sour stomach if you overindulged. He had a low maintenance style, usually wearing jeans and T-shirts. His buzz cut didn't require any styling, and he wore no jewelry other than a watch. I was suspicious of guys who decorated themselves more than I did.

The most attractive thing about him, though, was his laid-back confidence. It was confidence without cockiness, a rare delicacy.

"When does recruitment start for you guys?" he asked.

I had to think about it. I should know things like this, but it wasn't a priority. "I'm not sure. Probably in a week or two."

"Sororities have it lucky. The girls come to you. You don't have to actually recruit them. It's a pain in the ass trying to find decent guys to pledge."

"What about those guys from last week?"

He shrugged. "They might be all right. We have a lot of guys graduating though, so we need a big pledge class, at least ten."

"I guess you're in charge of it, huh?"

"Yeah, and then I'm the pledge master, too, so you could say I'm really invested in finding good guys."

"Well, Josh made a good impression tonight. That should help, right?"

"Maybe." Luke rested his head on the back of the couch. "The talent show helps the sororities more than the fraternities. Freshman guys are more interested in partying."

He had a point there. "What do you do to recruit?"

"We have recruitment meetings in the boys' dorms."

"Do other frats do that?"

"Yeah, they all do."

"Then how do you stand out?"

"That's the problem. There are too many damn fraternities on this campus."

I thought about the Greek community houses on campus, which were cookie cutter glorified dorms. Ours was nice, and the rooms were bigger than a regular dorm, but they were nothing special. "Your biggest asset is the house."

"Every frat has a house."

"Yeah, but most of them are on campus. They're not unique. Pick up the guys and bring them out here. Have a cookout or something."

"We tried that before, but it didn't work so well and it cost a lot of money. Plus once recruitment officially starts, we can't have any alcohol at an official recruitment event, or we could lose our charter. So we can't have guys out to the house like we did at the party last week."

"Let me ask you something—when those guys were here last week, how many of your brothers went out of their way to talk to them?"

He frowned. "I don't know."

"You should do what the sororities do."

He gave me a blank stare.

I explained. "When you get a guy who's interested, match him up with one of the brothers who has similar interests. Then the brother can get to know the guy and personally recruit him. When I rushed Alpha, I talked to the same girl every night. It was less intimidating coming in since I recognized someone. You just need a more organized strategy. Stop trying to impress the guys, and instead try to get to know them."

Luke considered. "Maybe. I don't know if the guys would go along with it. In the past, the pledge master has always done everything himself."

"But it sounds like that's not working, so this is worth a try," I said. "At the end of the day, people just want to belong, so make them feel like they belong."

Luke looked at me with raised eyebrows.

I looked down and fiddled with my fingernail. "I took psychology last year during recruitment. I made some connections."

Luke grinned, which gave way to a yawn. Then I yawned.

"What time is it?" I asked. "I should probably get Amber and head out."

He looked at his watch. "It's three a.m."

"Wow. I didn't realize how late it was. I really do need to go." I stood.

"How are you getting home?" Luke asked.

"Uh…" For as smart as I was acting tonight, I was pretty damn stupid because I hadn't thought about that. The Alpha DD stopped running an hour ago, and the town buses didn't run this far out. "Can your DD take me home?"

Luke shook his head. "He's been drinking in the party room for the last hour."

What, no last call? What was I going to do now? I calculated the distance in my head. It definitely wasn't walkable, especially in these heels. I couldn't believe I got myself in this situation. *Stupid, stupid, stupid.*

"Can you take me?" I asked, desperate.

He shook his head again. "I'm in no shape to drive." His lips slowly stretched into a smile. "You're stuck here."

A horrified expression formed on my face.

When I was hesitant to come out to the house, I was worried about awkwardness between me and Luke. The possibility of getting stranded hadn't even been on my radar.

"Sorry." The smile fell off his face and was replaced by a grimace. "That sounded really creepy. I don't mean it in a creepy way, I promise."

"Uh-huh. I'm just going to go check on Amber," I said and fled.

I rapped on Brad's door. When no one answered right away, I knocked again and called, "Amber! It's Cori."

Amber cracked the door and stuck her head out. "Hey, what's up?"

What's up? That's what she had to say?

And what was the deal with the cracked door? What was she hiding? I started to peek around, then thought better of it. I didn't even want to know.

"The DD isn't running," I informed her.

"Oh." Amber blinked, then realization dawned on her. "Oh," she said again, drawing out the word. "I decided to stay here, and when you didn't come back earlier, I figured you got a ride home."

I crossed my arms. "That's messed up, Amber. You think I would just leave without you? You're the reason I came out tonight."

A look of guilt flashed across her face. "I'm sorry. I wasn't thinking."

"No, you weren't." With a final glare, I turned on my heel and stormed down the hallway.

I leaned against the wall and cursed. Amber totally screwed me over on this one. Granted, I should have paid more attention to the time, but still. I was trying to be a good friend and let her have time with Brad, and look where it got me.

Stuck.

Fuck.

I had nowhere else to go, so I went back to Luke's room.

He had changed into plaid pajama pants and a white T-shirt. We were having a regular pajama party, except I didn't have my pajamas. My thoughts turned to last week when I slept in my clothes and woke up with my skirt practically around my neck. I looked down at my little black dress.

Double fuck.

Not that I'd be able to sleep. This situation was just plain awkward.

Fucking Amber. That was a shitty move she pulled.

"Do you want to borrow something?" Luke asked.

I weighed my options. Ending up with my dress up around my neck in the morning or wearing something of Luke's. The second option won, but just barely.

Spending the night wearing clothing that smelled like him was going to be pure delicious torture. My belly stirred in anticipation.

God, I needed to turn that off. But how could I turn off a gut reaction?

I shouldn't be having these feelings for Luke. It was too soon after Tyler. He'd died because of me, and here I was shacking up with another guy.

Okay, so I wasn't exactly shacking up, and it certainly wasn't by choice, but still. A small part of me said it was okay to get involved with Luke. Tyler's death was a tragedy, but our relationship was dead long before he was.

Then the larger, more reasonable part of me bitch slapped that small part in the face.

It was too soon.

Luke dug in his drawer and pulled out a T-shirt and a pair of athletic shorts. From another drawer he pulled out an unopened toothbrush.

He offered it to me. "I don't know about you, but I can't sleep unless I've brushed."

I relaxed a little bit. "Thanks." I somehow felt better clutching the plastic toothbrush in my hand.

I took the clothes and the toothbrush and traipsed down to the bathroom. It was not as clean as it was last week. Only a week, and the house was already beginning to fall apart. I was careful not to touch my bare feet to the ground and instead balanced on my high heels while I changed. I felt silly strutting down the hallway in my heels wearing athletic shorts that were rolled at the waist several times to keep them from falling off and a T-shirt that hit me mid-thigh, but it was better than contracting meningitis. I didn't even want to think about what was growing under my feet.

My fury at Amber burned a little bit when I passed Brad's door and I could hear her giggling inside. I gave the door the double one-fingered salute as I walked by. I felt mildly better.

When I got back to Luke's room, he was stretched out on the couch. I stood in the doorway, holding my clothes. Things were about to get awkward.

Luke looked up, noticing me standing there. "You can take the bed."

"No, that's okay," I said immediately. "I'll take the couch."

Luke's tall frame didn't fit on the short couch. He was lying on his back, and his feet were propped up on the arm. There was no way he could be comfortable. It wasn't fair to put him out because I was irresponsible.

"I insist," he said.

"I'm not going to kick you out of your own bed. That's just wrong. You've got to be uncomfortable. Let me take the couch. I fit on it better than you."

"That may be true, but I was not raised to let guests sleep on the couch."

"It's not like your mother's going to find out," I protested. "I highly doubt you're going to tell her about this."

He grinned, and I looked away, clearing my throat. I made it sound like there was something to talk about. There wasn't. Nothing to see here, folks. This was totally innocent.

Huh. Tell that to my nose that kept sniffing the T-shirt that smelled faintly of Luke. Or the tightening in my belly as a result of the lingering scent.

"Yeah," Luke said, "but you're still not sleeping on the couch."

Exhaustion was setting in, so I let him win this one and

climbed into his bed. The pillows smelled like him. I closed my eyes and inhaled, snuggling into them. Then my eyes snapped open.

What the hell am I doing? First the T-shirt and now the pillows? I vowed not to breathe through my nose.

In the darkness, Luke shifted on the couch, trying to find a comfortable position. It seemed like he shifted every thirty seconds or so. With every squeak of the couch, the guilt set in.

I sighed. "This is ridiculous. We can share the bed." It was out of my mouth before I knew I would say it.

Luke didn't respond at first. I wasn't sure how I felt about that. I was inviting the awkwardness I had been trying so hard to avoid. But what if he didn't want to share the bed with me? What would that mean?

I pulled the covers up to my chin and bit my lip. "Luke?"

"I'm thinking."

I waited for what seemed like an eternity, half expecting to hear the *Jeopardy!* music. I was in quite the predicament. I wanted him to want to sleep with me—and I meant *sleep* in the literal sense—but that might open a door that was best kept closed.

But what was taking him so long to decide? The longer he took, the faster my heart thudded and the tighter my fingers clenched the edge of the comforter.

Then he finally said, "Okay."

I shifted to the very edge of the bed as he climbed in. "Thanks," he said. "That couch is fucking uncomfortable."

I rolled my eyes in the darkness. Didn't I *just* tell him that?

Luke settled in on the other side of the bed, leaving a space between us, like the gentleman he'd been all night. That just made me like him more.

I paused, letting the realization sink in. I couldn't pretend anymore.

I liked him. It pained me to acknowledge it, but I liked him, and I meant *liked* him liked him. I shouldn't even be considering a relationship, though. On top of my academics, now I had to worry about the small problem of tuition money. If I didn't come up with that, I could kiss my college life good-bye. A relationship was a complication I didn't need and didn't have time for.

Plus, my last one hadn't ended so well. I squeezed my eyes shut and pushed the dark thoughts deep inside. Now wasn't the time.

The sound of Luke's steady breathing filled the room. He was asleep. I wished I could say the same for myself. I shifted into a more comfortable position and pleaded with my brain to silence and allow me to drift off.

I turned again and accidently grazed his leg with my foot. I stiffened and held my breath, but he didn't wake.

It dawned on me that this was the first time I'd slept with someone. I mean, I wasn't a virgin, but my experiences were when I was in high school and I was still living with my parents, so it wasn't like I could sleep all night with a guy.

Huh. I never thought my first time actually *sleeping* with a guy would be like this, strangely impersonal, yet oh-so-intimate at the same time.

I closed my eyes again.

I must have fallen asleep because I woke to find Luke gently shaking my shoulder.

"Hey, sleepyhead." Smiling, he propped himself up on his elbow.

I yanked the covers up over my head. "I'm still tired."

He pulled them back down. "I want to talk to you."

"Can't it wait?" I grumbled. Despite how cute Luke looked with his sleepy morning eyes, I still wasn't keen on being woken up. A morning person I was not.

He shook his head. "It's pretty important."

I sighed. "What is it?"

"I want to say good-bye."

I furrowed my brow. "What do you mean? Are you going somewhere?" I started to sit up, to get ready to leave—I wasn't going to stay here by myself—but his expression stopped me.

It was troubled, his eyes full of sadness. "You could say that."

Something wasn't right.

"Can I go with you?" I asked.

He shook his head again. "I don't want you to."

"Why not?"

"Because." He tucked a strand of hair behind my ear.

I didn't understand. What was he talking about? Where was all this coming from?

Then seemingly from out of nowhere, he pulled out a gun. It was silver and looked like one a cowboy would carry.

My eyes widened. "What is that?" It was a stupid question, born out of the fear that dominated my voice.

"This is my ticket out of here."

I clutched the covers, my knuckles whitening. "What are you talking about?"

"You'll see."

Before I could do anything else, he held the gun up to his temple. "Good-bye, Cori."

Chapter Nine

Screaming. Someone was screaming, a horrifying panicked scream, an I'm-being-chased-by-an-ax-murderer scream.

"Cori! Wake up!"

The screaming stopped as suddenly as it began.

"Don't do it! I'm sorry! I'm so sorry!" I felt someone squeezing my hand and my eyes popped open.

Luke was sitting up in bed next to me, concern in his eyes, my hand in his.

"Oh, God," I whispered. The screams were mine. I pulled my hand away from him and wrapped my arms around myself. Luke scooted back, giving me space.

"Are you okay?" he asked.

"Yes," I whispered. "It was just a nightmare."

My academic mind was taking over, insisting that the dream was just a result of stress. In the last seven days, my life had been turned upside down, smashed into bits with a jackhammer, and then beaten with a club.

Stress. It was just stress.

But knowing that still didn't stop me from shaking or dry

the dampness of my cold sweat.

Luke handed me a bottle of water and I gulped it down gratefully.

"You were pretty deep into it," he said. "I had a hard time waking you."

I clutched the water bottle, refusing to meet his eyes. I couldn't look at him right now. Not without seeing that silver gun pressed to his temple.

"What time is it?"

"Around six."

"Can you take me home now?" I whispered.

He hesitated like he wanted to say something, but wasn't quite sure what to say. "Okay," he said finally, getting out of bed and slipping on some shoes.

The ride to the Alpha house was painfully silent. Luke looked over at me a few times like he still wanted to say something, but ultimately thought better of it.

What could he say? I barely knew him, and I'd had a total freak-out while sleeping in his bed for an impromptu sleepover. The logical part of my brain registered embarrassment, but I didn't feel it yet.

Instead, I felt empty.

When we pulled up to the Alpha house, I immediately opened the door to get out of the car. Luke grabbed my hand, stopping me before I could get out.

"Cori."

"Thanks for the ride," I said stiffly, looking at my feet. I couldn't face him. Not yet.

He waited a few seconds before letting go of my hand and sighing. "You're welcome."

I ran into the house. It was not until I closed the door behind me that I heard him drive away. Luckily it was early enough that my sisters were still in their rooms. I didn't want to have to explain this walk of shame.

I stripped down and stepped into the shower. Sitting on the tiled floor, I pulled my knees to my chest. I squeezed my eyes shut, letting the scalding water rush over my skin. Sobs wracked my body.

Was it my fault? Was I the reason Tyler killed himself?

For about the millionth time, I remembered that last fateful conversation, the one I'd give anything to do over.

"You're being selfish, Cori."

"That's unfair. You're the one who decided to go to college thousands of miles away."

"I couldn't base my college decision on you."

"And you can't expect me to drop everything and jump on a plane whenever you beckon me. I don't have the money. Besides, I have a life here."

"What's so important? Another stupid sorority social with fucking frat guys?"

"You know what, Tyler? I can't do this right now. Call me back when you get your head out of your ass."

That was the last thing Tyler ever heard from another human being.

That's the thing about words. Once they're said, you can't take them back no matter how badly you want to.

What if I hadn't spoken to him that night? What if I'd said something different? What if I'd sucked it up and gotten on a plane to visit him?

Could I have saved him?

Would he still be alive?

We had already drifted apart by then. Our relationship was ending, but we were both stubbornly holding onto something that was broken because it was safe, comfortable. After five years together, it was all we knew. And what if he were still here? Maybe we could've fixed it, fixed us. At the very least, maybe we could've stayed friends. And that was just it.

I'd never know.

• • •

"Cori, wake up."

I pulled the covers over my face.

"I have doughnuts. Chocolate frosted with sprinkles."

I peeked out of my covers to see Amber shaking a bag from the local bakery. *Well played, Amber, well played.* I sat up and she perched on the edge of my bed.

She handed me a doughnut. "I'm sorry. I shouldn't have put you in that situation last night."

I broke off a piece and stuck it in my mouth. "What time is it?" I asked.

"Ten. I would have been home sooner, but Brad had to drop Josh off at his car, and then I had to get the doughnuts."

Yeah, the doughnuts were crucial. She definitely knew the way to soften me up first thing in the morning.

And honestly? Being mad at her didn't seem worth the energy anymore.

I swallowed the last of the doughnut. "It's okay. I'm over it."

"I still feel bad." Guilt filled her blue eyes. "I saw Luke this morning. He told me I should go home and talk to you."

I sat up straighter. "What did he tell you?"

Her brows furrowed. "That's it—just that I should go home and talk to you."

I exhaled and pulled my knees to my chest. "I'm not mad at you. I mean, I was, but I'm over it now. Honest."

She took in my ragged appearance. "Then what's wrong? Did something happen with Luke?"

I took a deep breath. "I had a nightmare."

"Well, that sucks." She waited for me to continue. She knew me well enough to know that wasn't the end of it. It was time to fill her in on what I should have told her days ago.

I sighed. "My parents told me a few days ago that Tyler's car accident wasn't an accident. It was suicide." Amber's expression went from disbelieving to horrified as I filled her in on the details.

"Is that what your nightmare was about?"

I shook my head. "Not exactly. Luke was in it, and he… he had a gun."

"A gun? Why did he have a gun?"

I made a gun shape with my hand and put it up to my temple.

She winced. "Did he…?"

"No. He woke me up right before it happened in the dream."

Amber sat with me in quiet solidarity for a few minutes. "I'm sorry."

Those two simple words were why I loved her. She got it. And she didn't give me a hard time about not telling her about Tyler sooner. She understood me enough to know it wasn't a reflection on our friendship.

I took a shaky breath. "Me, too."

"You know you can talk to me about it."

"I know," I said, and I knew she'd be as good as her word. She might be flighty sometimes and not able to keep her side of the room neat, but she was solid where it counted. I just didn't want to talk about it. So I changed the subject, knowing she'd understand and let it drop.

"I can't believe that it happened when I was sleeping in Luke's bed. Talk about bad timing."

"*What?*" Amber squealed, bouncing on my bed. "Give me details."

I rolled my eyes. "It's not like that. It was just *sleep*. We stayed on our own sides of the bed."

Amber's face fell. "Oh." She looked like a child who'd

gotten socks and underwear for Christmas instead of the pony she'd asked for.

"He was really nice about the whole thing, letting me sleep in the bed while he took the couch, but the couch was way too small for him, so to make a long story short, I told him we could share the bed." I leaned my forehead on my knees. "I'm so embarrassed."

"I'm sure he didn't think anything of it."

It was a nice thought, but I was skeptical. "Then why did he tell you to come talk to me?"

"Maybe he thought you were mad at me? You said you were at first. Did you say anything about it?"

I shook my head. "He let me borrow some clothes. You're going to have to return them for me. I can't face him."

"Honey, it's not that big of a deal. He seems to like you. It's sweet that he was worried about you."

"He probably thinks I'm deranged."

"I doubt that. Everyone has nightmares."

There was more to it than I was telling Amber. It was true I didn't want to face it, but only part of it was due to embarrassment. I was worried that every time I looked at him I would see him holding that gun to his head.

I broke out in a cold sweat just thinking about it. Another change of subject was needed. Pronto.

"Let's talk about something else. Tell me about Brad."

Amber's face lit up and she bounced on the bed again. "I *really* like him. He's cute. Funny, too." She yawned. "Sorry. I didn't get any sleep."

I raised my eyebrows suggestively.

Amber slapped my arm playfully. "No, not because of *that*. We talked all night. Well, we did a little more than talk, but we didn't do *that*." She yawned again.

"Go to sleep." I gently pushed her off my bed. "You can tell me about it later."

"Are you sure? If you want to hang out, I can jump in the shower real quick, and we can do something."

I shook my head. "I'm still pretty tired myself. I just want to lie in bed and read."

She looked at me doubtfully.

"I'm fine." I squeezed her hand. "Promise."

"If you're sure," she said, ambling off to the bathroom.

I spent the afternoon sprawled on my bed, alternating between reading for my classes and reading a romance novel. In other words, keeping my brain busy. My phone rang around two. It was a number I didn't recognize, so I didn't pick up. When it rang again at three from the same number, I answered it.

It was Luke.

"How did you get this number?" I asked in a clipped tone.

He hesitated a moment before answering. "Amber gave it to me."

I realized I sounded like a jerk. *Not cool, Cori.*

"Sorry. I'm just surprised to hear from you." *Lame explanation.* It was true, but it sounded weak.

"I, uh, just wanted to make sure you were okay."

I could picture him holding his phone with one hand and using the other to rub the back of his neck. I'd dubbed that his *bashful look.*

I smiled, despite the situation. Even though I was humiliated by what happened, it *was* sweet of him to call. "I'm fine, thanks."

"All right." There was silence for a few seconds. "I guess I'll see you later then."

"Yeah." I was about to say bye, but I felt I needed to say something about what happened. It was the huge white *thing* in the room. "Luke?"

"Yeah?"

"Thanks. You know, for being understanding."

"No problem."

I hung up feeling better. Some of the tension left my body. Maybe I wouldn't have to choose a new seat in criminology after all.

• • •

I scanned through the list of scholarships offered by the university. Most were major specific, which meant they didn't apply to me. The few that did apply to me had spring deadlines, which meant the money wouldn't be awarded until next fall.

I would have to cast my net wider. I did a general search for scholarships on the internet and found a database that might be helpful.

I clicked on the first scholarship that looked promising. Minimum GPA requirement? No problem. Essay? Check. Letter of recommendation? Can do. Minority status? *Fuck*.

Almost every scholarship had some kind of requirement that disqualified me from even applying. I wasn't at least ten percent Native American, my parents weren't in the blacksmiths' union, and I wasn't willing to teach in Africa for three years after graduation. The list went on and on.

I'd heard all through high school that thousands of dollars in scholarships went unclaimed every year. Now I knew why.

My computer chimed, signaling an incoming email. I opened my email program, grateful for the distraction.

I stared at the sender name on the email, blinking to make sure I was seeing straight, but there it was in pixelated black and white. *Charles Pullman*. Tyler's elusive father. I'd met him twice in the five years that Tyler and I had dated. Why was he contacting me now?

I opened the email to find one line: *Call me at your earliest convenience*. No *please* or anything. There wasn't even a personal signature, just the standard signature at the bottom that went out on every email.

Irritation swelled within me. *Unbelievable.* He couldn't find the time for his son while Tyler was living, and now that he was dead, Mr. Pullman thought he could issue commands to me, his late son's girlfriend.

Screw that.

I drummed my fingertips on the desk. What could he possibly want? It made no sense.

I hovered over the delete button. Then I thought, *what would Tyler want me to do?* I sighed. He'd want me to call his dad. Despite Mr. Pullman's absence, Tyler had always strived to develop a relationship with him, something I'd never understood.

I dialed the number in the email. As it rang once and then twice, I swallowed hard.

"Chuck Pullman." His tone was curt, a busy businessman's voice that screamed of self-importance.

I took a deep breath. "Mr. Pullman, this is Corinne Elliott."

It was silent on the other end except for the sound of papers rustling and people talking in the background.

I cleared my throat. "Cori, you know, Tyler's—"

"I know who you are," he interrupted.

"Okay."

The background noise on his side got quieter. He must have stepped away from wherever he was. "I'd like to see you."

I frowned. That was not even close to anything I expected him to say.

"Why?"

There was a silence again, but this time, I resisted the urge to fill it. Finally, Mr. Pullman said, "I didn't spend much time with my son. I'd like to try to get to know him a little better."

"Through me," I said flatly.

"Obviously."

I clenched my fist. This man was unbelievable. I couldn't believe… There were no words.

"I don't know," I said. "My schedule is pretty busy."

"I'll make it worth your while."

My nostrils flared. *What the hell does that mean?*

I ran my hand over my face. I owed this man nothing. I wanted to tell him where to stick it, but I held my tongue. I might have owed him nothing, but I owed it to Tyler to see his dad at least once.

"Fine."

He was going to be in Roanoke later that week on business. That was only an hour away, so I grudgingly agreed to meet him for dinner.

Fan-frigging-tastic.

Chapter Ten

My feet were dragging on the way to criminology Tuesday morning. I hadn't spoken to Luke since he called on Sunday, and I was an emotional salad bowl, full of insecurity, embarrassment, and hope.

He was sitting in our usual spot when I arrived. He didn't notice me at first, so I was able to observe him. God, he was gorgeous. He was sprawled in the chair, his long jean-clad legs stretched out in front of him. I couldn't see his eyes from this angle, but I could only imagine how his light blue T-shirt would make his eyes seem even bluer.

I took a deep breath and approached slowly. His eyes met mine. Yup, I was right. Blue as a cloud-free sky. My stomach turned over.

He smiled. "Hey."

"Hi." I set my stuff down and slid into my seat. Going through the routine of taking out my notebook and lining up my pens calmed me a little, but my palms were still sweaty. I wiped them on my jeans, hoping he wouldn't notice, which was a long shot. Luke noticed everything.

"Okay, I have to know," Luke said, his expression serious.

I braced myself. If I wanted things to return to normal—whatever that was—I had to expect him to have some questions. "What?"

"What's the deal with the pens?"

I breathed a sigh of relief, laughing a little. "What do you mean?"

"I've watched you take notes for the last two classes. Is there a system? Do different colors mean different things? Or do you just use whatever color strikes your mood?"

"All of the above. I use a different system for each day, depending on what mood I'm in."

He reached over and flipped my notebook back to the notes from the last class. "Okay, so explain this system."

"The purple is the main headings, obviously. The green is what was written in the PowerPoint, and the blue is what she said."

He pointed to the page. "What about the pink?"

I scooted my notebook over so he couldn't read it. "Those are my own thoughts."

His eyes lit up. "Let me see." He reached for my notebook again, but I blocked him by throwing out my elbow, which hit him solidly in the chest.

"Ouch." He rubbed his chest. "You have bony elbows."

"That's what you get for snooping."

He looked down at his black pen. "I suddenly feel inadequate."

I laughed. "Trust me, you're more than adequate."

He tilted his head, a cocky grin spreading wide. "Oh, yeah?" Then the cocky grin changed into something much more dangerous, much more tempting. Something that almost made me forget we were in the middle of a classroom. *You're more than adequate.* I couldn't believe I had said that. Where was the rewind button when you needed it? Luckily

Tanya came in and started the class. *Saved!*

Luke turned his attention to the lecture, and I watched him out of the corner of my eye. I admired that about him. He took his studies seriously.

I caught him peeking at my notes halfway through the class, so I elbowed him gently on his arm. He feigned pain. I wouldn't have minded kissing all the hurt away—faked or not—but self-control had me shaking my head and rolling my eyes. I tried to peek at his notes, but he shielded them with his arm. He shook his finger at me and mouthed, "No, no."

Yes, yes. If he kept looking at me like that, I was going to fail this class. I already had a hard time paying attention with him inches away from me as it was.

Diversion needed.

I rooted around in my backpack until I found an extra blue and green pen. I placed them on the table and nudged them over toward him. I didn't look at him, but I saw him grin out of the corner of my eye and snatch up the pens. He uncapped each of them and started switching between them.

He gestured to his notes, seeking my approval. I shrugged and mouthed, "Not bad."

Not bad, indeed.

. . .

That night, Amber dragged me out to the Beta house. Brad had invited her, so by extension that meant he'd invited me, too. Or that was how her logic worked anyway.

We were hanging out in the party room watching Brad and Josh play a lazy game of beer pong. I wasn't playing because I had biology bright and early tomorrow morning. Bio was hard enough without a hangover.

Luke was nowhere in sight. I was disappointed. Though I wouldn't admit it to anyone, I hoped he'd be here. That was part of the reason I'd agreed to come. That and to shut Amber up. She got whiny when she didn't get her way, and even after years of being friends with her, I still wasn't immune to it.

Brad had his left arm around Amber and was throwing the ball with his right hand. Josh had his new flavor by his side as well. Her name was Brittany or something like that. I was getting the impression he changed girls so often that it really didn't matter if I remembered their names. Chances were I'd never see them again.

I was totally the fifth wheel. I sat on a metal folding chair and watched the game, trying to look more entertained than I felt. I would rather be in bed.

Suddenly, my chair started to tip back, throwing my stomach up into my throat. I shrieked and threw my weight forward, firmly planting my feet on the floor.

"Gotcha," Luke said in my ear, his breath tickling my neck.

Placing my hand over my heart to slow it down, I spun around in my chair. He was wearing a wifebeater and jeans, with a tool belt slung low on his hips. Drool threatened to fall out of my mouth, and my cheeks flushed. His shoulders and arms were muscled and well-defined, his skin smooth and tan. Yum. I attempted to cover up my ogling with a glare. "You almost gave me a heart attack."

He tweaked my nose and grinned. Then he walked away. *Wait. That's all I get?*

My face fell, but I recovered quickly, carefully returning it to a neutral expression. My heart did a little pitter-patter when Luke walked back over with a chair. He set it up next to mine and stretched out in it, crossing his feet at his ankles.

"You want in?" Brad asked him.

Luke shook his head. "Nah. I've got to finish writing this damn paper." He turned to me. "I have this professor who's already assigned a ten-page paper. Can you believe that? It's only the second week."

"Maybe he's trying to weed people out."

"Could be. Hopefully after the drop period ends, he'll ease up a little. Because, damn, I do not want to write a paper every week."

"You should get Cori to help you," Amber chimed in, her arm in the air, practicing the throwing motion. She had one of her eyes closed, which was probably supposed to help her aim. "She helps me with all of my papers." She winked at me when she thought Luke wasn't looking, except I'm pretty sure he was.

Real smooth, Amber. She launched the ball and missed. *Serves her right.*

"Um, sure," I said, running my toe along a crack in the concrete floor.

"Don't sound too excited about it, Miss Valedictorian," Luke said.

I made a face, but I was pleased he remembered that little detail about me.

I gestured to the tool belt. "What's up with that?"

He glanced down as if he had forgotten he was wearing it. "Oh, this. I was fixing the deck stairs. I'm the house manager."

I raised my eyebrows. "I didn't know you were a handyman."

He shrugged. "Pays the rent and keeps me from having to get another job."

Sitting next to the beer pong table with Luke's prize trophy in view, I couldn't help but wonder at the juxtaposition of his personality. He liked to party and have a good time. I could certainly attest to that in the short time I'd known him, but he also bore responsibilities and seemed serious about his schoolwork, much more so than Brad and Josh, who were currently setting up cups for another game. Yet the guys didn't give him shit for not playing, showing they respected him.

Something had to give. Nobody was that perfect.

I looked over at him out of the corner of my eye, then guiltily looked away. I shouldn't be looking for flaws. If they were there, they'd surface eventually.

Probably.

He nudged me with his foot. "I'm going to propose your idea for recruiting pledges at our next meeting."

"It's worth a shot."

"I agree. Hopefully my asshole brothers will get on board."

I raised my eyebrows.

"Some of the guys are assholes," he said. "There's bound to be at least one in every group. Don't you have some in your sorority?"

Since our sorority was so big, I didn't know all of my sisters very well. In the group of about a hundred girls, there were several smaller cliques. This may seem to go against the notion of sisterhood, but it actually kept the peace. There were bound to be girls who didn't get along, and this way they didn't have to interact.

Luke took my silence as a refusal to speak ill of my sisters. "Okay, take the high road. Make me look like the asshole."

I waited a beat. "Do you even need my help for that?"

"Very funny." He stretched and looked at his watch. "Shit. It's almost eleven. I better go finish this paper. See you later, Cori."

Disappointment washed over me. I appreciated that he wanted to get his paper done, but why did his damn professor have to assign it in the first place? Now his professor was pissing *me* off.

I waited another ten minutes, and then I motioned to Amber that it was getting late. She held up five fingers. *Five more minutes.* I sighed, sitting back in my chair. We had taken her car, and I had no other option for getting home. Buses didn't run this far and the DD didn't run on weeknights.

Twenty minutes later, I gave Amber a look that meant *let's get out of here*. She held up five fingers again. Yeah, right.

I sat in my seat, tuning everyone out. I was tired. I wanted to go home. And the loud music was giving me a headache.

Ten minutes passed. I looked up just in time to see Amber accept a drink that Brad pressed into her hand. So much for five more minutes.

Irritation flared within me. I should have known better than to go out with Amber where a guy was concerned. I guess I didn't learn my lesson last time.

I decided to wander upstairs to Luke's room. Maybe he wouldn't mind if I dozed on his couch while I waited for Amber to decide she was finally ready to leave.

We were friends, right? I was still navigating this new friend thing. Sure, I had guy friends, but never ones like Luke, ones who made my heart palpitate and my palms sweat.

His door was ajar, but I knocked anyway. He was sitting at his computer with his back to the door. When he didn't respond, I noticed he had earbuds in.

I leaned against the doorframe and observed him for a moment. His long fingers danced over the keyboard, and I could see the muscles flex in his arms as he typed. He paused, putting his hands on the back of his head. Then he deleted a line of text and started typing again.

I don't know how long I watched him. One minute? Two? I was definitely indulging in some creeper behavior.

I knocked again, but he still didn't hear me. How loud did he have his music turned up? Geez, he was going to blow out his eardrums.

"Luke?" I said loudly. I was about to give up and return to the party room when he finally turned around, hitting the pause button on his iPod.

"Sorry," he said with a smile. "I was in the zone."

"Oh." I fiddled with my necklace. "I'll just leave you alone then." I turned around to leave, feeling stupid. Of course he didn't want company—he was working. I didn't like to be bothered when I was working, either, so I should know better.

"No, that's okay. Stay."

I hesitated, then walked across his room and sat on the edge of the couch. "I don't want to bother you. It's just that I have a headache and the music is loud down there."

"Yeah, try living here. That's why I use the earbuds."

"How is that any different from what's downstairs?"

He blushed a little, the pink hue spreading from ear to ear. Straight from sexy to adorable. I was definitely intrigued.

He motioned for me to come over. "I'll let you in on a little secret."

I crossed the room and he handed me an earbud, which I put in my ear. He hit play, and classical music filled my ears. I didn't recognize it, which meant that it probably wasn't Beethoven or Mozart. My knowledge of classical music was lacking.

"My older sister had a baby a few years ago, and she always played classical music for him both before and after he was born," he explained. "It's supposed to make him smarter or something. So, I figured, why not? It sure as hell can't hurt. Now I'm hooked on it. It's the only way I can study, especially living here."

I handed back the earbud. "Did it work?"

He gave me a blank stare.

"For your nephew," I clarified. "Is he smart?"

"Oh, yeah. He's three, and he's a hellion. Here." He opened a file on the computer and up popped a picture of a little boy. I leaned in to get a better look. The kid had dark brown hair and a twinkle in his light blue eyes.

"He looks like you," I commented.

"That's what everyone says."

"He's a cute kid."

"Thanks."

I didn't realize how close I was to Luke until I went to back up. If I moved a few inches to the left, I would be sitting in his lap. I thought back to the last time I was in his lap—in the DD's car. I could faintly smell his cologne, and my stomach immediately tightened.

I stood up abruptly. "I can go so you can finish your paper."

"No biggie. You can hang here if you want," he offered. "I do have to work on my paper, though."

"That's fine." I sat on the couch. "You won't even know I'm here."

His gaze traveled the length of my body slowly before landing on my eyes. "I doubt that."

My insides warmed, and I was half a second away from jumping into his lap, but he put his earbuds in and turned back to his computer.

I took a deep breath. *Get it together, Cori.* Friends don't jump each other's bones. We weren't *those* kinds of friends.

I took off my shoes and curled up on the couch. Might as well make myself comfortable. Who knew how long I'd be here?

I must have dozed off because I was startled awake by the chime of my cell phone. It was a text from Amber.

In Brad's room. Where r u?

I texted back. *Luke's room.*

WHAT! Give me details!

I rolled my eyes. *Not like that. You ready to go?*

Five minutes.

You said that over an hour ago!

She didn't respond. I sighed, looking at the time.

Luke spun around in his chair. "I can take you home if you want."

I hesitated. I felt bad making him go out, but it was super late, and I needed to get home. Amber probably couldn't drive, and I could always take her car, but it was stick shift and I wasn't too confident in my shifting abilities. I could probably get by in a pinch, but I didn't want to try it in the dark if I didn't have to.

Luke stood and grabbed his keys. "Come on."

"Thanks," I said gratefully.

His car was a Jeep with no doors or top and ginormous tires. I clambered up into the passenger's side.

The wind made it pretty loud on the ride home, so that meant no small talk. I texted Amber on the way to let her know I left. I was no hypocrite.

When we pulled up to the Alpha house, Luke put the car in neutral.

I quickly undid my seat belt and prepared to exit the Jeep, hoping I could do so more gracefully than when I got in.

"Thanks again," I said.

"Anytime. Hey, Cori?"

I turned. "Yeah?"

"You want to go out this weekend? Maybe dinner and a movie or something?"

My mind whirled. My immediate gut reaction was *YES!* Then reality set in. How could I even think about a date when I was planning to have dinner with my dead boyfriend's father tomorrow night? It just seemed...wrong.

Because it *was* wrong.

But I liked Luke.

I hadn't planned to. In fact, a relationship did not fit in

my life plan right now, not in the least. I had more important things to deal with, like tuition. Getting involved with Luke would only add another complication to my life.

But I couldn't deny my attraction to him. Even now at nearly one in the morning when I probably looked like I'd been run over by the Jeep instead of ridden in it, he looked like he walked out of a cologne ad, sexy stubble on his face and all.

And what if things went wrong? If the past two weeks were any indication, it seemed like I would be seeing him a lot over the next few months. I didn't want to set myself up for a semester of awkward encounters.

"You can pick the movie, if that makes a difference." His hand remained on the shifter, but his thumb tapped rapidly.

I realized I was taking too long to respond.

Wait, was he nervous?

He looked out the windshield instead of at me. He *was* nervous. That realization made me giddy. He *liked* me.

What the hell. Amber was always telling me I was too uptight. So I went with my gut. "Yes."

"Friday?"

I nodded and hopped down out of the Jeep. It was more of a falling hop, but still.

Right before I shut the door, he said, "Cori? Don't pick a chick flick, okay? You're cooler than that."

I grinned. "I guess you'll find out." I slammed the door and walked to the house. I didn't turn around until I got to the front door. I gave him a little wave. He waved back, but he didn't drive off until I was safely inside.

I leaned against the door and hugged myself, sighing like a heroine in a silly teen movie.

I felt like one.

I hadn't been on a first date since I was fourteen. Not since Tyler— No. I wasn't ruining this. For the first time in a while, I was happy. Ridiculously, deliriously happy. I didn't realize how *unhappy* I'd been.

"You're allowed to be happy."

The therapist my parents had sent me to after Tyler died used to tell me that all the time. I hadn't understood until now.

I still had a lot of crap going wrong in my life, like lack of tuition and a dead boyfriend, but for tonight, I was allowing myself to be happy.

Chapter Eleven

I checked my face in the rearview mirror and pulled out my compact for a touch-up even though I didn't need it.

I was ten minutes early for my dinner with Mr. Pullman. I glanced at my cell phone. No new messages since two minutes ago.

Yup, I was using every stall tactic in the book. I was so not looking forward to this dinner. At least I would get a good meal out of it. The restaurant looked like the type that required coats and ties and had real linen tablecloths. I was glad I'd changed into a skirt.

I hadn't seen the man since graduation. And I'd only met him one time other than that in five years. So forgive me if I didn't have much sympathy for him. True, he'd lost his son, but he hadn't been a real father to Tyler.

When I got down to two minutes left, I gave in to the inevitable and left the safety of my car. I never should have agreed to this meeting.

The restaurant lobby was dimly lit with rich wooden paneling and thick maroon carpet. The furniture was heavy and had ornately carved patterns. A maître d' stood erectly at a podium. I gave him my name, but Mr. Pullman hadn't arrived yet, so I sat down to wait in a chair that could have doubled as a throne.

When Mr. Pullman walked in, he glanced around. His gaze rested on me for a moment before passing me over.

He didn't recognize me.

I stood and smoothed down my skirt. "Mr. Pullman."

He smiled a smooth businessman's smile and crossed to me. "Cori, of course. It's been too long."

I shook his hand and in his face I saw the ghost of the boy I once loved. If Tyler had lived, I imagine he would have eventually looked just like his father. Sandy hair, brown eyes, an aristocratic nose—the Pullman men were handsome in a posh sort of way.

My hand lingered in his a moment too long and I noticed the shape of it was eerily similar to Tyler's. I yanked my hand away, taking a step back as my heart hammered. This was definitely a mistake.

Slight shock shone in his eyes before his face returned to a carefully polished expression. He smiled tightly. "Shall we?"

I followed the maître d' to our table where he pulled my chair out for me and placed my napkin in my lap. While I could appreciate fine dining, I was more of a peanuts-on-the-floor restaurant type of girl. I was right about linen tablecloths. There was also more silverware than I knew what to do with.

Mr. Pullman perused the wine list. "I hear they have a lovely merlot from a local winery. Have you tried it?" He looked up from the wine list and peered at me over his reading glasses.

"I'm nineteen," I replied flatly. "The same age as your son."

He cleared his throat and focused his attention on the wine list again. "Yes, of course."

I opened my menu with shaking hands and used it to block my face while I regained control of my emotions. The bastard didn't even know how old his own damn son was.

After the waiter poured the wine and took our orders, I could no longer hide behind the safety of the menu. I straightened my spine and set my hands in my lap. I wouldn't let him see me squirm.

Mr. Pullman held up his wine glass, rotating his wrist so that the liquid swirled. "Tell me about yourself, Cori."

I blinked, caught off guard by the question. "What do you want to know?" There was no way I was making this easy for him.

"For starters, what's your major?"

"Political science, pre-law."

"That's much different than Tyler's." The intonation of his voice indicated that he didn't know if this should be a question or not.

I leaned forward. "Do you even know what his major was?"

"Of course," he said dismissively. "Science."

I shook my head in disbelief. "You don't know, do you?"

He placed his wine glass on the table and steepled his fingers. "Why do you think I asked to see you?"

I gritted my teeth, looking away. I'd known going into this he barely knew Tyler. Seeing it first hand, though, irked me. Tyler had deserved better.

"Biochemistry," I said.

"Interesting. What did he plan to do with it?"

I wasn't sure I could answer the question. In high school, Tyler had wanted to do medical research, like finding a cure for cancer. That could have changed in that last year, and I wouldn't know.

I fiddled with my fork. "I'm not sure I'm the best person to help you get to know Tyler. That last year, he and I weren't... as close as we used to be."

"Yet you still wear his necklace around your neck."

My hand flew to my throat, where the silver necklace had freed itself from under my blouse. "How did you know he gave me this?"

Mr. Pullman smiled smugly, and I hated him a little more. "I was with him when he bought it. I did see my son occasionally."

"Why only occasionally?"

He looked away. "I'm not here to discuss that."

"Don't you think—"

He slammed his fist on the table, rattling the silverware. "That's between me and my son."

The other patrons in the restaurant looked over at us curiously.

I leaned back in my chair. "Your son is dead." I threw my napkin on the table and stood. "This was a mistake."

Whatever problems Tyler and I had had, I'd loved him. I couldn't say the same for this man. I refused to be disloyal to Tyler's memory by discussing him with his sham of a father.

Mr. Pullman grabbed my wrist as I walked past. "Please, stay." I started to pull free, but his pleading eyes, so much like Tyler's, weakened me. I returned to my seat and crossed my arms.

"I'm a very busy man." He took a deep breath, showing a crack in his armor. "I always thought I would have time for Tyler later. I was never good with children, so I figured when he became an adult, we could develop a relationship."

I frowned and shook my head. "It doesn't work that way."

Our conversation was halted as the waiter placed salads in front of us and offered fresh ground pepper.

Mr. Pullman poked at his salad, a grimace on his face. I

clenched my fork, knuckles turning white. Tyler used to do the same thing. He always ordered salad as a starter even though he didn't seem to like it, only ever taking a few bites.

Mr. Pullman looked at me expectantly, and I realized he must have said something. "I'm sorry. What?"

"Can you share one of your favorite memories of Tyler?" he asked. His voice somehow seemed small, like he'd lost some of his authority, his power. He was asking me to take pity on him.

I leaned back in my chair, pondering. Tyler and I had been inseparable all four years in high school, plus we were still together our first year in college, even if it was rough. Five years' worth of memories was a lot to sift through.

The most recent memories came to mind first, like the last time we saw each other—familiar and awkward at the same time. We had both known things had changed but neither of us had been willing to admit it. Stubbornness was a trait we shared.

I went back further and smiled as one memory came to mind. "I had a pageant the same night as Tyler's semi-final soccer game. The pageant was in Hudson Hall, so it was a pretty formal affair. Even the audience was expected to dress for it. Anyway, Tyler always came to my pageants. He never missed one. At the end of the opening number, there was a scuffle in the audience. It was so loud we heard it from backstage. I peeked through the curtains to see Tyler arguing with a security guard. He was wearing his soccer uniform, which was covered in mud and grass stains. He didn't have time to go home and change first, and he refused to leave. I don't know what he did, but eventually he must have convinced the guard to let him stay, because there he was sitting in the front row, grass stains and all, when I went onstage to do my talent."

My chin quivered and tears threatened to spill over. I

sucked in my lip and blotted the tears out of my eyes with my napkin.

Mr. Pullman smiled, his salad long forgotten. "He sounds like he was very devoted to you."

A knot formed in my throat, and I bit my lip to keep from crying. "He was a great boyfriend."

• • •

I sat in my car in the parking lot long after Mr. Pullman had left. I hadn't looked forward to this meeting, but I also hadn't realized exactly how difficult it would be.

I tried not to think about Tyler often. It was the only way I was able to move forward. Or so I had thought. Recently I'd realized I hadn't been moving forward at all—I'd just been treading in place, barely keeping my head high enough to continue breathing.

The fact was that if he had lived, we'd probably be broken up by now anyway. But it was the *probably* that killed me. I didn't know what might have actually happened. Maybe we would have worked things out. Maybe not.

But I would never know.

And there was nothing to be gained from wondering about it.

I took a deep breath. Closing my eyes, I willed the thoughts of Tyler back into the recesses of my mind. I pictured a steel door and shut those memories behind it.

I looked down at the plain white envelope sitting in my lap. Mr. Pullman had handed it to me before we parted ways. I opened it now and found a check for one thousand dollars.

My mouth formed an O.

What…the…hell.

I guess Mr. Pullman meant it when he said he'd make it worth my while.

I crammed the check back in the envelope and stuffed the envelope in my purse, out of sight.

I couldn't accept the money, could I? There was something that seemed wrong about it, like I was selling out or something, like I was cheap.

Mr. Pullman was loaded, so it wasn't a financial hardship for him. I didn't know exactly how much money he had, but this was probably just a drop in the bucket for him.

For me, this check would go a long way toward my tuition for next semester.

My hands gripped the steering wheel, and I stared at the corner of the envelope sticking out of my purse.

I hadn't done anything wrong. Having dinner with my deceased boyfriend's father was not wrong. And if he wanted to make an investment in my education, so be it.

It's not like I'd asked for the money. It wasn't a condition of my meeting him. I hadn't put a price on my memories of Tyler.

And each day that passed was one day closer to my spring tuition being due. So far my search for scholarships had turned up next to nothing.

I didn't have time for sentimentality where my spring tuition was concerned. I needed money, and I needed it now. It was practical, pure and simple. I would be foolish not to take advantage of this gift.

I swallowed my lingering doubts and started the ignition. I needed to get to the ATM to deposit this check before I changed my mind.

Chapter Twelve

Luke slid into the seat next to me in criminology. "Did you pick the movie yet?"

I gave him what I hoped was a coy smile. I wasn't necessarily trying to flirt with him. I just hadn't chosen a movie yet. It'd totally slipped my mind between dinner with Mr. Pullman and working on two scholarship essays.

He rapped his fist against his forehead, closed his eyes, and groaned. "You picked a chick flick, didn't you?"

I smiled serenely. The truth was that I didn't even know what was playing. I was a little out of touch.

"If you did, that's okay. I'm a man of my word. I'll watch it." The look on his face was pained, like he'd just hit his thumb with a hammer or something. It might be worth it to choose a chick flick just to see his expression during the movie.

"What's so bad with chick flicks?" I asked with a straight face. "They have happy endings. Everyone likes a happy ending."

"Action movies have happy endings."

"Everything blows up in action movies. And people get killed…a lot."

"Yeah, all the bad guys. The good guys always win in the end."

"Which is completely unrealistic."

"And chick flicks aren't?"

"Girl meets boy. Girl falls in love with boy. They live happily ever after. Seems pretty realistic to me." The irony of what I was saying struck me. If only it were that simple. Still, I had started my argument, so I was seeing it through. "Much more realistic than one guy beating up, like, what, a hundred guys or something like that?"

He waved his hand dismissively. "Details."

I raised an eyebrow. "You know, you're all about the details until they go against your purpose."

Luke opened his mouth to reply, but he was saved from spouting what would have undoubtedly been a lame response by Tanya's arrival. She promptly started class. That was one of the things I liked about her. She didn't mess around.

I was pleased to see that Luke continued to use multiple color pens to take notes. I wondered if he did the same thing in his other classes. It would be easy enough to find out the next time I was at the Beta house. I knew where he kept his binders.

Class also ended promptly, a little earlier than normal actually.

Luke put his binder in his backpack and zipped it up. "Is six good for tomorrow night?"

I nodded, gulping a little. This was really happening.

Grinning, he reached out and playfully tugged on a lock of my hair that was hanging on my shoulder. "See you then."

• • •

"What are you wearing?" Amber said.

"Huh?" I looked down at my clothes, confused. I was wearing shorts and a T-shirt. We were in our room, Amber hunched over her toes, painting each one a different color, me reading my criminology textbook with highlighter in hand. I would be getting a lot more done if Amber would stop talking to me.

She rolled her eyes. "Not now, silly. Tomorrow night."

Surprisingly, this was the closest she'd gotten to grilling me about my date with Luke.

"I haven't thought about it."

And I hadn't. On purpose. I was trying to stay cool, calm, and collected about this. So what if it'd been almost six years since I'd been on a first date?

Except when I put it that way, I started to hyperventilate a little.

"Where's he taking you?"

"Dinner and a movie."

"I *know* that." She sighed. "*Where* are you going for dinner?"

"I didn't ask."

"So you don't know?" A look of horror crossed her face.

"No. Is that a problem?"

"Uh, yeah." Her expression clearly said *you're an idiot*. "If you're going to a fancy restaurant, then you need to dress up. If you're just going to McDonald's, then that's something else."

"I highly doubt he's taking me to McDonald's," I said drily.

"You know, I never would have thought that was possible on a first date, but after that one guy last year..." She shuddered. "I don't even remember his name. I've blocked it out of my memory." Another guy from Amber's sparkling track record. And speaking of her track record—

"When is Brad going to take you out on a formal date?"

"That is an excellent question," she huffed. "Let me know if you figure out the answer to that one, because I sure as hell don't know."

"Uh-oh. Trouble in paradise?"

She screwed the top on her nail polish. "Yes. No. I don't know. Maybe I've been too forward."

"You haven't...?"

She shot me a dirty look. "No, I haven't slept with him." She gestured to herself. "This milk ain't free. I at least need some dinner or something first."

She had my sympathy. They could make a sitcom based on her dating experiences.

"And you're changing the subject," she said. "This isn't about me. *You're* the one with a date. Decide what you're going to wear, and I'll tell you if it's acceptable."

I looked longingly at my textbook and highlighter. "Now?"

"Yes."

With a sigh, I closed the book and went to stand in front of my closet. The sooner I got this over with, the sooner I could get back to studying. There was a reason I hadn't picked an outfit yet. I didn't want to obsess over this whole thing. I had a track record of being *weird* where Luke was concerned.

And besides, he'd already seen me in everything from jeans to party clothes to my performance dress. Heck, he'd even seen me in his clothes. It wasn't like I needed to make a first impression. It was much too late for that.

I pulled out a baby blue button-down shirt at random.

"Eww, no." Amber made a face. "This isn't a job interview."

I gave her an insulted look. That was a nice shirt. Still, I shoved it back into the closet and pulled out another. This one was also met with rejection.

"What do you suggest?" I asked. She might as well just cut to the chase and tell me what to wear now rather than us going through this song and dance of me suggesting things she was just going to inevitably reject.

"A dress."

"I don't know. That seems so formal."

"When's the last time you went on a first date? Weren't you, like, fourteen or something?"

"So?" I said defensively. Cue the hyperventilation. *See?* That's why I hadn't done this.

"Relax. I'm not criticizing." She paused. "Well, not much anyway. The point is you're out of practice." She stood and waddled over to my closet, careful not to smudge her toenail polish. She looked through my closet until she spotted some black fabric in the back. "What's this in the back? A little black dress?"

It was a black dress, but not the kind she was thinking of. She pulled it out, and I immediately snatched it out of her hands and hung it back up.

"Is that what I think it was?"

If she thought it was the dress I'd worn to Tyler's funeral, then she thought correctly.

I nodded stiffly.

"Why do you have that here?" she asked incredulously.

I crossed my arms, refusing to answer her. It was a question that I had often asked myself, but when it came time to pack my stuff up at my parents' house, I couldn't leave it behind.

She looked at where it was hanging in the closet, barely visible, her confusion evident. "Are you planning to wear it?"

"Of course not."

"Then why do you have it?" At my angry look, she hastily added, "I'm not judging you, I promise. I'm just trying to understand. Why do that to yourself?"

Before I knew what I was doing, I reached out and touched the fabric with my fingertips. It was scratchy, just as I remembered. Scratchy and suffocating.

"I don't know." I was unable to explain my actions. "If I left it at home, my mom would probably get rid of it."

"Would that be a bad thing?" she asked gently.

She had a valid point. The dress was a memento from one of the worst days of my life. I had sat in the front of the church right behind Tyler's family, one of the best seats in the house. The view was— I took a shaky breath, remembering. I could see the casket clearly from where I was sitting, a rich mahogany. People told me afterward that the service was *beautiful*. How could a funeral be fucking *beautiful*? It didn't matter anyway. How could I listen to what anyone was saying when all I could look at was that box and think about who was inside?

I balled the dress up in my hands. Tears started to gather in my eyes.

"Okay, okay," she said quickly. "Let's not talk about it anymore. This is a happy thing we're doing—picking an outfit that will drive Luke crazy." She took my hands in hers and shook them, like she was trying to shake off the somber mood. "Let's be happy here."

I leaned my head back and closed my eyes, taking a few deep breaths, each one burying the memories. When I was done, I opened my eyes and righted my head. "Okay."

"You good now?"

I took another deep breath and nodded.

She smiled. "Good. What other dresses do you have?"

I pulled out a spaghetti strap dress in a navy print with pink and yellow flowers and a ruffled bodice. It fell to mid-thigh.

Amber clapped her hands. "You've been holding out on me! This is *perfect*. Wear it with heels."

"I don't want to be too tall." At five foot six, I wasn't overly tall, but add three inches to that and I started to feel like an Amazonian.

She snorted. "I wish I had that problem." Even in four inch heels, Amber barely came up to my nose when I was in flats. "Anyway, Luke's tall. You won't be taller than him."

"I don't know." I hesitated, trying to come up with an excuse to wear jeans. "It might be cold at the restaurant and in the movie theater."

Amber hopped over to her own closet and pulled out a cropped jean jacket. "Problem solved."

I stood in front of the mirror holding the ensemble up to my body. *Not bad.* Then the realization set in that I was really and truly going on a date with Luke.

Cue the obsessing.

• • •

Luke was right on time. He'd even put a top and doors on his Jeep, thank goodness. Amber spent a good thirty minutes curling my normally stick-straight hair, and I'd hate to see it ruined in the first five minutes.

I waited at the front door for him, so I ran out to meet him before he had even turned the ignition off and quickly clambered up into the passenger seat. I wish he'd installed a step when he put the doors on. At least the door handle gave me something to hold onto while I hoisted myself up.

He smiled. "I was going to get out and open the door for you."

I folded my hands in my lap. *Shit.* Had I screwed up already? Amber had been right when she pointed out how long it'd been since I'd been on a first date. I didn't know the rules anymore. But wasn't chivalry supposed to be dead? Luke must not have gotten the memo.

We sat idling in the parking lot. I shot him a confused look. "Are we going?"

"Buckle up."

I blushed. "Oh, yeah." I pulled the seat belt across my body and we were off.

Luke had the radio tuned to an interview with the university football coach, which suited me just fine. Small talk was overrated.

He took us to a steak house. True to his word, he hopped out and came around to my side of the Jeep to open my door. He held out his hand, which I took, and I tried to climb down without showing off my business to the world. Easier said than done.

There was already a crowd of people waiting, so I found a corner to stand in while he put our names on the list. The restaurant was the type that gave out buckets of peanuts and people threw their peanut shells on the floor. Somehow one got lodged in my sandal. I was considering the best way to get it out when Luke came over with a buzzer and a bucket of peanuts.

"It should be about thirty minutes," he said.

I nodded and shifted. That damn shell was really digging in. I shifted again and then inhaled sharply as the shell dug into my skin.

Luke's expression was alarmed. "What's wrong?"

"The peanuts—"

"Oh, shit. Are you allergic to peanuts?"

I shook my head.

He exhaled. "Thank God. I didn't even think to ask about that. Is this place okay? If not, we can go somewhere else."

"I like this place. It's just—" God, this was embarrassing. "There's a peanut shell stuck in my shoe."

He laughed. "Is that all?" Kneeling, he handed me the

bucket and buzzer. He patted his knee.

I looked at him in shock. "You don't have to do that. I mean, it's on my foot."

"Come on, Cinderella. Give me your foot."

I hesitated. That damn shell was really hurting me, though, so I put my foot up on his knee, careful again to hold down my dress. He slipped the shoe off my foot and shook it out. Then he replaced it and even re-buckled the strap in the right hole. Impressive.

"Better?" he asked.

I put the weight back on my foot and sighed with relief. "Much."

I handed him the peanuts, but held onto the buzzer. He grinned.

He nodded with a gleam in his eye. "Make sure you include that in your report tonight."

"What are you talking about?"

"Isn't that what you girls do? The entire Alpha house will know about our date by tomorrow."

I raised my eyebrows. "Is that what you think I'm going to do? Give my sisters the play-by-play as soon as you drop me off?"

"Oh, yeah." He grinned. "Right before the pillow fight in your lacy underwear."

I rolled my eyes. "You are so delusional."

He popped a peanut into his mouth. "Not delusional. Just hopeful."

"Sorry to shatter your hopes and dreams, but this dress is more revealing than my pajamas."

He gave me the once-over with his eyes. I smoothed down the dress self-consciously. I'd all but invited him to check me out and he'd accepted. "It is a very nice dress," he assured me, his tone naughty.

My thoughts were equally naughty. I silently thanked

Amber for convincing me to wear this.

"Thank you."

He fingered one of my curls. "This is nice, too." His finger grazed my throat, lingering there briefly.

"Thank you. Again."

He looked at me expectantly. "Come on. Don't leave me hanging. It's your turn to say something nice about me."

I stood back and put a hand up to my chin, making a show out of checking him out. He was wearing dark jeans and a blue polo shirt, which brought out his eyes. I wondered if he did that on purpose. He was clean shaven, and he didn't wear any jewelry other than a watch. I liked that about him. He was low maintenance.

"Very nice," I said.

"I feel like such a piece of meat."

I laughed. "You loved it."

He smiled. "You want a peanut?"

I took a peanut out of the bucket and cracked it open. Our buzzer went off then, and we waded through the crowd of people to get to the hostess station.

Over dinner I learned a lot about Luke. He was from northern Virginia. He told me about growing up as the middle child. He'd played baseball in high school and had hoped to play in college, but then he injured his shoulder his senior year, ruining his chance at a scholarship. He didn't seem bitter about it, though. He was graduating with a business degree next year, but had no idea what he wanted to do with it. He was considering getting his MBA while he figured it out.

While we were waiting for the server to return with his credit card, Luke leaned back in his chair and sighed. "Okay, hit me with it. What movie are we seeing tonight?"

"There's a new Reese Witherspoon rom-com," I gushed.

He flinched, but recovered quickly. "Okay."

I laughed. "I'm just kidding. There's that new Marvel movie."

His eyes lit up. "Seriously?" He was way too excited for this.

It was my turn to lean back in my chair. I raised my eyebrows. "Are you a closet comic book nerd?"

"First of all, superheroes are cool. And second of all, I'm not a closet anything. My life is an open book."

"An open book, huh?" I racked my brain, trying to come up with something I wanted to ask about that open book. Our server came back with his credit card, and I missed my window of opportunity. *Damn.* Too slow.

He guided me out of the restaurant with his hand on the small of my back, even carrying my doggy bag. He was definitely playing the gentleman card, and I couldn't deny that I enjoyed the chivalry.

"Are you going to the game tomorrow?" he asked once we were in the Jeep and on the way to the movie theater. Tomorrow was the first home football game of the year.

"Nope."

"Why not?"

I shrugged. "I don't know. I'm just not."

He glanced over at me. "Do you want to go?"

"Are you already asking me on a second date when this one's not even over yet?"

If so, yes please!

"No, I'm doing you a favor. Even though our team sucks this year, you should still go."

"Why?"

He looked at me like I'd grown a second head. "Because college football is awesome."

"I went to a few games last year. It was okay."

"You must have been doing something wrong."

I laughed. "How can you do that wrong? You go to the

game, you watch the game. Done."

He shook his head sadly. "Cori, this is just sad. You don't even know what's wrong with what you just said. Do yourself a favor and come to the game with us tomorrow."

"I don't have a ticket."

"We have extras."

I still wasn't convinced. And I'd planned to go to the tutoring center to see if I could get a work study position or something. I didn't know if they did that, but I was getting nowhere with the tuition situation. Getting a job was not part of my plan, but a position at the tutoring center on campus wouldn't be the worst thing ever.

The theater wasn't far from the restaurant, so we were already in the parking lot, looking for an open space. He found one in the last row and pulled in.

He turned to me. "Even if you end up regretting going on this date with me, you won't regret going to the game with the Beta Chis tomorrow."

"I don't regret this date," I said quickly.

"Your hesitation here is making me wonder."

"Sorry," I said, looking down at my lap. "I haven't been on a date in a while."

"Really?" he questioned, surprise in his voice.

I looked up sharply. Maybe I shouldn't have told him that. I didn't want him to think I was a social leper, but I wasn't ready to share the truth with him, either. That wasn't a subject easily broached, but I'd have to tell him eventually.

Maybe.

"Sorry," he said. "I'm just surprised, that's all. You're hot, you're fun, you're nice, and you're smart. I would keep going, but I want your ego to fit in the theater."

I smiled. Who wouldn't after a guy like Luke said something like that?

Still, I used the opening to change the subject. "Speaking

of which, we'd better go or we'll miss the beginning."

He glanced at his watch. "Shit." He hopped out and jogged around to my side of the car to help me out.

He bought our tickets and nodded at the snack bar. "You want something?"

I looked at him incredulously. "Half of my dinner is in your Jeep."

"I know. Just being a good date." He grinned. "Make sure that goes in your report tonight at your pajama party."

I just shook my head and he laughed, grabbing my hand and pulling me toward the theater. We easily agreed on seats—about a quarter of the way down from the back on the aisle. Thank goodness for that. That was the only place to sit in a theater as far as I was concerned.

The lights dimmed and I was suddenly all too aware of his presence next to me. I'd just spent the last two hours with him at the restaurant, but that was different. We were sitting across from each other at a table, talking. We talked several times a week in class and when we hung out with the other Betas and Amber. That was nothing new.

Sitting close together in the dark in a theater where a hundred clichéd date things could happen threw me for a loop. For instance, the armrest between us was the kind that could be raised up. Should I have asked if he wanted to raise it?

I looked over at him out of the corner of my eye. He seemed perfectly relaxed with his left foot propped up on his right knee. Why was he so relaxed? Why wasn't he nervous like I was? Was it because he had a lot of experience with dating? How many girls had he gone out with? He was surprised I hadn't dated more. Did that imply that he went on a lot of dates?

And I was obsessing.

Tighten up, Corinne.

A reminder came on the screen to silence cell phones. I pulled mine out, happy to have something else to focus on. I checked to make sure my phone was on vibrate and saw that I missed several texts from Amber. She apparently couldn't wait until I got home to find out how my date went.

Maybe Luke's theory about girls and the after-date report was truer than I realized. As everyone seemed to be reminding me lately, I had been out of the game for a while.

I tucked my phone back in my purse and settled in to watch the previews. I *loved* the previews, sometimes even more than the actual movie. They brought the promise of something great. Previews were a conglomeration of the best five minutes of a film, designed to leave you wanting more. It was rare that a movie could ever live up to its preview.

The movie itself started with a bang, literally. I jumped as a car exploded unexpectedly on the screen.

Luke looked over at me, then grabbed my hand and squeezed as if to reassure me. He didn't let go.

Heaven.

The movie was pretty good. I liked superhero movies. My younger brother was into superheroes as a kid, and I'd always watched the cartoons with him. It was the one thing we still did together—watch superhero movies.

When the lights slowly came back up as the credits were rolling, some people around us started gathering their things and exiting the theater while others stayed put.

Luke and I didn't move, him still holding my hand. That was fine with me.

As the people filed down the center aisle toward the exit, a girl looked at me, her face a mix of contempt and disgust. I looked behind me to see if there was someone she was shooting the visual daggers at. Did I know her from somewhere? I didn't recognize her, and I never forgot a face. So why was she looking at me like I'd skinned her cat?

I squirmed in my seat as she and her date passed. It was a good thing she didn't fire lasers out of her eyes like the villain in the movie or I'd be dead. Yikes.

I glanced over, and thankfully Luke didn't seem to have noticed. He was looking in the opposite direction.

After almost everyone had cleared out of the theater, Luke said, "You ready?"

I nodded, and he let go of my hand to stand and stretch. I was a little disappointed when he shoved his hands into his pockets instead of reaching for mine.

"Did you like the movie?" I asked. It was silly, but I was looking for reassurance. I'd picked it and I wanted his approval.

What the heck was up with that? I wasn't one of those girls who fished for compliments or cared overly much what anyone else thought.

But I cared what Luke thought.

"It was good," Luke said. I waited for him to elaborate, but when he didn't, I crossed my arms and fell in step behind him.

When we reached the car, Luke opened the door for me and gave me a hand getting in, still silent.

I stared at him, but he kept his eyes on the road, his brow furrowed. The tension in the car was thick. I didn't get it. What had happened between us holding hands throughout the entire movie and now?

I thought back over what I'd said. Nothing. I'd said nothing. With the exception of that chick shooting death rays out of her eyes, nothing out of the ordinary happened.

After several minutes of silence, I couldn't take it anymore. "Why are you being weird?"

He looked over at me with a shocked expression on his face, almost like I'd startled him with my question, like he'd forgotten I was there.

His eyes met mine, and as he smiled, the tense muscles on his face relaxed. "You don't have a monopoly on being weird."

"*You* held my hand for two hours. *I* threw myself at you for an uninvited make-out. I think my reason is better." I couldn't believe how brazen I was being, bringing that up. I focused on my breathing, trying to keep the blush that was threatening to erupt at bay.

He glanced over at me.

When we pulled to a stop at a red light, Luke leaned over, wrapping his hand lightly around my neck to pull me closer, then he brushed his lips over mine. *Soft.* That was all I could think. Why were his lips so soft?

I leaned in, putting my hand on his shoulder, and he parted my lips with his tongue.

I moaned slightly. Sober kissing Luke was a million times better than drunk kissing him.

The car behind us honked. Luke pulled away, but not before kissing me one last time.

As he put the car in gear and pulled off, he glanced over at me with a sly grin. "I think we're even now. And for the record—no make-out with you is ever uninvited."

Chapter Thirteen

"You want ice cream?"

My mind was buzzing. "Uh, sure." I touched my lips with my fingertips, feeling the warmth where Luke's lips had covered mine. Then I hastily placed my hand in my lap, hoping he hadn't seen that. *Don't be pathetic.*

At the ice cream parlor, Luke ordered a sundae topped with strawberries. I ordered a proper sundae, with hot fudge and nuts.

We found a table outside on the patio, which was packed. I noticed a few people from the theater who must have had the same idea as us. To our left sat a young mother who was ineffectively trying to corral her two young children who were literally running circles around her and the table. Not that I was an expert on children or anything, but what did she expect loading them up with sugar at nearly midnight?

"You want a bite?" Luke offered, holding up a spoon dripping with ice cream and strawberries.

I eyed it suspiciously, my lips curling.

He looked down at his sundae and then back at me.

"What?"

"How can you mix your food groups like that?"

He looked down at his sundae again. "What are you talking about?"

I pointed at the offending strawberries with my spoon. "That. You mixed health food with your dessert."

"The strawberries? What about your peanuts? Isn't that like protein with your dessert?"

"Peanuts are a staple in many different types of confections." I counted them off on my fingers. "Snickers, Peanut M&M's, Reese's cups, Reese's pieces, Mr. Goodbar, Payday... Do I need to go on? I've already run out of fingers on one hand."

He laughed. "I forgot I shouldn't argue with you."

I grinned, swirling my spoon around in the chocolate syrup. "At least you're a quick learner."

"I'm also hardheaded. You still haven't agreed to go to the game tomorrow."

"I thought you'd forgotten about that."

"Come on. It'll be fun."

"All right."

I could check out the tutoring center any day, but I could only go to the game tomorrow. It made perfect sense, but deep down, I knew I was BS-ing myself. And constantly putting off dealing with the tuition wasn't going to make the problem go away. I just honestly didn't know what to do. If I did, the bill would already be paid.

"All right?" He seemed a little surprised that I'd agreed so readily this time. "Be at the house at ten."

"Wait. Isn't the game at two?"

"The pre-game before the tailgate starts at ten."

"Whoa. Pre-game *and* tailgate?"

He put his forearms on the table and leaned forward. "Can you handle it, Corinne?"

Chills went down my spine at him saying my full name. No one except my mother called me that, but I liked it. I liked the sound of my name on his lips. I liked the thought of his lips mixed with anything of mine.

Oh, geez. *Get a grip.*

I hunkered down over my ice cream, hoping its coldness would calm my thoughts. Once I had my thoughts under control, I snuck a peek at him.

Bad idea. Thoughts were right back in the gutter.

Sigh.

• • •

Amber had also been invited to go to the game with Brad. She was still hung up on not going on a formal date with him yet, though, so she hadn't planned to go. Once she found out I was going, she changed her mind.

Having learned my lesson about letting Amber drive, I drove. I didn't want to get stuck like last time. It was going on ten thirty by the time we left our house. Neither Amber nor I were morning people. Plus, I had trouble coming down from my post-date "Luke" high last night, so I didn't get much sleep.

After we had finished our ice cream, Luke drove me home and walked me to the door. He'd taken my chin in his hands and kissed me gently. That one kiss rocked my consciousness just as much, if not more, than the steamy kisses we'd shared in the Jeep. While I'd told Amber about kissing in the Jeep, I'd kept this one to myself. And the memory of it kept me awake for hours. When I finally fell asleep, my dreams involved Luke, ice cream, and whipped cream.

Enough said.

• • •

The parking lot at the Beta house was packed, forcing me to park on the grass. Hopefully my poor old car wouldn't get stuck. Oh well. If it did, I'd deal with it later. Besides, Luke could probably hook a chain up to his Jeep and pull me out.

The weather was cooler today, perfect jeans and T-shirt weather. For once, Amber had approved of my chosen attire—jeans, T-shirt, tennis shoes, and a hoodie—even though she opted for the dressier look of skinny jeans and knee-high boots.

Brad met us in the parking lot, immediately picking Amber up and swinging her around. She squealed.

"She's so little. I love it." Brad gave a lopsided grin.

She peered at him closely. "How long have you been drinking?"

He shrugged. "Not long. Just a few hours."

She looked at me, her mouth wide open and laughter in her eyes. He grabbed her hand and pulled her toward the deck where three kegs were chilling in huge tubs of ice. "Let's get you a drink."

That left me alone in the yard. I'd met a lot of the guys, but I wouldn't say I was friends with any of them except for Josh and Brad. And Luke, of course.

Well, I didn't know what I was with Luke.

As if on cue, he came up behind me and wrapped his arms around me, nuzzling my neck. I closed my eyes and soaked in the moment.

Having his arms around me felt right. How could I feel so comfortable, so safe with him after such a short time?

"You're late," he said. "I thought you'd stood me up."

"Ten is early on a Saturday."

"Not on game day. Come on." He led me over to the deck where there was quite a spread—finger sandwiches, chips, veggies, dip, doughnuts, pastries, fruit salad. In addition to kegs, they also had mixers for various cocktails. "Something with orange juice?" he asked. I nodded and he whipped up a concoction. I didn't pay close attention to what he put in it, but it was yummy.

I sat down on the deck steps and he sat behind me, his legs straddling me. My, wasn't he being affectionate this morning. Of course, if he had been drinking with Brad all morning, he probably had a nice buzz going.

I'd put my hair in a ponytail, and he toyed with the school-colored ribbons I'd tied in it. "Nice touch."

"I try."

I sipped at my drink. Noticing my restraint, he asked, "Don't you like it?"

I held up my keys. "I'm driving."

He snatched them out of my hand and tucked them deep in his pocket. "Not anymore you're not. We've got DD's, so have fun." He pointed over to two guys sucking on Cokes and looking miserable.

I laughed. "How'd they get the short straw?"

"They're the newest brothers. They've got to pay their dues."

Brad and Amber claimed the steps next to us.

She poked Brad in the chest. "You are a bad influence on me. I never drink before noon. *Never.*"

"I make no apologies," he said. "I was a nerd in high school. I've got some years to make up for."

I caught Amber's eye and we burst out laughing.

"What?" Brad asked, confused.

Amber whipped out her phone and pulled up his Facebook page, showing everyone the picture of him in his bow tie posing with the tuba.

"Shit." The normally suave Brad blushed. "I didn't know that was on there."

"It's okay," Amber reassured him. "If I could, I would reach into that picture and pinch your chubby little cheeks."

She pinched his cheeks. "These will have to do."

"Aw, thanks, babe."

Luke looked at me suspiciously. "Is there anything on my Facebook account that I should be worried about?"

"I haven't looked at yours."

"Yeah," Amber chimed in. "We're not friends. Here, I'll friend request you."

He wrapped his arms around me and whispered in my ear. "What about you? Any embarrassing Facebook photos you want to confess to?"

"I don't really use Facebook," I said lightly. It was true. I'd even deactivated my account and hadn't been on it in months, not since the spring. Since the posts left on my wall became conciliatory. Since the photos posted there became haunting reminders. Since I couldn't bear to update my relationship status. They didn't have one for "deceased boyfriend."

I took a swig of my drink, pushing my thoughts into the furthest place in my mind—the place reserved for forgetting.

Josh wandered over and plopped down on the step next to me. *Saved from myself.*

"Why haven't you been in class this week?" I asked him, grateful for the diversion.

He was unconcerned. "Don't worry about me. I've been studying plenty of women."

"Too bad they can't say the same for you," Brad said.

"Whatever. You'd still be working up the courage to talk to a girl if it weren't for me," Josh said. "I changed your life."

Brad wrapped his arm around Amber and raised his cup. "And I thank you for that."

"When this guy moved in with me freshman year, he was hopeless," Josh told Amber.

"I know." She giggled. "I've seen the pictures."

Brad sulked. "I'm going to kill whoever posted that picture."

Amber tapped her finger on her phone. "Tina Highland."

Brad groaned while Luke and Josh burst out laughing.

"Count on Mama Highland," Josh said. "Did you know she sends him cookies every month? Chocolate chip, his favorite."

"Aww," Amber said. "That's sweet. You're a mama's boy."

Brad's face turned red from his blond roots down to his neck.

"It's almost noon," Luke said, looking at his watch. "We should probably head over to the tailgate."

Brad quickly jumped up. "Thank God. I'll find the DD."

The tailgate was fun, better than I expected. Some Beta alumni had a prime spot next to the stadium. There were mountains of food: chicken, ribs, potato salad, coleslaw, chips and dip, cupcakes—you name it, they had it. Luke introduced me to several alumni he knew, simply saying, "This is Cori."

Very smooth, introducing me without having to put a label on our relationship. Would I be friend or girlfriend?

But what did I want to be? All I knew was that I was *where* I wanted to be—with Luke.

• • •

The game was awesome, just as Luke had promised. We lost, but it was a close game. The spirit of the Beta Chis was infectious, and I found myself joining in the lewd cheers and heckling. Afterward, we headed back to the Beta house for more debauchery. Someone ordered about a dozen pizzas. I offered to pay my share, but Luke wouldn't let me. I was grateful. Impromptu pizza didn't fit in with my new penny pinching routine.

As twilight began to fall, the guys started up the bonfire. I found myself sitting next to Josh and his guitar in a déjà vu moment of a few weeks ago. Had it only been a few weeks? My life had been turned upside down since then. In a good way, though.

For the first time in months, I exhaled. The tension left my body. And I realized...I was ready for the next chapter of my life—a chapter that included Luke.

Until the last few weeks, I'd only been existing, not living, only going through the motions. I filled my time with so many responsibilities that I had a built-in excuse for standing still, not moving forward.

I looked at where Luke was sitting on the other side of the fire. The light from the fire made the blue in his eyes look even lighter, more like frozen ice. Even though he'd been attentive the entire day, he didn't keep himself glued to my side, letting me stand on my own. He noticed me looking at him and smiled at me. He mouthed, "You okay?" I smiled and nodded back.

Yes, I was definitely okay.

Chapter Fourteen

Luke drove me home the next morning. I'd spent the night with him, and this time we didn't stay on our respective sides of the bed, instead having a good old-fashioned make-out session before we fell asleep spooning.

When he pulled up to the Alpha house, he turned off the ignition and walked around to my side to open my door. He helped me down, but instead of walking me to the door, he put his arms on either side of me, trapping me against the Jeep. He gave me a playful smile and then leaned down to press his lips to mine. I grabbed his shirt and pulled him closer. Our tongues tangled and I drank in the scent of him, something that never failed to affect me.

He pulled away after a few moments. "Did you have fun yesterday?"

I nodded, barely comprehending the question. My lips were swollen, and the taste of him was on my tongue.

He tweaked my nose playfully. "Told you."

"Am I supposed to be eternally grateful?" I somehow managed to say this with a straight face.

He considered. "Maybe not eternally, but remember this the next time I do something stupid."

My jaw dropped in mock surprise. "*You* do something stupid?" Even though I was exaggerating with my reaction, I honestly couldn't imagine it. I'd hit the boyfriend jackpot with Luke.

His eyes roamed over my face. "You're a good girl, Cori."

"You're not so bad yourself," I said, pulling him in for another kiss.

• • •

Amber's nose entered the kitchen first, followed by the rest of her body. "What is that smell? Are you baking something?"

I glanced up from where I was crouching in front of the oven, watching the cupcakes rise. "Yup." I wasn't an experienced baker, but I figured I could handle some cupcakes out of a red box.

Amber appeared utterly confused. "Why? Shouldn't you be studying or writing a paper or, well, doing anything else but this?"

I glared at her through slitted eyes. "What's that supposed to mean?"

"In the ten years I've known you, I can count on one hand the number of times I've seen you bake something. Maybe even on one finger."

I slipped oven mitts on my hands. "That doesn't mean I can't do it." I pulled the cupcakes out of the oven and set them on the stove. A toothpick stuck in the middle of one determined they were perfectly done. *Thanks for the tip, Pinterest*. I gave Amber an *I told you so* look.

Amber slapped her palms together and rubbed, a gleam in her eyes. "When do we eat?"

"We don't," I said firmly. "These are for the Beta Chi

pledges."

Amber raised her eyebrows. "Oh?"

I busied myself with checking the cupcakes to ensure that each one was cooked through, even though I knew they were. "Luke is the pledge master. I thought this would be a nice treat."

Amber hopped up on the counter and grinned. "You've been spending a lot of time together."

I nodded, still not meeting her eyes.

"And?"

I sat down at the kitchen table where I'd put my homework. She was right on the money about me doing homework. It annoyed me that I was so predictable.

She nudged me with her foot. "Uh-uh. You aren't getting off that easy. I've given you space this entire week. I can't take it anymore. Spill."

Luke and I hadn't seen each other outside of class this week, but we'd talked on the phone every night, if only for a few minutes, and exchanged texts back and forth. He'd been busy getting ready for the new pledge class which had its first meeting tonight. I'd jokingly volunteered to be the "pledge mom" and bake cupcakes, even though as Amber had so *helpfully* pointed out, I wasn't an experienced baker. Despite my lack of experience, I was pleased when Luke took me up on it.

I wasn't sure what the status of our relationship was. We were more than friends, but I wouldn't quite consider him my boyfriend yet—we hadn't had "the talk." Knots formed in my stomach whenever I thought about that. Absently, I toyed with my necklace. I felt like I shouldn't be ready to take that next step. It felt wrong, disloyal. But the truth was I wanted to move forward. Why else would I be *baking*, for goodness sake?

I picked up my highlighter and focused on my textbook,

not meeting her eyes. "We're friends."

"What kind of friends?" Amber prompted.

"Friendly ones."

She threw up her hands in exasperation. "You are impossible!" She hopped off the counter and leaned over my shoulder. "What are you working on?"

"Stupid biology," I muttered.

She wrinkled her nose. "I'm so glad I didn't take that. Guess what?"

I sighed and put down my highlighter. "What? On second thought, why don't you guess the number of chapters I have to get through tonight?"

She stuck out her tongue. "Two. You've mentioned it a few times. Seriously though, guess what?" I waited half a beat for her to rush on like she normally did. I never actually got to guess. "Brad asked me out. On a real date!"

Good thing I wasn't the guessing type.

"That's great, Amber. When?" I didn't have to fake my enthusiasm. I was happy for her.

"Tomorrow. I thought about telling him I was busy. I didn't want to give in too easy, but then again, we're getting too old for games, don't you think? I mean, I do like him. You and Luke aren't playing any games, are you?"

I ignored her last question, a lame attempt to get me to talk about Luke. "Where's he taking you?"

"Dinner somewhere. I'm not sure. I don't really care. I'll eat anything. I'm just glad he finally got around to taking me out somewhere. Hanging at the house is fun and all, but my college years are ticking. I don't want to waste any more time on scumbags."

I rose and walked over to the stove to take the cupcakes out of the pans so they could finish cooling.

Amber looked longingly at them. "Are you going to decorate them?"

I pointed to a can of chocolate frosting I'd bought with the cake mix.

She shook her head. "What? No sprinkles?"

"They're boys. They don't care about sprinkles."

"Well, not specifically," Amber huffed, "but you've got to make them look appealing." She grabbed my arm. "Come on, let's go buy some blue sprinkles. Isn't blue a Beta color?"

"Wait." I stopped and glanced at the cupcakes lined up in neat rows on the counter. "Do you think these are safe here?" I didn't trust leaving the cupcakes unattended in a house full of girls.

I cringed as Amber ripped a sheet of paper out of my notebook. If she'd asked, I could've gotten her a sheet of paper out of my bag instead of her tearing up my notebook. *Sigh*.

She scribbled on it and slapped it down on the counter in front of the cupcakes. The paper read DO NOT EAT UNDER PAIN OF DEATH!!!

"That should do the trick."

By the time we went to the store and came home with blue sprinkles in hand, the cupcakes were cool and ready to frost. Amber helped me frost and decorate them. Then I packaged them up in a plastic container I'd found in the kitchen and loaded them into my car.

Butterflies were in my stomach as I sat in the Beta Chi parking lot. I gripped the steering wheel with my hands, even though I had already turned off the ignition.

"Stop being stupid," I told myself. "Get out of the car."

Fuck. What was I doing?

Cupcakes, I told myself. *They're just cupcakes*.

It didn't feel like that, though.

My phone rang. It was a number I didn't recognize, but the area code was from home, and I was desperate for an excuse to stall.

"Hello?"

"Is this Cori Elliott?" The woman's voice sounded vaguely familiar.

"Yes."

"Thank goodness! This is Mrs. Talbot."

It took me a second to remember she was the pageant coordinator at my high school. "Hi, Mrs. Talbot."

"I'll cut right to the chase. I'm in a bit of a situation. Our pageant is this weekend and I'm short one judge. I was hoping you could fill in."

I balked. "I've never judged before. I don't think I'm qualified."

"You're a former Miss Forrest Creek, which means you're automatically an approved judge. Besides, with all of your pageant experience, you're more than qualified."

I hesitated. This was really last minute. Granted, I didn't have any plans for this weekend, but still, it was almost a six-hour drive.

"Please, please, please!" Mrs. Talbot pleaded with desperation in her voice. "I'm begging you. I'll even pay for your gas money."

I sighed. "Okay, I'll do it."

"Yay! The pageant starts at seven. Interviews are at four. Try to arrive no later than three. Oh, and wear a suit."

"Yes, ma'am."

"You're a doll."

That's what I get for stalling.

I popped the top off the cupcake container. I grabbed one and stuffed my face.

Brushing the sprinkles off my shirt, I opened my car door. With a smile on my face and a box of cupcakes in my hands, I threw my shoulders back and walked into the Beta house.

Those were some damn good cupcakes, if I did say so

myself.

• • •

It was startling to wake up in my room at my parents' house, almost like I'd gone through a time warp instead of driving across the state. Sheet music for the songs I used to perform was tacked all over one of the walls. In the bookcase, binders from my high school career were neatly alphabetized. The clothes I'd left behind when I went away to college were in uniform stacks in the back of the closet right where I'd left them. The bulletin board was still covered with the white sheet I'd put over it this summer. My heart had caught in my chest when I'd awoken and seen the sunlight streaming through the window onto it. I could vaguely make out the shapes of the photos and other things pinned on it. When the light threatened to reveal too much, I'd gotten up and headed to the shower.

As I was standing under the spray, I realized that this could be my future. If I didn't figure out my tuition situation, I'd be waking up every day in my childhood room.

Good-bye Alpha Delta.

Good-bye Amber.

Good-bye Luke.

I hadn't been focusing on the problem like I should. But now that I was back in my parents' house, the possible consequences became very real.

I might actually have to come home.

Everything I'd worked so hard for just…gone.

Tuition just got moved to the top of my priority list. I was an idiot not to have it there in the first place.

Even though I'd slept in, I had several hours to kill before I was due for pageant judging. I poured myself a bowl of Lucky Charms and laid my criminology notes and textbook out on the breakfast table.

My mom joined me. I spared her a glance before returning to my notes.

"Should I come to the pageant?" she asked.

Shoveling a spoonful of cereal in my mouth, I shrugged.

"Do you want to go out to dinner?"

"I won't be home until late."

"Oh, okay." She fiddled with the edge of the placemat. "What about breakfast before you leave tomorrow?"

I shook my head. "I want to get on the road early."

She sighed. "All right. Let me know if you change your mind."

It might have been cruel, but I wasn't ready to forgive her for how she handled my financial aid situation. I wasn't going to address it with her, either. That was the way with my family. We each lived in our own orbits that happened to intersect from time to time.

I arrived early at the school, and Mrs. Talbot was nowhere to be found, so I wandered around a bit. I hadn't been back since I graduated. Not much had changed. Same gold colored lockers, same cream cinderblock walls, same scuffed speckled tile floors. It was the same, yet it seemed so different.

I was different.

There by the main office was my locker from freshman year, where Tyler had asked me out for the first time. I smiled, remembering the way his Adam's apple had bobbed up and down as he swallowed from nervousness. He'd been an attentive high school boyfriend, bringing me a rose each month on our anniversary for the first year. We held hands between classes and kissed when we had to go our separate ways. For Valentine's Day, he always brought me the biggest, most obnoxious stuffed animal and balloon arrangement he could find. Back in the day, those things were important.

All the girls had been so jealous.

I slipped into the girls' bathroom on the main hallway. The same bad fluorescent lighting illuminated the forest green stalls. Most of the graffiti had been scrubbed free over the summer, but the requisite "so-and-so is a slut" scrawls peppered the walls. I checked the second stall and yup—the lock was still broken. Amber and I had hid in it once when we skipped gym class my sophomore year. That was the first and only time I ever skipped a class. I chewed every nail on my fingers down to a nub in the hour we huddled there. I just knew a security guard was going to fling open the door at any moment and drag me to the principal's office.

I pulled out my lip gloss for a touch-up. In my black suit and teal blouse with my copper locks pulled into a sleek low ponytail, I looked a lot more grown-up than the last time I'd touched up my makeup in this mirror.

It felt like decades had passed.

"Corinne?"

My back stiffened, and I turned to find two high school girls gaping at me.

"Corinne Elliott?"

I pasted a smile on my face. "That's me."

The girls wore green and gold FC cheering uniforms and held rolls of raffle tickets in their hands.

"Oh my God, they said you were coming, but I can't believe you're actually here," the first one gushed. Her long blond hair was curled and pulled back into a ponytail. The star on her skirt indicated she was the captain of the squad. That meant she was probably a senior, so she would have been a sophomore when I was a senior, but I didn't recognize her.

My smile tightened, but to my credit, it remained on my face. "It's great to be back." I sounded like a damn politician.

"We've never met," the second one said, "but I am like, *so* sorry for your loss. You and Tyler had to be the most perfect couple I've ever seen." This one also had her blond hair curled and pulled back into a ponytail. They could have been twins.

"It's just so sad," Captain Blondie said, tears actually forming in her eyes.

You have got to be freaking kidding me.

Blondie Two wrapped her arm around Captain Blondie's shoulders. "Tragic. It was tragic. How do you go on? You are so brave."

Captain Blondie nodded emphatically. "You're like a tragic heroine, like Juliet or something."

Not really. Juliet killed herself. I hadn't gotten there yet. But I might if I had to talk to these two any longer.

My smile was so tight my face was in danger of cracking. "I do the best I can." It was the standard line I always gave to questions like these. I'd learned in the beginning that no one wanted to hear an honest answer. No one wanted to hear about the sleepless nights or, worse, the nightmares.

Blondie Two's bottom lip started to quiver, and I fought the urge to punch her in the mouth. Instead, I said, "It was nice to meet you both," and hurried out of the bathroom.

No more trips down memory lane, especially if it meant more encounters like that.

I probably shouldn't have come. I wondered what Amber and Luke were doing, then I remembered that Amber had her date with Brad tonight. Then they'd probably end up at the Beta house.

Even though I didn't have formal plans, I probably would have ended up there, too. I would much rather be there than here.

I headed toward the library where the interviews were taking place. A smartly dressed man in a charcoal suit was waiting there. I remembered him as one of the judges from when I competed in the pageant. After briefly introducing myself, I sat on a bench to wait.

I thought back to my conversation with the Blondies. They compared me to Juliet. Was everyone waiting for me to make one last tragic show of devotion?

If Juliet hadn't killed herself, would she ever be forgiven for moving on with her life?

I was scared to know the answer.

Chapter Fifteen

Judging the pageant was actually fun. There were a few contestants whose talents were painful to watch—after all, this *was* a high school pageant—but there were some genuinely talented girls. It was hard not to reminisce about my own pageant days—the preparation, the anticipation, the feeling of accomplishment when I knew I had nailed it. Being crowned the winner wasn't so bad, either.

After the winners were announced and the audience had rushed the stage, I craned my neck from where I sat at the judges' table, trying to find Mrs. Talbot to let her know I was leaving.

"Oh my God, Cori, it *is* you!" a high-pitched male voice said.

I turned to see Dante, my former pageant coach, strutting his way over to me, hips swinging in his signature swagger. He was wearing white skinny jeans, black leather boots, and a black button-down shirt. Black eyeliner lined his deep brown eyes and his black hair was slicked back. It totally worked for him.

I grinned. "Were you coaching one of these girls?"

He pursed his lips and jerked his head toward the stage. "Blue taffeta."

My eyebrows shot up. Her performance had been mediocre at best.

He flipped his hand out and popped his hip. "Tell me about it. But what are you going to do? The money was good. Not everyone can be a starlet like Miss Corinne over here." He flashed a smile and put a hand on my arm.

I blushed.

"So girl, tell me, what are you doing with yourself?"

"Studying mostly."

"Uh-huh. What new titles have you added to your impressive resume? I've been so busy with local pageants I haven't had time to follow any others."

I shook my head and stepped aside to let someone pass. "I'm not doing them."

"Say what?" Dante put his hands on his hips, a look of befuddlement on his face.

"I'm not doing them anymore," I said again. "I'm too busy with all my classes."

"Puh-lease. That's an excuse if I've ever heard one."

I laughed. It was nice to see some things hadn't changed. "I've missed you, Dante."

He gave me an affectionate smile. "You're one of the best girls I've ever had. You know that, right?"

I nodded.

He whipped out his phone. "Give me your email. My friend is directing the New River Valley pageant. It's only a month away, but they're low on contestants. I bet I can get you in."

"I told you, I'm done with pageants."

"Uh-huh. What's your email?"

I gave it to him. I knew him well enough to know he would

nag me until I gave in. He could send me the information, and once I was a couple hundred miles away, I'd tell him I wasn't going to do it.

He slipped his phone back into his pocket. "Done." He looked at the stage and sighed dramatically. "I'd better go console my girl." He leaned forward and air-kissed my cheeks.

• • •

I hefted my suitcase to my car bright and early the next morning, eager to get back to school, back to my life.

The on-ramp to the interstate was just ahead when I looked down and noticed the gas gauge was dangerously close to E. "Shit." I cut through two lanes of traffic and pulled into the last gas station on my side of the road before the interstate. Other people must have had the same idea as me, because all the pumps were occupied. I pulled behind a pick-up truck to wait.

I scrolled through my email on my phone while I waited. There was one from Dante. *Damn, that was quick*. My finger hovered over the delete button, but I opened it instead, just out of curiosity.

The pageant was in a little over a month. There was the standard information about scoring, talent length requirements, costumes, blah, blah, blah. At the bottom, the scholarship amounts were listed.

My eyeballs nearly jumped out of their sockets.

The rumble of the pick-up truck in front of me driving away caught my attention, and I pulled up. I quickly got out, swiped my credit card, and shoved the gas nozzle into my car.

As it gassed up, I leaned against my car and looked at the email again. The scholarship would be available immediately, and it was almost enough to pay my spring tuition.

I bit my lip as a battle waged within me. The rehearsals

were extensive, not to mention the extra time I'd have to put in on my talent since I was out of practice. I already had a lot on my plate with my heavy course load.

But if I didn't come up with money, and fast, worrying about heavy course loads would be a thing of the past. At least at this university. I wrinkled my nose at the thought of moving home. This wasn't where my life was anymore.

How hard would it be to resurrect one of my old performances? I had everything I needed packed away in the closet at my parents' house. It would just be a matter of dusting off the dresses and brushing up on my song. It'd be like an encore of the last pageant I won, right?

Right.

The gas nozzle clicked, signaling it was done. I secured it back on the gas pump and grabbed my receipt.

I slid into my seat and clicked the seat belt. This was crazy. I couldn't possibly prepare for a pageant in a little over a month and keep up with my classes. I was scheduled to start volunteering at the women's center for my Women's Studies class. And if I did the pageant, I could kiss the possible internship with a local law office that I was applying for good-bye.

I pulled up to the traffic light in front of the gas station with my right turn signal flashing to go toward the interstate. The light turned green, but I didn't go, my hands paralyzed on the steering wheel.

Drivers laid on their horns behind me, snapping me into action. I flipped my left turn signal on.

I needed to retrieve some dresses out of storage.

• • •

When I walked into my room, Amber had her purse on her arm and was applying lip gloss. She raised her eyebrows at the sight of the bulky dress bags I carried in.

"Don't ask," I told her, hanging them on the outside of the closet.

"I'm heading out to see Brad. You want to go?"

I hesitated. I wanted to see Luke, but I didn't want to show up unannounced. What kind of a message would that send? I'd been so busy this weekend I hadn't had time to call him, and I didn't like to talk and drive.

Amber looked at her watch impatiently. "Yes or no?"

My desire to see him won out. "Give me five minutes."

At the Beta house, we found Brad and Josh in Josh's room. Amber climbed over Josh's legs to squeeze in next to Brad. She smiled and gave him a peck on the lips. *Guess the date went well.*

I perched on the arm of the couch next to Josh.

Disappointment must have shown on my face.

"Aren't you happy to see me?" Josh teased. "Luke's down the hall, working on the wiring in one of the bedrooms."

I stopped myself from sprinting down the hallway and instead walked at a respectable brisk pace.

Luke was right where Josh said. He had the faceplate pulled off the light switch and wires were hanging out of the hole in the wall. Hmm, electrical surgery.

Luke's lips curved into an easy smile when he saw me.

I let out the breath I didn't know I was holding. My weekend trip put miles between us, literally and figuratively. I wasn't sure what to expect when I saw him again. Had he missed me? That was silly, I chided myself. It's not like our relationship was hot and heavy. We'd gone days before without seeing each other.

He held the wires secure in one hand and wrapped his other arm around me in a hug.

I closed my eyes and let myself enjoy the moment. I had missed him, more than I realized. More than I wanted to admit.

"How was your trip?" he asked when I stepped away.

"Okay."

He shoved the wires back into the wall. "Just okay?"

Between the cheerleaders in the bathroom treating me like a tragic widow and Dante's ambush, yeah, it was just okay. Not that I was going to tell him about either of those things, especially the former. That was a conversation I'd like to have, oh, I'd say never.

"What'd I miss around here?"

"We had a lame party on Saturday. Some girl puked all over the party room, so there was that."

I wrinkled my nose. "I'm sorry I missed it."

He screwed the faceplate back on the wall. "Let there be light," he joked, and flipped the switch.

I looked up at the ceiling light, which was indeed shining. "I'm impressed."

"It'd be more impressive if I could convince these asswipes to stop screwing things up around here. Then I wouldn't have to spend so much time fixing everything."

We joined the others in Josh's room, squeezing onto the couch next to Brad and Amber. Luke ran his fingers up and down my arm absentmindedly, giving me chills. I cuddled closer to him, inhaling his scent. He always smelled good, but I was yet to figure out what kind of cologne he wore. The scent was so light he might not wear any at all. It could just be his soap and shampoo. I lifted my nose slightly and took a whiff of his hair.

He craned his neck to look at me. "What are you doing?"

I blushed furiously. "Smelling you." What else could I say? I'd been caught yet again. Suave, I was not.

"I hope I passed your sniff test."

"Don't worry," I assured him. "You always do."

He caught my eye, and his smile turned a little less

innocent. His eyes darkened, and I licked my lips. He nodded his head toward the door with a question in his eyes. *You want to get out of here?*

I nodded.

As we were leaving, Brad said, "Hey you guys, you want to grab something to eat later?"

Luke looked at me again, putting the ball in my court. I shook my head.

I traveled the now familiar path to Luke's room, walking behind him down the narrow hallway, my hand reaching forward to hold his hand. When we entered the room, he crossed to his desk, taking his cell phone out of his pocket to plug it in the charger. I shut the door behind me with a deafening click. I don't know which was louder—the sound of the door or the thud of my heart hammering against my rib cage.

I was doing this. I crossed the room to where he stood messing with his cell phone with a frown on his face. I took the phone out of his hands and placed it on the desk. Wrapping my arms around his neck, I stood on my toes and pressed my lips to his.

He responded immediately, wrapping his arms around my waist. His tongue tangled with mine. His hands slid under my shirt and my skin burned at the feel of his palms and fingers on my bare flesh.

He turned me around so that I was against the desk and lifted me up on it. I spread my knees so that he could stand in between my legs and scooted to the edge of the desk so that the length of our torsos were pressed together. Our kisses were slow at first, sweet, before becoming hotter and more urgent. He pulled away, leaving me wanting more.

He ran his thumb along my lower lip. "I think you missed me."

I nodded, forcing myself to look into his ice blue eyes.

"Did you miss me?"

He kissed me gently. "I did."

I wrapped myself around him and pulled him to me, my mouth hungry for his. I grabbed at his shirt, pulling it up until he pulled it all the way over his head. My shirt joined his on the floor, and I thanked my lucky stars I'd taken the time to change out of the plain white cotton bra into a sexy lace one.

He ran his hands up my sides, grazing my breasts. My breath caught, and I let out a small moan. His mouth left mine to grace my neck with kisses. I ran my fingertips along his back.

In one smooth motion, he lifted me. My legs were already wrapped around his waist, so I tightened them. He set me down on the end of the bed, and I scooted backward so that I was at the head of the bed. He crawled up to meet me.

And that, as they say, was that.

Chapter Sixteen

I arrived at criminology a full fifteen minutes early on Tuesday. Other than a few irrelevant texts, Luke and I hadn't spoken since Sunday. I told myself it was normal to be nervous. It was normal to come to class super early just to claim home field advantage.

Who was I kidding?

I was exhausted. I hadn't gotten more than a few hours' sleep last night. I couldn't turn my mind off. Would things be weird between us? I felt like we were just getting to a good place. Did my actions on Sunday ruin that? Would he think less of me? We hadn't known each other that long. Was it too soon?

"Boo," Luke whispered in my ear.

I nearly fell out of my chair. As it was, I knocked my notebook and my set of carefully arranged colored pens on the floor.

He kneeled and picked up my fallen things, then settled into the chair next to me, laughing. "Sorry. You looked like you were somewhere else. I couldn't help myself."

I smiled nervously. I didn't know what to say. I was tongue-tied. Two days ago I was naked with this guy, and now I couldn't speak if my life depended on it.

He glanced over at me. Then he leaned closer. "You're not being weird again, are you?" he whispered with a smile.

I playfully shoved him. "No."

"Good." His eyes had a wicked twinkle. "Because I like the you from Sunday."

I did, too.

"You're such a guy," I said, keeping it light.

"Thanks." He glanced at my notebook. "What's the color scheme today?"

I smiled.

• • •

"I told you we were going to be late."

Amber sipped her coffee. "I needed caffeine."

"I'm getting you a Keurig for Christmas," I muttered. Except I probably couldn't. Those darn things were expensive. I wasn't a coffee drinker myself, and good thing since I was on a spending lockdown. I couldn't believe how much Amber regularly shelled out for her cup of designer coffee.

I circled the mini-golf course parking lot for the second time, hoping things would be different this time around and I'd find an empty parking space. No such luck. Looks like we'd be hoofing it.

The closest space I could find on the street was at least a quarter mile away. This sleepy mini-golf course only saw this much action once a year—it was time for Chi Omega's annual mini-golf philanthropy event to raise money for the Make a Wish foundation. Amber had signed me up to be on a team with Brad and Josh without asking, of course, because that was her style. Luke was spending the day at a retreat for the

Beta Chi pledges.

By the time we hiked up to the course, the guys were already waiting for us, taking practice swings with their putters, but their swings were huge, like we'd be playing regular golf.

"This is mini-golf, right?" I asked Josh.

He handed me the putter and a yellow golf ball. "Just testing it out for you."

We looked over at Brad and Amber who were wrapped around each other.

"Hey!" Josh used two putters to separate them. "None of that. This is a family venue."

Amber grinned. "You're just mad you're here with Cori."

"Wait…what? Hey!" I protested.

"I didn't mean it like that," she said quickly. "I just meant poor Josh has no one to make out with."

Josh put an arm around my shoulders. "I respect Cori too much to make out with her."

We all looked at him. "What?" he asked.

"We should get started," Brad said, taking Amber's hand and pulling her toward the first hole. "We're the last team."

"Sorry we're late," I said. "Someone—*Amber*—made us stop and get coffee."

"You should have called me, babe," Brad said. "I would've brought you some."

"Aww, you're so sweet," Amber cooed. *Cooed*, like she was an infant or something. What happened to my best friend? I was glad Amber was finally having some luck when it came to love, but I missed the Amber who wasn't into PDA and didn't *coo*.

My phone rang and I pulled it out of my pocket.

"Sorry, guys," I said when I looked at the number. "I need to take this."

I walked up the path a little ways into a semi-private area

and answered it.

"Cori, this is Diane Hadnot, the contestant coordinator for the Miss New River Valley pageant."

"Yes, hi." I chewed on my cuticles. I'd sent in my paperwork earlier in the week, and I'd been waiting for this call to find out if I'd be allowed to compete in the pageant since rehearsals had already started. I had mixed feelings. I didn't really want to return to pageants, especially since at this level there was a bathing suit competition, but I needed that money. A minimum wage position at the tutoring center wouldn't be enough, even if I worked every day.

"I spoke with the director, and she's agreed to let you compete."

"Thank you—"

"There is a condition."

My heart sank. Conditions were never, ever good.

"You will have to attend private rehearsals with her until she feels you have caught up with the rest of the girls." The woman's voice had an apologetic tone to it. "And if you don't catch up in time, you're out."

That was more than reasonable. I'd expect nothing less than that, actually. So why did the woman seem so apologetic? I must be missing something.

"Come on, Cori!" Amber yelled, motioning for me to come back to the group. I held up my finger to indicate I'd be another minute, and I wrapped up the call.

With each step I took back toward the group, I added another item to my "to-do" list. Reserve time in the student center music rehearsal hall, review interview questions, practice the evening gown walk, develop a workout routine to prep for the swimsuit competition... The list went on and on. And this was on top of all of the other things I already had going on.

I should be running out to my car to get started on this

stuff, not spending the morning at mini-golf. My college tuition depended on it.

Josh handed me my putter again. "It's your turn."

I put the ball on the rubber mat and smacked it with the putter. It hit a wall and ricocheted off an obstacle to land back at my feet. *Pathetic.*

Josh and Brad groaned simultaneously. "Come on, Cori," Brad said. "We want to win."

I shot him a weary look but didn't say anything. He was right. Even though this was just a charity event, I owed it to my teammates to pay attention and at least try. Beta Chi boys took competition seriously, whether it be mini-golf or beer pong. I'd never hear the end of it if I was the weak link on the team.

I squared my shoulders and hit the ball again. This time it landed in the vicinity of the hole. It took me two more shots to make it in. Not perfect, but better.

"How's class been?" Josh asked me.

"You'd know if you actually came," I said.

"I never should have signed up for that class," he admitted. "It seemed like a good idea at the time."

"It's not so bad."

He set his ball down to take his turn. "There should be Men's Studies. I'd probably get an A in that."

I cocked my head. "What would that class be about?"

He hit the ball, nearly making a hole-in-one. "Man stuff."

"Care to elaborate on that?"

He knelt down to get a better look at his shot and grinned up at me. "Do you really want me to?"

"Yeah, probably not. Speaking of that class, though, you know there's a huge test this week."

"Really?"

"Yes, really. You might want to come take it. I think it's like twenty percent of our grade."

He furrowed his brow, actually looking a bit concerned. "What's it on?"

"Everything we've covered for the last month." I sighed. "Do you want me to come by this week and get you caught up?"

I really didn't have time to tutor him, but he looked so lost, like a stray puppy. How could I not offer?

"Yeah, that'd be good," he said. "Thanks."

I pulled my ball out of my pocket, and as I was rising from setting it up, the hair on the back of my neck stood up.

From two holes up, a girl was staring at me with her arms crossed and her eyes narrowed.

She was tall, blond, and in a word, gorgeous.

She also had a fierce look about her that made me nervous.

I turned away and glanced over my shoulder to see if maybe she was looking at someone behind me. When I turned back, she was still glaring at me.

She seemed familiar, like I had seen her before, but I didn't know her.

I took my first swing, botching it.

The girl was still staring at me like I was at the top of her hit list. Where the heck had I seen her before? If I'd done something to deserve that evil stare, I'd hope I'd at least remember it.

The movies. That's where I knew her from. After the movie with Luke, she also looked at me with hate beams shooting out of her eyes.

Her group moved on, so she left with them, but not before giving me one final dirty look.

That was twice now. I wasn't imagining it.

What…the…hell.

I kept my eye on her as we continued on to the next hole. When I saw her chatting with some guys I thought were Beta

Chis, I nudged Josh.

"Who's that girl?"

He looked up. "Who?"

"Over there." I jerked my head in her direction. "Talking to your brothers."

"Oh, yeah. Her."

So he did know her.

"She keeps giving me these dirty looks, but I don't think I know her."

"Huh," Josh said, still not enlightening me.

"Josh," I said, grabbing his arm. "Who the heck is she?"

He hesitated a moment. "Luke's ex-girlfriend."

I let go of his arm, reeling back. Luke had never mentioned a supermodel-esque ex-girlfriend.

Then again, I hadn't mentioned a dead boyfriend, either.

"What happened?" I asked.

"They broke up."

"No shit."

"You'll have to ask him," Josh said. "There's no way I'm getting involved in that mess."

"It's not *getting involved*. You're just answering a question."

Josh shook his head. "Uh-uh. Not doing it, chick. Ask Luke."

That was one thing I certainly wasn't going to do. So far we hadn't done the whole delving into each other's dating history thing, and that was exactly what I had wanted. I'd been so worried about my own past that I hadn't even considered that Luke might have a past of his own.

Which was stupid. *Of course* he did. He was a gorgeous twenty-one-year-old college guy. Based on the evil looks that girl was giving me, it was safe to say their relationship did not end well. There was definitely some bad blood there.

So maybe what's-her-name—Josh hadn't even given me

that little bit of info—still had a thing for Luke. Maybe *he* broke it off with *her*, and she still wasn't over it.

That had to be it. Yeah, that was it.

Geez, I wasn't even kidding myself. Nothing was ever that simple. But there was no way I could ask Luke without opening a door to my own past.

I craned my neck to watch her a little bit. She hugged one of the Betas she had been talking to and rejoined her group.

She was definitely stunning—Victoria's Secret model gorgeous. She and Luke must have made—

Stop it—just stop right there.

I was not doing this. I was not getting jealous over something that didn't exist anymore. She was his *ex*-girlfriend, emphasis on the *ex*.

If it mattered, then Luke would have told me about it.

Faulty logic! my brain screamed at me. Tyler definitely mattered, and I hadn't even mentioned him.

But it was a non-issue. It didn't affect my and Luke's relationship. If it did, I would definitely tell him. Right?

"Earth to Cori," Amber said, grabbing my arm and shaking it a little. "It's your turn, girl. Is everything okay?"

"Of course."

Focus on the now, Cori. I had a good thing going here. Luke and I were solid, and I had great friends, some of whom were right here with me. Sure, my life had some issues, but I didn't need to add to them by inventing problems where they didn't exist. Sometimes I was too neurotic for my own good.

I needed to get out of my own head.

Chapter Seventeen

I drove out to the Beta house, once again resenting the rule banning guys from the Alpha house bedrooms. I was going to help Josh cram for tomorrow's test in Women's Studies. I didn't have high hopes for his test grade, but maybe I could at least help him pass.

I didn't understand how people could spend so much money on college tuition and then just blow off their classes. Even if they didn't necessarily want to learn anything, shouldn't they at least want to do enough to get the credit? Otherwise, it was just wasted money and time.

I parked my car in the lot and was disappointed to see that Luke's Jeep wasn't there. I would be lying if I said I wasn't hoping to see him, too.

I climbed the stairs to the second floor and found Josh in his room strumming on his guitar with headphones on and a football game blaring on the TV.

When he saw me he pressed the mute button on the TV remote. "Hey, girl. What's up?"

I dropped my Women's Studies textbook and notebook

on his coffee table with a thud and looked at them pointedly. "Time to educate you."

Josh pulled the headphones off his ears and rested them around his neck. He slapped his hands together gleefully. "Let's do this."

I pulled the test review guide out of my notebook and handed it to him. "How much of this do you know?"

He scanned over it and laughed. "Not much. Um, the definition of feminism, that's like, *go women*, right?"

I closed my eyes and groaned.

He grinned sheepishly. "I guess I should've gone to class."

I bit back a snippy retort and reminded myself that one of the things I liked about Josh was his carefree attitude. He could be just a little too carefree, though.

I opened my notebook to the notes from the second day of class. We didn't have time to go over the textbook or all of the lectures that were posted online. If he could learn all of the material in my notes, then hopefully he'd know enough to pass the test.

As I went over it with him, I found that he wasn't stupid at all. In fact, Josh was rather intelligent. I figured he had to have some brains or he'd never have gotten into this school, but I didn't expect him to be as smart as he was. He simply wasn't motivated and didn't care. Not a good combination.

Josh's room faced the parking lot, and I couldn't stop myself from looking out the window every few minutes, hoping to see an oversized black Jeep roar down the drive. It must have been obvious, because Josh commented.

"Is there something out there?"

"Er, no," I stammered, blushing.

"You're looking for Luke, aren't you?" he asked, totally calling me out.

I did the only sensible thing—denied, denied, denied.

He just laughed. "It's okay."

I fiddled with a loose string on the couch. "Does he ever talk about me?"

"A little, I guess. I dunno. I never really pay attention." He paused. "The guys give him shit about you, though."

My eyes widened and my breath caught. "What do you mean?"

"Nothing bad. Don't worry. They just give him a hard time, like they do with any guy who has a new girl."

I waited for him to elaborate, not wanting to ask any more questions. Josh didn't take the hint.

So much for sophisticated intel. Still, I wasn't about to incur Amber's wrath. So I asked, "What about Brad? Do the guys give him shit about Amber?"

"Yeah..." He picked up his guitar and played a few chords. "So do you think I'm gonna pass this test?"

I gave him a bland look. "Do you remember everything we covered in the last hour?"

"Yeah." He laughed. "For now, anyway. Tomorrow might be another story."

I sighed. "Let's finish this section. Then you're on your own." Honestly, if he couldn't pass after I tutored him, then he was beyond help at this point.

Then I heard the sound I'd been waiting for—the crunching sound of gravel made by huge Jeep tires coming up the drive.

I jumped up. "I...I'll be right back." It was pathetic. I knew it, but I didn't care.

I jogged down the hall, but when I stepped out on the deck, I stopped short. Luke was standing next to his Jeep with a girl. And not just any girl—a gorgeous girl. Tall, long legs, curvy, and long blond hair that fell in waves down her back. I couldn't see her face, but I'd seen enough of it and her evil stares lately.

Why was Luke's ex here?

And what in the hell was she doing with Luke?

I retreated a few steps and flattened myself against the wall so I couldn't be seen, not that they were looking at me. They shifted, and I could see her face.

She was standing close to him, that bitch, with wide eyes and a pouty mouth. I'd never wanted superhero powers so much in my life—I'd kill to hear what they were saying. I couldn't see his face, but his shoulders and neck looked stiff. And were his arms crossed? Or was that wishful thinking on my part?

I watched them for a few minutes. She did most of the talking.

Had they come here together? I had flown out of Josh's room so fast I couldn't say for sure if she had been in the Jeep with him. I searched the parking lot for any unfamiliar cars. Nope, I'd seen all of the cars before, and I most certainly had *not* seen her here before.

My hands were shaking. Luke didn't strike me as the type of guy who would date multiple girls at once, but what did I know? As Amber frequently reminded me, I had been out of the game for a long time. Maybe my perception of him was way off.

Except in my heart, I really didn't believe that.

Then I saw something that made my blood run cold. He hugged her. That was *not* a friendly nice-to-see-you hug. That was a— Well, I didn't know what it was, but it wasn't entirely innocent. Her hands were all over his shoulders and back.

I would like to think I wasn't the jealous type, but Tyler and I had been together so long that jealousy hadn't been a factor. What I was feeling right now could only be described as a cocktail of jealousy, rage, and hurt.

When he released her, he opened the passenger side door for her and offered his hand, helping her up as he had done for me when I'd ridden with him.

Tears blurred my vision, but I didn't need to see any more. As I hurried down the hall to Josh's room, I heard the roar of the Jeep's engine.

Fucking asshole.

How could I have been so stupid?

I barreled into Josh's room and ran right into him.

He grabbed my shoulders to steady me. "Whoa, sorry. I was just going— Wait, are you crying?"

I wiped my eyes with the backs of my hands and turned my head so he couldn't see my face. "No."

"Yeah, you are."

I sniffled and took a deep breath. "I'm fine. I just need my keys. You can borrow my notes."

He looked at me skeptically. "Now I know you're not all right. You would never trust me with your notes."

"I need to go," I said firmly.

Josh looked uncertain as to what he should do. I could tell he was battling with himself. As my friend, he felt like he should talk to me. As a guy, he didn't want anything to do with a crying female. *Whatever.* He was in my way. My purse with my keys was behind him.

"I'm fine," I said, looking him right in the eye.

"Okay." He stepped aside, his expression still uncertain but also relieved.

I shoved past him and yanked my purse by its strap. It twisted around and all of the contents fell on the floor.

"Fuck." I kneeled down to gather my things. Sitting right next to my purse was a breath mint from the steak house Luke had taken me to. I grabbed it and threw it across the room. "*Fucking asshole!*"

"Something tells me you're not talking about me," Josh said.

I stuffed my belongings into my purse, but my keys were missing. I got on all fours and looked under the couch, then I heard a jingle behind me. Josh was holding them up.

I snatched them out of his hand. "See you tomorrow."

Once I was in my car, I threw it in reverse and hit the gas, narrowly missing the car parked behind me. "*Fuck!*" I banged the steering wheel with my fist and took a deep breath, willing myself to calm down so I could drive. I was slightly calmer when I shifted into gear.

As I turned out of the driveway, the big black Jeep was turning in. I averted my eyes and sped away.

• • •

I pulled into a space on the far side of the Alpha house parking lot, needing to pull myself together before I went inside. Amber would be all over me, and I didn't want to talk about it.

How could I be so stupid? Even though Luke and I hadn't had *the talk*, I thought our status was somewhere in the neighborhood of exclusivity. Apparently I was wrong.

At least I hadn't made a big deal about our relationship to anyone. I hadn't called him my boyfriend and the most anyone knew was that we were seeing each other. So aside from Josh, I should be spared the public humiliation. Josh and Luke were fraternity brothers, but Josh was my friend. I didn't think he'd make a big deal out of my freak-out in his room. Or so I hoped, anyway. Josh didn't make a big deal out of anything, so this shouldn't be any different.

It was time to think about damage control. I might as well move on now. My relationship with Luke obviously wasn't what I thought it was.

What I'd hoped it was.

That was the real pisser.

It was just as well. This would make my life a lot less complicated. No more guilt.

Except I didn't feel guilt right now. Realizing that, I felt guilty for not feeling guilty. How fucked up was that? I'd paid attention in psychology, and I'd actually read the self-help and grief counseling books my parents and therapist forced on me. Not that they helped me at all. Now I could just psycho-analyze myself more expertly than before.

Oh, God. I'd fallen for him hard and fast. I thought it was mutual, but what if it was all in my head? What if Luke really felt nothing for me at all? My heart clenched.

Fresh tears streamed down my face and I cursed. I had just stopped crying, and now I'd started it up again.

I needed to get out of my damn head.

I fumbled around in my car searching for a tissue and came up with a Burger King napkin. That would just have to do. Yanking down my mirror, I blotted my face, trying to remove the smeared makeup without causing any more damage. My room was on the far side of the house, and there was no way I was feeding myself to the gossip mill.

After stealthily sneaking through the house to avoid the other girls, I lay on my bed, staring up at the ceiling with my feet propped up.

I wondered what he was doing. What he and the blonde were doing. Were they—

Fuck. Fuck. Fuck.

Why was I still thinking? I needed my brain turned off.

The door swung open and Amber appeared in the doorway. "What are you doing?"

I tried to neutralize my expression. "What do you mean?"

She strode over to my purse and pulled out my cell phone. "You have like a million missed calls. Is it on silent?"

I grabbed my phone out of her hands. Sure enough, I had four missed calls from Luke, one from Josh, and two from Amber. There were also several texts from each of them. I tossed the phone on my desk without looking at them.

Amber raised her eyebrows but didn't comment on it. "Anyway, Luke's here. He has your notes. You left them in Josh's room or something."

"I don't want them."

"That's a good one. Seriously, Luke's downstairs in the foyer."

I lay back down on the bed and stared at the ceiling.

Amber cleared her throat. "Did I miss something?"

"Tell him I'm not here."

"Um, he already knows you're here. I told him you were, and besides, your car's out front."

I rolled to my side so I didn't have to face her. "Just get rid of him."

"Seriously?"

"As serious as ever."

Amber sighed, but I heard her footsteps and the click of the door closing. I rolled onto my back and stared at the ceiling again. A few moments later she returned with my notebook, which she tossed on the bed next to me. She pulled my desk chair next to the bed and straddled it.

"What's going on?"

"Nothing," I whispered.

"Obviously it's something."

"It's nothing. It was always nothing, except I didn't know it."

"What are you talking about?"

"Nothing."

"Stop talking in riddles and tell me what's going on."

My lower lip trembled and a tear escaped despite my best efforts to hold it in. *Fuck. Fuck him.* I had my first pageant rehearsal tomorrow and now my eyes were going to be swollen and my face blotchy.

Amber moved from the chair to the edge of my bed. "Oh, honey." She pulled me up and hugged me. Her sympathy released the floodgates and I sobbed in her arms.

"I saw him with another girl. His ex." I managed to get out a few words at a time.

"When?"

"Just now at the Beta house."

She looked at the clock. "Like two hours ago?"

I nodded and told her what I saw.

She scrunched up her eyebrows, a sure sign I wasn't going to like what she was going to say.

"I think you should talk to him."

I shook my head.

"I'm on your side, but Luke doesn't strike me as someone who would cheat on you."

"That's just the thing," I said bitterly. "Who's to say we were ever together?"

"Are you serious?" Amber laughed in disbelief. "It's obvious you two are together. Have you seen yourselves?"

"No, but I saw him with his supermodel ex-girlfriend wrapped around him. I can't ignore that."

Amber shook her head. "I'm not telling you to ignore it. I'm telling you to ask him about it."

"I have nothing to say to him."

She snorted. "That's not true. Let's say he was up to no good, not that I think he was. Wouldn't you at least want to tell him off?"

I propped myself up on my elbow. "No, I just want it to be done, like it never happened, like we…"

I trailed off, remembering our time together after my weekend home. His hands on my skin, his lips on my collarbone, his body pressed against mine. I'd felt something, and I could've sworn he felt it, too.

I balled my hand into a fist and pressed it against my mouth to hold in the sob that was threatening to escape.

I needed something, anything, to take my mind off this. I

jumped off my bed and yanked my shirt off.

"What are you doing?" Amber clearly thought I'd lost my mind.

I pulled a sports bra out of my drawer. "I'm going to the gym."

I had pageant dresses to fit into and a guy to forget.

• • •

In criminology, I did something I had never done, something I didn't think I would ever do. I sat in the back. I wasn't about to skip class, but I wasn't ready to face Luke, so I slipped in at the last minute through the back door.

Cowardly, I knew, but I never claimed to be otherwise. Cowards were often the survivors in life. They did what they needed to do.

Luke was in his usual seat, next to my vacant one. I watched him throughout the class. He wore his usual jeans and T-shirt and looked as good as he ever did. I felt a warmth in my belly, my body reacting to the sight of him, and I was pissed at my body for betraying my heart.

I watched him throughout class as he took notes and switched between red and black pens. I smiled in spite of myself.

When class was over, I threw my notebook in my backpack and tried to make a quick exit. Next to me, two girls having a lengthy conversation about hair extensions of all things were blocking the aisle while they packed up their stuff. I crossed my arms and tapped my foot, but they were oblivious. *Stupid back rowers.*

I kept an eye on Luke the whole time. Right before he left the room through the front exit, he pulled his phone out of his pocket to check it for messages. Then he looked straight up to where I was standing, and our eyes met.

My lower lip trembled and I pulled my gaze away. "Excuse me," I said, pushing past the two girls.

"Hey!" one protested.

"So rude," I heard the other one say.

I didn't care. I had to get out of there. There were two different stairwells I could take. Since the classroom had stadium seating, the front entrance to the classroom was on a lower floor than the top. I took a gamble and picked the stairwell on the right.

I picked wrong.

Luke was waiting for me at the bottom, leaning against the wall with his arms crossed. His expression was perturbed.

I stopped in my tracks, causing the people behind me to run into me, and stumbled down the last step to stop right in front of Luke.

"We need to talk."

Chapter Eighteen

"I can't," I said, not meeting his eyes, afraid of what I'd see there. "I have to go—"

"That's fine," he said, his tone hard. "But we're going to talk. I'm coming over tonight. Don't send Amber to get rid of me this time."

He shifted to allow me to pass. I scurried past him, still avoiding his eyes.

I should have just talked to him then. I was useless in my next class. A rhino in high heels and a tiara could have come through and I wouldn't have noticed.

Later that afternoon back in my room, I was still useless. Luke had said he was coming over, but he hadn't said when. I even nuked a Hot Pocket instead of going to the dining hall with Amber. I didn't want to risk not being here. Now that I knew this confrontation was happening, I didn't want to put it off any longer than I had to.

Turned out I didn't have anything to worry about as far as dinner was concerned. It was after eight when my phone buzzed with a text telling me he was outside.

His Jeep was parked next to my car, and he was leaning against it, arms crossed. His eyes were hard, his expression dark. I'd never seen him angry before, but from the looks of it, he was pissed.

My nerves morphed into anger. Why was he pissed? *I* was the wronged one here.

I leaned against my car opposite him and crossed my arms. Under any other circumstances, our mirror-image postures might have been amusing.

"What the fuck, Cori? You ignore my texts and calls, you leave me waiting in your house for twenty goddamn minutes and then get Amber to send me away. Then today you try to avoid me in class."

I stared back at him, fury barely contained in my eyes. I was *not* the one at fault here. "That's right," I said, my voice dripping in venom.

"Like I said, what the fuck?"

I looked away for a moment, trying to keep my lip from trembling while I got the words out. "I saw you yesterday."

Confusion replaced the anger in his eyes. "What?"

"With your ex. At your house," I spat. "You drove off with her."

"*Fuck.*" He looked away, clenching his jaw, not even trying to deny it. Even though I'd seen the evidence with my own eyes, I had still hoped he'd deny it, that he'd be able to say something that would erase that image. It was stupid.

"So I guess we're done here." I turned to walk away.

He grabbed my arm. "Wait."

I eyed his hand on my arm and he quickly dropped it. He ran both hands over his hair, sighing.

"Lindsey came out to the house to talk to me."

"Then why'd you drive off with her?"

"Her friend dropped her off earlier. She's still friends with some of the guys, so she was hanging out, waiting for me. I just took her home."

"What'd she want to talk to you about?"

"She wants to get back together."

No hesitation at all. He just put it out there.

I was silent for a moment. I bit my lip and looked away, trying to mask the tears that were filling my eyes. *Shit.* I didn't want to cry in front of him.

Luke closed the distance between us. "Hey. Why are you crying?" He wiped away a stray tear with his fingertips.

I jerked my face away. He held his hands up.

"Do you think I got back together with her?"

I looked at him, the tears freely falling. "What else am I supposed to think? I saw you two wrapped around each other."

He shoved his hands in his pockets. "Fucking Lindsey." He sighed. "She's been trying to get back together with me since we broke up last spring. I said some harsh things to her so she would get it through her thick skull that I don't want anything to do with her. She started crying, so I hugged her. I'm not a complete dick." He laughed bitterly. "Or maybe I am. I've managed to make two girls cry in the last twenty-four hours."

"Why did you break up?" I wanted to know. Now that we were having this conversation, I might as well get all the dirt.

His gaze met my eyes. "She cheated on me."

I sniffed. "That sucks."

He kicked at the ground with his feet, and I knew there was more to it than that. I waited.

"You have to understand, Cori, I'm not the same guy I was with her. She was like an infection or something. God, it was toxic, you have no idea. But I was like addicted or something."

I raised my eyebrows and wrapped my arms around myself, taking a little step back.

"*Shit.* I didn't want you to find out like this." He sighed. "She cheated on me first. So I cheated on her. It was a vicious cycle that went on for about a year. She'd cheat on me, then I'd cheat on her. It was like some sick game she liked to play. I finally woke up to what I had been doing, how shitty it all was. So I ended it right before summer break."

I took a minute to process everything he'd said.

Toxic, infection, vicious cycle.

Cheat, cheat, cheat.

None of that sounded anything like the Luke I knew. The Luke I knew listened to classical music while he studied and showed me pictures of his baby nephew. The Luke I knew acted like a big brother to the pledges he was in charge of. The Luke I knew respected me, wouldn't cheat on me.

But here he was in front of me admitting he had a history of cheating, that he'd once been *addicted* to the girl I'd just seen him with.

He looked me in the eye. "I'm not going to apologize because I didn't do anything wrong, not to you anyway. I swear to you that what you saw was innocent." He took a breath. "But I am sorry that you had to find out about everything like this. I probably should have told you, and that's the only thing I will apologize for. It messed me up for a while, so I don't like to talk about it. And I know how it makes me look. I was a complete dick. But I swear, Cori, I swear to you that's not me. I wasn't like that before her, and I'm not like that now."

Luke looked like he wanted to come to me, close the distance between us, but I kept my arms wrapped around myself, a definite sign he needed to stay away.

I gazed up at the sky. I didn't know what to do. What Luke had just told me about himself shattered my perfect image of him. I mean, I'd known he couldn't be *perfect*—no one is—but he was pretty damn close to it.

Everything he'd told me didn't match anything I knew

about him. If I hadn't seen him with Lindsey, I'd never have believed him. In fact, if he had tried to tell me about his sordid past last week, I probably would have laughed, thinking he was joking.

But any girl who's ever read *Cosmo* knows the rule when it comes to guys who've cheated—once a cheater, always a cheater. If he were planning to cheat, though, why would he tell me about his past? He'd said it himself—he knew how it made him look.

I couldn't blame him for not telling me about this. It had never come up, and no one wants to offer up dirty details that made themselves look bad.

And who was I to punish him for his past?

I let out a breath. "Okay."

"Okay?"

"Okay. I wish you had told me sooner, but okay. I get why you didn't."

"I'm sorry, Cori. I was such a fucking dick last year. I'm so glad I didn't meet you then. I swear I'm not that guy anymore."

"I know." I smiled a little. "You're not a dick."

He stepped forward, taking my smile as a good sign. "Are you sure about that?"

"About ninety percent sure."

He reached for my hand. "Are we okay now?"

I took a deep breath and nodded. "I think so."

He looked down at me. "Because if you want to, we can hash out all our old relationships and crap. I'm an open book. I'll tell you anything you want to know." He grinned a little. "Do you have any secrets you want to share? Any old boyfriends waiting in the wings?"

Not in the wings, just in a grave.

He'd made the comment to ease the tension in a tense situation, but I stiffened, then forced myself to relax so he wouldn't realize something was off.

This was it. The question had been asked. I'd told myself I would tell him about Tyler if he asked. I just never thought he would.

I needed to tell him.

I should tell him.

But I couldn't.

Our relationship had just suffered a blow with his past. I didn't need to add to it. I shouldn't add to it. It was in his and my best interests not to tell him.

Lie. But it was a lie I was willing to believe.

"No," I said. "We don't need to talk about all that stuff. It's in the past."

He sighed with relief. "Thank God. I hate talking about all that shit. I'd rather focus on the now, you know?" He pulled me into his arms and kissed me gently, hesitantly at first, his lips soft and gentle. When I deepened the kiss, I could feel the tension leave his body and his lips devoured mine hungrily.

"I'm sorry I freaked out," I said. "I should have talked to you first."

"And then freaked out?"

I grinned. "Yeah, obviously."

He chuckled. "Cori, you're it for me."

I closed my eyes, smiling. "Say it again."

"You're it for me, Cori. No one else."

As far as "the talk" goes, it was perfect.

He kissed me again, then he pointed to the second floor of the house. "I think we've been entertaining your sisters."

I twisted to see who was peering out the window. All I caught was a blur of blond hair as whoever it was ducked. Probably Amber.

I wrapped my arms around Luke's neck and smiled mischievously. "I'd hate to disappoint them." I pulled his lips to mine.

• • •

"We're supposed to be studying." I playfully pushed Luke away. We'd been "studying" for an hour already, but so far that had mainly consisted of Luke nuzzling my neck.

"I am studying." He pulled my hair back and his lips began a lazy trail down my throat.

I tilted my neck to give him better access and enjoyed the sensation for a few moments. Then I came to my senses and pushed him away again. I stood, putting distance between us. That was the only way we were ever going to get any studying done.

"What are the approaches to restorative justice?" I narrowed my eyes at him.

"Individual orientation," he recited dutifully.

"And?" I prompted in my best teacher voice.

"Community orientation."

"Good. Now tell me what each one focuses on."

"Individual focuses on crime problem. Community focuses on social justice."

I closed my notebook with a snap. "Okay, so maybe you are ready for this test."

"I told you that an hour ago. Besides," he said, reaching into his pocket, "I have this." He held up a white furry rabbit's foot on a little chain.

I wrinkled my nose. "Where did you get that? And more importantly, why is it in your pants?"

"Hey, don't hate on the rabbit's foot." I could tell by his tone that he was mildly offended. "My dad gave it to me when I was eight. I hit my first home run that day. It's *definitely* lucky."

I snorted.

"Don't tell me you don't have a good luck charm."

"I don't need luck. I prefer preparation."

"Bullshit. Everybody needs a good luck charm."

I stuck my tongue out at him. A wicked gleam appeared in his eyes.

I looked at him hungrily, wondering what he was thinking. My thoughts began to go naughty before I pulled myself out of it. "There are only four grades in the whole class, so neither of us can afford to fail this test."

"We're not going to fail. Or in your case, get a B, which *isn't* failing, by the way."

"There's nothing wrong with having high standards."

"I never said there was. You obviously have high standards in your love life." He grinned.

I grabbed a pillow from his bed and threw it at him. It caught him off-guard and hit him in the face. I laughed at his surprised look.

He smiled and stretched out on the bed, folding the offending pillow in half and putting it under his head. "Would it make you feel better if I told you I also have high standards?"

"That goes without saying."

He raised his eyebrows. "Cocky, aren't we?"

"Not cocky, just confident."

"What's the difference?"

"Cocky has a negative connotation. Confidence is a positive trait," I explained.

"Your know-it-all voice is sexy."

I smirked. "That explains the attraction then because I always know it all."

"Correct me if I'm wrong, but that statement falls on the cocky side of things."

"It's not cocky if it's true."

He just laughed and held his arms open. "Come over

here."

An hour later, I peeled myself off the bed and away from him "I need to get home."

He pouted, actually *pouted*. Somehow he managed to pull it off while still maintaining an air of masculinity. And sexiness. "Why?"

"I need to get a good night's sleep tonight." As if on cue, I yawned. "Too many late nights at the Beta house make me a tired girl."

"You could just spend the night."

It was tempting, but grades came first. "Not on a school night."

He sighed. "If you insist."

I slipped into my hoodie. "That's the way it's gotta be." I wondered who I was trying to convince with that line—me or him. It wouldn't have taken much persuasion for him to talk me into staying.

He stood. "I'll walk you out to your car." Although part of me was disappointed, this was one of the things I loved about him. He respected my dedication to my grades.

I turned toward the door and smiled to myself, zipping my hoodie. Luke patiently waited at the door to walk me to my car as promised. That was another thing I loved about him; he was a gentleman.

My thoughts jerked to a stop. I loved things about him. Just *things*, though, right? I couldn't love *him*. We so weren't there yet in our relationship. Were we?

I didn't think so. We'd only been dating for two months. Surely that was too soon.

Luke put his hand on my lower back to guide me out of the room and down the stairs.

Did I love him?

The question troubled me.

• • •

Straight to bed. That's where I was going. I hadn't lied when I said I'd spent one too many late nights at the Beta house. I'd been over there almost every night for the past two weeks. Sometimes Amber came with me to see Brad, but the status of their relationship was rocky. They were hot and cold. Frankly, I couldn't keep up.

Amber was lying facedown on her bed sawing logs. One arm was hanging off the bed and she'd kicked the covers down around her ankles. I quickly brushed my teeth and donned my pajamas, slipping in earplugs before I climbed into bed.

Then I tossed and turned. I stared at Amber across the room. How could anyone so small create such a loud, obnoxious noise? I contemplated crossing the room to shake her, but in the end I threw the covers off and turned on my laptop. Even though my body was tired, my mind was too busy to sleep anyway.

Things with Luke were moving fast. But *too* fast? That I wasn't so sure of. Luke was a great guy. I liked him a lot. And I really cared about him. We had fun together, and with the exception of the situation with his ex-girlfriend, the relationship was drama-free.

What more could a girl want?

Nothing.

I smiled into the darkness. I was a lucky girl.

I scrolled through my email for a few minutes, but there was nothing important. A few games of solitaire later, I shut down my computer.

I grabbed a novel from my nightstand and curled up in bed with plans to read myself to sleep. It only took two pages for my eyes to start drooping, but then I realized I'd forgotten to plug in my cell phone.

I groaned and flung the covers off, grabbing the phone.

A light was blinking, indicating I had a voicemail. It would drive me crazy if I didn't check it, so I punched in my code and put the phone up to my ear.

"Cori, this is Chuck, Chuck Pullman."

His voice was unsteady. Could he be drunk? Did he actually drunk dial me?

I covered my mouth with my hand, stifling a giggle. Was that funny or pathetic?

I hadn't heard from him since our one dinner, so I figured he'd gotten what he wanted. Good. Everything about that situation was complicated.

"I was just sitting here thinking, you know, about cake. What kind of cake would my boy like? I like pound cake, but what does he like? Vanilla? Chocolate? Carrot? Hell if I know. Shouldn't I know this? Shouldn't I know what kind of cake to get my son for his birthday?" His voice caught on that last line and the message abruptly ended.

Frowning, I stared down at my phone. Then I noticed the date in the upper left-hand corner.

Oh, fuck.

I gasped, quickly covering my mouth with my hand. How could I forget?

I'd been too busy thinking about Luke to remember what day it was. Tyler's birthday. He would have been twenty.

All the air had been sucked out of my lungs. I inhaled sharply, trying to fill my chest with air, but even still, the emptiness remained.

I couldn't breathe. I put my head between my knees and gasped, my breaths coming in short. I pulled my knees up to my chest and rocked.

Spice cake. Tyler's favorite cake was spice cake with cream cheese frosting. It was so odd—what person under the age of sixty liked spice cake? In some ways, he'd had the tastes of an old man. I teased him about it mercilessly, but the truth was I always thought it was kind of cute.

He'd had so many endearing traits, like calling his teachers *ma'am* and *sir*, even when they were barely older than we were. His mother had raised him right. He was chivalrous when most of his friends were trying to figure out the fastest way into a girl's panties.

After we went our separate ways to college, though, things changed. *He* changed. I saw it, but I didn't take the time to figure out why. Now it was too late.

I wondered what he'd think of Luke. I never thought about both of them at once—they were carefully kept separate in my mind. I purposefully didn't compare them. It seemed wrong, not fair. Luke wasn't a substitution for Tyler.

Still, I had to admit there were similarities, but so what? That just meant I had a type. Most girls did, right?

Most girls didn't drive their boyfriends to commit suicide, a dark voice inside me countered.

I climbed back into bed and pulled the covers up to my neck. "I'm sorry, Tyler," I whispered to the dark. "Happy birthday."

Chapter Nineteen

I turned in my Scantron for the criminology test. As usual, I had stressed over nothing. It was easy, and Luke and I had studied all of the right material. There was only one question that I was a little iffy on, and I was pretty confident I'd guessed correctly. Either way, I aced it.

Luke had finished his test fifteen minutes before me. I was horrified that he'd turned it in without even double-checking his answers. I double-checked and *triple*-checked mine.

He was waiting for me outside the classroom, leaning casually against the wall with his backpack slung over one shoulder. He smiled when he saw me. "How'd you do?"

"Easy peasy."

He snorted. "Then why did it take you so long?"

I huffed. "I was being thorough."

He threw an arm around my shoulders and said suggestively, "I like it when you're thorough."

I gave him a tight smile. Normally, I would have come up with a retort for his innuendo, but I wasn't in the mood. I was still morbidly singing "Happy Birthday" to Tyler in my mind.

He looked at me quizzically, his eyes studying my face. "Are you okay?"

As if on cue, I yawned. "I didn't sleep well last night."

"How come?"

I shrugged, not answering the question.

"You weren't seriously stressing over this test, were you?"

I didn't answer, which he took for a confirmation.

He shook his head. "Cori, you are the smartest person I know. I bet nobody's GPA even came close to yours in high school."

"One person's did," I said without thinking. Tyler and I had been neck and neck with our GPA's all throughout high school. We took a lot of the same classes, which is actually how we met. The competition was fierce and good-natured at the same time. We were always heckling each other over grades. It came down to our final semester to determine I would be valedictorian and he salutatorian. I had been appropriately modest on the outside, but I was secretly thrilled.

Thrilled to beat him in what turned out to be our final competition.

I stumbled.

"Whoa," Luke said, grabbing hold of my arm to prevent me from falling.

"I'm sorry," I said, feeling the tears coming. I used my hair as camouflage and trotted ahead. "I've got to go!" I called back to him. As soon as I got out of the building, I broke into a run and just made it onto the shuttle to Greek housing before it pulled away.

It was a short ride to our house. I ran into the building, almost knocking over one of my sisters on the way up the stairs. I called an apology over my shoulder.

I curled up on my bed, wrapping myself in my comforter. How could he have done it? How could he have ended his life at nineteen? Could I have prevented it? We'd been fighting a lot, sure, but so did a lot of couples in long-distance relationships. It was stressful. It didn't help that we were both type-A personalities.

If only I'd known where he was heading, I might have been able to talk him down from that ledge. But like so many other things, I'd never know. I was too dense to see the signs. They say hindsight is twenty-twenty, but even now, I didn't see it. Surely there had to be signs. Or maybe I was too involved with my own life to be bothered.

Amber strolled in and dropped her backpack in the middle of the floor, true to form. "What are you doing here? Don't you have class?"

I looked up. "Yesterday was his birthday."

Confusion clouded her eyes at first, then realization hit her. "Oh, honey." She crossed the room to me and wrapped her arms around me. "Why didn't you tell me?"

"I forgot," I whispered. "I just forgot."

"That's good."

I recoiled as if she'd hit me.

She moved to my desk chair. "Don't take that the wrong way. It's just that's how it's supposed to work. You're supposed to move on."

"It's my fault." I shook my head again, pulling my knees up to my chest. "I should have known."

"How? No one knew! You can't beat yourself up over this."

I put my head down on my knees, smearing tears and mascara on my comforter. My phone beeped, indicating a text message.

I heard Amber pick up my phone. "It's Luke." She held it out to me.

"I...I can't right now."

"He wants to know if you're okay. Should I text him back

for you?"

"Sure."

She pounded out a quick text and then tossed the phone back on my bed. "You know, you're going to fuck this up if you're not careful."

My neck jerked up. The anger in her eyes surprised me.

"That's right," she snapped. "Luke is like, perfect, but you're going to fuck it up if you don't get your head out of your ass."

My jaw dropped open. My disbelief turned to anger, then to hurt. I didn't even know what to say to her. She was supposed to be my best friend. She'd always been so understanding about Tyler. Her new attitude was catching me off-guard.

Amber stomped back to her side of the room and rummaged through her backpack. "Any girl would kill to have a guy like Luke. You probably ran out on him today or something, didn't you?"

The look on my face was the confirmation she needed.

"You're so busy living in the past that you're pushing away the here and now, and everyone in it."

"I can't believe you're saying this to me," I stammered. "You obviously don't get it."

Amber threw up her arms in frustration. "I get it! What happened was terrible. But life doesn't have to keep being terrible. You couldn't control what happened then, but you're in control of now, and I'm telling you—you're messing it up."

My hurt transformed to fury. What did she know about relationships? She'd never managed to develop a healthy one. With the guys she usually picked, they were DOA. She had no room to be shoveling out relationship advice.

"How can you say that to me?"

Amber yanked on the zipper on her backpack and slung the strap over her shoulder. "I say it because you need to hear it." She opened her mouth as if she was going to say something else, but the beep from my phone cut her off. She just shook her head. "That's probably Luke. I'll see you later."

The slam of the door echoed in my ears long after she was gone.

. . .

I eyed Amber across the party room at the Beta house as she planted a kiss on Brad's cheek. Her hot and cold thing with Brad must be in a hot period. I wouldn't know. We'd avoided each other all week. I kept waiting for her to apologize, but it was becoming painfully obvious she wasn't going to.

I wasn't in the wrong here. She'd been way out of line. Right? Right.

I mean, *what the hell*. She was supposed to be my best friend. If our roles were reversed, I never would have lashed out at her like she lashed out at me. But that was just the problem. Our roles weren't reversed and it was unlikely they ever would be. I *hoped* they never would be.

She just didn't get it.

A ball sailed into the cup sitting in front of me, splashing beer onto my shirt. I fished out the ping pong ball and shook it off, then downed the cup. Ugh. Warm cheap beer.

Luckily, it was Luke's turn next, and he sank the next shot, winning the game. I still didn't get the whole beer pong obsession, but I was glad we won for his sake. I didn't know why he insisted I play with him. My skill level had gotten worse, not better.

He wrapped an arm around my waist. "Do you want something decent to drink?"

I smiled, figuring if I faked a good mood long enough, it might actually become reality. "Sure."

"I'll be back." He kissed my cheek and started toward

the hall that led to the bedrooms.

I grabbed his arm. "You stay and play. I'll go."

"You sure?"

I nodded.

He smiled and kissed me. "You're the best."

I wandered down the hall and up the stairs to his room. His mini-fridge was well stocked with beer. I searched, but couldn't find any liquor other than whiskey. I don't think I'd ever be that desperate. Beer it was.

I grabbed two bottles and headed back to the party room. Josh had joined the group with his flavor of the month. She was a leggy young-looking blonde he introduced as Tiffani, spelled with an *i*, she informed me. It took all the self-control I had left not to roll my eyes to her face. I immediately looked to catch Amber's eye, but then I remembered we still weren't on speaking terms.

I dropped into an empty chair several feet away from the beer pong table. Close enough so as not to be anti-social, but not close enough to have to socialize.

Luke sank into the chair next to me. "You doing okay?"

"Yeah. Just a little tired."

"Are you still not sleeping well?"

I picked at the label on my bottle. "Not really."

"Should you see someone about that?"

I shrugged. I had prescription sleeping pills, but I never took them. I figured if I got tired enough, I would sleep.

That wasn't the whole problem, though. Between practicing for the pageant, working out, and actual pageant rehearsals, not to mention keeping up with my normal schoolwork, there wasn't much time left for sleeping. So when I didn't get to bed until way after midnight most nights, taking an hour or more to fall asleep, it meant I was lucky to get three or four hours a night.

So far, I hadn't told Luke about the pageant. He was so

busy with the pledges that it'd been a non-issue—he hadn't noticed how much time I'd been away doing pageant stuff. I couldn't put into words why I was reluctant to tell him. Probably because I was reluctant to do the thing in the first place.

"I'll be fine." I put my bottle between my knees and rubbed my temples.

"Headache?"

"Yeah. Drinking this"—I held up the beer and shook it—"probably isn't helping."

Luke stood, taking the bottle out of my hands. "I'll drink that, then. I'll be right back with some water and Advil for you."

He gave me a peck on the lips before he left, and I smiled at his retreating form. It was nice having someone who wanted to take care of me.

I tapped my fingers on my thigh, tuning out the conversations around me while I waited for Luke to return. Then something Tiffani said caught my attention.

"My roommate is such a bitch," she complained. "The world would be a better place if she just killed herself."

All the breath left my body. I clenched my fists and I ground my teeth. Amber quickly looked over at me to see if I'd heard, her eyes wide as the ping pong balls.

"She can't be that bad," Josh said, laughing. "I could tell you some stories about my freshman roommate that would put this girl to shame."

Brad threw a ball at him and it bounced off his forehead. "Hey, asshole. That was me."

"No, no, no," Tiffani insisted, waving around her hands adorned with fake nails. "This girl is pathetic. She seriously should just kill herself."

I stood up so fast my chair fell over backwards. "Don't say that."

Tiffani flipped her hair over her shoulder and put a hand on her hip. She looked at me scathingly. "Whatever."

"No," I said firmly. "Not *whatever*. Don't say that."

"I wasn't talking to you," she said, rolling her eyes. "Mind your own business."

Brad and Josh stood watching with their mouths open, neither one making a move toward us. They didn't seem to know what to make of the situation.

Amber grabbed my arm and gently pulled me away. "Let's go. Just let it go."

I gave Tiffani one last dirty look, but allowed myself to be led away. It didn't matter, I told myself. She's just a stupid girl.

"Maybe *you* should go kill yourself," Tiffani muttered to my back.

I spared a split-second glance at Amber before I turned and lunged at the stupid bitch. All I could see was red. Blood pounded in my ears.

"I told you. *Don't say that.*"

I pushed her, hard enough to make her stumble. "Fucking bitch!"

Her eyes opened wide. Then she grabbed a cup of beer off the beer pong table and threw it on me.

I didn't think. I just reacted.

I charged at her, and we both fell to the ground. I cracked my knee hard on the concrete floor, but I ignored the pain that shot up and down my leg.

It was like all the rage I'd ever swallowed down had been unleashed all at once.

The little twit got hold of my hair and yanked. I felt a burning in my scalp, which only fueled my anger. I balled my fingers into a fist and punched her in the nose. Surprise at the pain in my knuckles only registered for a brief moment before I was going at her again.

I felt hands pull me back. I flung my fist out one last time, clocking her on the cheek. "Fucking bitch!" Then I was hauled up and carried away.

"Let me go!" I screamed. "She deserves it!" I clawed at the person carrying me. Rage consumed me.

When we got outside, I realized it was Luke carrying me. He put me down once we were outside in the parking lot. "What the fuck?" He put a hand up to four long scratches on his neck.

Amber pushed past him to hug me. I started sobbing.

"Did you hear what she said?" I choked out. "How could anyone say that?"

Now that I was away from the situation, the rage gave way to anguish. I knew the effects of suicide firsthand. I couldn't believe someone would wish that on another human being.

Amber made comforting sounds in my ear, the way someone might for a baby. I collapsed into her and sank down to my knees. The sobs came so thick and heavy I could barely breathe.

Luke stood back with his hands on his hips wearing his *what the fuck* expression, but he didn't go back into the house.

Amber stroked my hair. "Honey, calm down."

I struggled to breathe.

"Is she okay?" Luke asked gruffly.

"Does she look okay?" Amber snapped.

Luke cursed. "I mean physically."

"Honey, are you hurt?"

I shook my head, my breaths starting to come in a normal rhythm.

"Is that blood on her arm?"

I numbly looked down to see a streak of blood on my arm. That bitch must have gotten her claws into me.

Luke paced around the parking lot for a few moments, then sighed. "Bring her up to my room."

Amber looked at me with a question in her eyes. I knew she was asking what I wanted to do. I nodded to let her know it was okay.

"I'll meet you there." He stalked off to the party room.

Amber helped me up and guided me back toward the house and Luke's room. He wasn't there when we got there.

"I couldn't stop myself," I said, dropping onto his couch and resting my head in my hands. "I literally saw red." I laughed bitterly. "Who knew that expression was for real?"

"Josh has seriously bad taste in women." Amber propped a hip up on the desk.

"*Fuck. Fuck. Fuck.* I can't believe that just happened."

It was almost like an out-of-body experience, like some rage-fueled monster had taken control of my body. I'd never thrown a punch before in my life.

Amber raised her eyebrows. "*You* can't believe it? Have I mentioned I'm sorry for yelling at you earlier this week?"

I snorted. "Don't worry. I'm not going to attack you in your sleep or anything."

"That's a relief. You've got a mean right hook…I think. Is that what that was? She'll probably have a black eye."

I laughed, a little hysteria returning. "You think so?" I wasn't too proud to admit the thought pleased me.

"I hope so," Amber said. "Look, I'm sorry about earlier. It was tough love, you know that, right?"

I nodded just as the door opened. Luke entered holding a wet washcloth to his neck. "Josh is taking her home."

Amber nodded, mouthing *should I leave?* to me. The truth was I didn't want her to leave. I didn't want to be left trying to explain to Luke why I'd acted the way I had.

It was totally not me, but strangely, I didn't regret it.

I nodded to Amber and she slipped out, pointing to the phone in her pocket to let me know to call if I needed her.

Luke sank into the chair opposite me and dropped the

washcloth on the coffee table, giving me a clear view of his neck.

Yikes. The bleeding had subsided, but it looked like he'd gotten mauled by a tiger cub. The scratches were red and angry.

"Let me see your arm," he said in a controlled voice, not meeting my eyes. I realized then that I'd crossed some kind of line in his mind. I'd done damage that might not be reparable. I laid my arm on the table on top of the clean washcloth he'd just put down and he inspected it. Then he pulled a plastic kit out of his desk drawer. In one swift motion, he twisted the cap off a bottle of peroxide and poured it on my arm.

I hissed, and he held my arm down before I could yank it away. He blotted the skin with a paper towel, then applied antibiotic ointment and Band-Aids to the worst part of it, where it looked like her nails had dug in.

Only then did he lean back in his chair and his eyes met mine.

I stared up at him. His face was a mix of emotions—disbelief, confusion, but mostly anger. How must it look to him? "I'm sorry," I whispered.

His eyes were hard. "What the fuck, Cori?" He stood up and paced the short length of the room.

"I can explain—"

He cut me off. "You'd better."

I cringed a little. He was so pissed.

"I didn't know you were the one who grabbed me. I would never try to hurt you."

He let out a breath. "You think that's what I'm worried about? I can handle myself. I'm more worried about the fact that you attacked a guest in my house. You do know I'm house manager, right? I'm responsible for everything that happens here."

"I'm sorry." My voice was small.

Luke's normally calm demeanor was gone, replaced by anger and coldness. There was a chill in the air. Then his eyes met mine, and they softened a bit.

He sighed and sank back into the chair. "Why did you go after her?"

"She said some things," I said meekly.

The muscle in Luke's jaw twitched. "What things?"

"She said her roommate should kill herself. After I yelled at her for it, she said I should kill myself."

Luke exhaled. "Okay." He looked at me expectantly, waiting for me to continue. When I didn't, he said, "That's a shitty thing to say, but there's got to be more to it. Why would you do something like that? I'm trying to understand here, but you've got to talk to me."

I fiddled with the loose strings surrounding the hole in the knee of my jeans. There were a few drops of dried blood there. "My... I..." I took a deep breath. "My high school boyfriend committed suicide last spring."

The hardness slowly faded from Luke's eyes. He leaned his forearms on his knees. "Fuck. I'm sorry. Were you still in touch with him?"

I realized he was under the impression that by "high school boyfriend," I'd meant only high school. He didn't understand that Tyler and I had still been together last year. Now would be the time to set the record straight. Now would be the time to fess up about Tyler.

That I might as well have killed him myself.

But I couldn't. I knew it was wrong. Luke had told me about the darkest side of him, his time with Lindsey, but I couldn't bring myself to tell him that I was the reason Tyler died.

"Yes," I said. "We were still in touch." I spoke the truth, just not all of it. Omission wasn't the same as lying. Or so I made myself believe. "So when that girl... I couldn't stop myself. I'm so sorry, Luke. I couldn't even think. I just reacted."

"I guess you're still pretty torn up about it—his death."

"And now I've messed everything up." Realization set in. Amber was right. She told me I was messing everything up, and here I was, sitting in a huge mess of my own making.

Luke lifted himself out of the chair and settled next to me on the couch. He put his arm around me. "I wish you had told me about this."

"I don't like talking about it," I said.

He took a deep breath, but said nothing.

"I'm sorry," I said again. "I'm so sorry."

He took another deep breath. This was it. He was going to send me packing. A fresh wave of tears threatened to spill over, blurring my vision. I wiped at my eyes with my fingertips.

"There's just one thing left to do." *Oh, God. Here it comes.*

He smiled half-heartedly. "You'd better tell me what your hot button issues are. You have a mean right hook."

I let out the breath I didn't know I was holding. Then I started laughing.

He gets it.

God, I loved him.

Chapter Twenty

"Stop laughing."

Luke lay on his back on his bed, you guessed it, laughing at me.

"This is why I didn't want to tell you." I poked him in the side. "I mean it. Stop laughing."

"Poking me in the side isn't going to make me stop laughing."

I raised my eyebrows. "Are you ticklish?"

I quickly straddled him, tickling him all over. He convulsed with laughter, his face turning deep red before I took pity on him.

"How can you be so ticklish?"

"Even Superman has his Kryptonite," Luke said defensively, catching his breath.

I rolled my eyes. "Somehow I don't think Superman would make it very far if all the bad guys had to do was poke him in his side." I stuck out my fingers menacingly.

Luke held his hands up in surrender. "Truce."

I flopped onto my back next to him.

"Honestly, I think it's great." He chuckled. "I've never dated Miss New River Valley before."

I sighed. "Trust me, if it were up to me, you wouldn't."

I'd finally told him after he noticed my weight loss. I was down four pounds, but I would like to lose another four. The bikini I'd been given for the swimsuit competition was practically non-existent.

I also needed to step up my game at the gym. I didn't want my butt and thighs jiggling in the spotlight.

"If you don't want to do it, then why are you?" Luke asked.

"I need the scholarship money."

"You know you could always get a student loan. I've got them."

I didn't want to explain my prejudice against student loans. "I'd prefer to get scholarships."

He leaned up on his elbow and tucked a stray strand of hair behind my ear. "You'll be great." A droll expression crossed his face. "You're not going to turn orange with all the tanning, are you?"

I rolled my eyes. "No. My skin doesn't tan, anyway. I'll have to get a spray tan the week before."

His eyes opened wide. "Seriously? Like spray paint?" He laughed.

"Fine, laugh, Mr. Hawaiian Tropic. Some of us weren't blessed with your golden complexion." I bit my lip. "Will you come?"

A look of surprise crossed his face. "Of course I'll be there."

My face relaxed into a smile and some of the tension left my body.

"Just let me know if you need me to oil you up for the swimsuit competition."

I poked him. "You're impossible."

I yawned. I was exhausted. Keeping up with my classes, attending pageant rehearsals, doing my own personal rehearsals, and working out were taking their toll on me. I was counting down the days until I could go back to a normal lifestyle.

And that was why all my preparations were so important. If I didn't do well in the pageant and win that scholarship money, then I wouldn't have a normal life to go back to. I'd be heading home next semester.

As far as motivation went, it didn't get much better than that.

Luke yawned in response to my yawn. "Stop that. You're making me tired." He kissed me lightly on the lips. "I'd better get going. The pledge meeting starts in five minutes."

He rose and held his hand out to help me up.

"How are they coming along? I haven't seen them in a while."

"And you're not going to, either. You bringing snacks and cupcakes made them soft."

I raised my eyebrows. "I don't recall you turning away any cupcakes."

He grinned. "I didn't want to hurt your feelings." He pulled me toward him.

I kissed him. "Such a gentleman."

He grabbed my ass, pulling me closer to him. "Always." He kissed me, his tongue teasing mine. Then he groaned. "I wish I didn't have this meeting now, but I can't be late. It sets a bad example."

I bit his lower lip gently.

"Okay. Maybe I can be a little late."

• • •

I looked at the paper in horror. Then I blinked. And blinked again.

No matter how many times I blinked, the grade scrawled in red Sharpie did not go away.

B-.

What the hell.

I slapped the paper facedown on my desk so I wouldn't have to see the offending grade.

With one final glance at the paper, I slipped into my jacket. I was meeting Amber at the dining hall for dinner. I still had over half an hour, but I decided to walk instead of taking the shuttle. I needed to clear my head.

Anything less than an A in Women's Studies was unthinkable. For starters, it was an intro level class. And second, the material wasn't that difficult. So when I'd run short on time and had to cut corners with my schoolwork, I'd chosen to focus on other classes rather than that one, thinking it would be okay, and now I was paying the price.

I stuffed my hands into my pockets and hunched my shoulders. Fall was late in coming this year, but now that it had arrived, it was here with a vengeance. I probably should have broken out my heavy parka, but I was delaying that as long as I could bear it. Once the parka came out, it would be months until warmer weather prevailed again.

That class was supposed to be an easy A, my slacker class. I quickly did calculations in my head, averaging the paper grade with the other grades I had received so far. An A- would be doable, but a solid A would take near-perfect or perfect scores on *all* the remaining assignments.

Like the one I should be working on tonight.

Sigh.

After dinner, I only had about an hour to do schoolwork before I had to leave for pageant rehearsal.

I stopped in my tracks and contemplated for a moment, earning the stares of a few passersby who must have thought I was one color short of the full set. Then I pulled out my phone to text Amber. She was going to be pissed, but I didn't have time for dinner. I turned around and trudged back toward the house.

Crackers and diet Pepsi it was, the dinner of champions.

· · ·

"No, no, no, no!" The pageant director's nostrils flared. She spoke with a French accent and kept her hair pulled so tightly in a bun that Botox was rendered unnecessary. I couldn't pin down her age—she could be anywhere from forty to seventy.

"Again!" Madame Yancy clapped her hands above her left shoulder.

Dante had led me astray. His friend was *not* the director. George was Madame's assistant, and he was as cowed under as the rest of us girls. The first time I'd met her, I knew immediately why the contestant coordinator sounded so apologetic about my having to do extra rehearsals.

We scurried offstage to take our places as the lights dimmed. This was our seventh, no, eighth time running through the opening number, "Luck Be a Lady."

We each glided onto the stage at our cue, arms open, smiles wide. *Step, glide, glide. Step, glide, glide. Turn!*

"No sloppy turns! Make them sharp! Sharp turns!"

I gritted my teeth—not an easy feat while maintaining a smile—and sharpened my turns. Any sharper and they'd be lethal.

We finished the dance and stayed frozen in our final positions. Madame slowly walked up onto the stage, one heel click at a time. She stopped at each contestant, pursing her lips and scrutinizing while she circled like a vulture going in for the kill.

She poked the girl to my left in her stomach with glasses

I'd never actually seen on her face. They'd only ever been used as a cattle prod.

"Suck it in!"

I sucked in my breath and held it while she looked me over. She made a little *hmph* sound and moved on. I considered it a victory.

Down the row, she jabbed another girl in the butt with the glasses. "Jiggly. That's all I see when you turn. Jiggles."

She sauntered down the row once more, somehow managing to look down her nose at everyone, even those of us who were taller than she was.

"Dismissed," she announced. "Talent in five minutes."

The girls scattered, some to the wings to stretch while others slipped on headphones. I slipped out into the hallway and sat at a piano to warm up with scales.

Jiggly Butt Girl—bad, I know, but I hadn't learned anyone's names—slipped out the same door. She wore guilt on her face and held a Twinkie in her hand.

"Jiggly, my ass," she muttered and stuffed a piece of Twinkie in her mouth.

Oh, the irony. I stifled a laugh.

She looked up when she saw me. "Hey, are you doing scales?" In went the rest of the Twinkie.

I nodded.

"Do you mind if I warm up with you?"

"Sure." I scooted on the bench to make room. See, that's the thing about pageants. Contestants are usually nice to one another. It's not the cutthroat catfight people think it is. And directors like Madame Yancy are rare. But I wasn't going to complain. Her dour demeanor was the reason there were so few contestants in the pageant, which allowed me to get in at the last minute.

The girl sank onto the bench and opened another Twinkie, taking a bite. Putting her hand up to cover her chewing, she said, "Go ahead and I'll join in. I don't want to hold you up."

I started at middle C. After a few scales, she joined in.

She was good. *Really* good. Good enough for me to realize I had stiff competition. Still, I complimented her.

"Thanks," she said, picking the crumbs off her shirt. "I would *kill* for another Twinkie. You don't have one, do you?"

I shook my head.

"I didn't think so. You're so skinny." She wasn't skinny, but I definitely wouldn't label her as plump. "I know I need to lay off the Twinkies, but every time that *woman* pokes me in the ass with those damn glasses, I can't help myself. This pageant's going to make me diabetic." She sighed. "I'm Sarah, by the way."

"Cori," I said. "Have you done many pageants?"

"More than I'd like to admit. This will probably be my last one. I'm about to age out."

My eyebrows shot up. If I'd had to guess, I would have pegged her at eighteen. With her full freckled cheeks and baby blue eyes, she didn't look old enough to have a license. I couldn't believe she was twenty-four.

"Have you done this one before?"

She nodded and held up two fingers. "Twice. That's why Madame Yancy singles me out."

"Has she always been this awful?"

"Believe it or not, she's actually mellowed. There were some complaints last year, so she's had to tone it down."

I laughed. "That's her toned down?"

"You should have seen her two years ago when she was going through her divorce." She sighed. "I don't even like these stupid pageants."

"Then why do you do them?"

Now the irony was on me. Luke had recently asked me the same exact question.

"My mother was runner-up for Miss Georgia, and

she never got over it." She shook her head. "So here I am competing in pageants. Twenty-four years old and I still can't tell my mother no." She nodded to the keyboard. "Can you play a few more scales?"

I'd gotten into pageants by chance. My mom's co-worker was involved in them and convinced my mom it would be fun to enter me in a Little Miss pageant when I was ten. I was second runner-up, so I kept doing them until I won one. I was never pressured into doing them; they were just something I did because I could. It's stupid to quit something you're good at, right? Some kids played fall and spring soccer; I did the fall and spring pageant circuit. And then once I started winning scholarship money, it would have been pure idiocy to quit.

Sarah wandered off after a while, leaving me alone at the piano. Absently, I played the notes to the chorus of "My Favorite Things." I couldn't play the piano properly, but I could tap out the melodies for a few songs.

I went backstage to see how far along they were and was surprised to see they were only up to contestant number four.

Each girl's talent was easily taking four times as long as it should have. Madame was no doubt being relentless with her *suggestions* yet again. I yawned. It was going to be a long night.

It was past eleven by the time the girl before me was up. My vision blurred with exhaustion. I stepped out to splash cold water on my face in the hopes that it would wake me up.

By the time I took the stage, Madame, George, and I were the only ones left in the auditorium. The other girls had left as soon as they were done with their talent.

My stomach clenched and unclenched as I stood in the center of the darkened stage waiting for the opening notes of my music. It was a familiar but not welcome feeling.

As my cue came, I pressed my palm flat against my

abdomen and filled my diaphragm. Before I could even get the first note out, Madame interrupted me.

"No! Why is your hand on your belly, girl?" Contempt filled her voice. "You look like you're groping yourself for heaven's sake. Again."

I blinked, my fingers clutching at my T-shirt. That was my routine, my ritual. I *always* put one hand on my abdomen. Feeling the air entering my body calmed me so that I could get those first notes out.

The curtain closed, shrouding me in darkness and I returned to my starting position. The music started again, the curtain opened, and I moved into position. It took all my willpower to keep my arm at my side as I drew my first breath.

"Stop, stop, stop! Are you a skeleton? Why is your arm so stiff at your side? Again!"

So we went through it all again. This time I was allowed to sing the first line before she stopped me.

"No, no. That note was hideous."

She was right. I was so concentrated on my right arm looking natural that I slid into the first note rather than hitting it full on.

When the curtain closed, I rolled my neck a few times and took several deep breaths. *Get it together, Corinne. Don't let that crazy bat get to you.*

I made it as far as the chorus.

She crooked her finger at me. "Come closer, girl."

I walked to the edge of the stage.

"You need to rehearse before entering my stage again. I will not tolerate mediocrity in my contestants. And you, my dear, are mediocre." She sneered. "Dismissed."

I wanted to run offstage. I wanted to yell and scream. I wanted to cry. Instead, I calmly gathered my belongings and exited the building.

The breakdown hit me in the car. I drove a quarter mile

down the street and parked in a McDonald's parking lot so I wouldn't risk Madame seeing me cry.

I hugged the steering wheel, the sobs shaking my whole body. I had known my performance wouldn't be stellar, but I didn't expect it to get massacred.

It didn't deserve that. Did it?

Was I still in danger of being cut out of the pageant? Madame Yancy had placed conditions on me when I joined late. I thought I'd proven myself and that I stood a strong chance of winning. Otherwise what was all of this for? Now I was worried about just being allowed to compete.

I was so tired. *I couldn't... I wouldn't...*

"Fuck!" I slammed my fists on the steering wheel.

I would just have to work harder, practice more. There was too much at stake.

And I'd be damned if I'd give Madame any reason to lay into me again.

Chapter Twenty-One

Luke pulled to a stop in front of the Alpha house. As I slipped on my jacket, I checked my watch. He was actually a few minutes early.

Got to love punctuality in a man.

I ran out—well, not really. In four inch heels, the best I could do was scramble out to his Jeep and climb in, careful to keep my skirt down. I wrapped my arms around myself and shivered. Fall was losing its battle to winter. Dr. Dunnall's moon boots might make an appearance sooner than I would like.

My cousin lived about an hour away, and today was her wedding. My parents were supposed to come, but my dad caught the flu, so I was representing the family.

I can't say I was disappointed my parents would be absent, giving me a stay of execution from the awkward meet-the-parents scenario. Maybe I could actually enjoy the wedding. It'd been a while since I'd done the Electric Slide, and everyone needs the Electric Slide in their life once in a while.

I twisted, leaning my back against the door so I could have a better view of Luke as he drove. His posture was relaxed.

"Did I tell you my parents aren't coming?"

"That's too bad." His ambivalent tone surprised me.

"Do you want to meet my parents?"

He glanced over at me before checking his rearview and switching lanes. "Do *you* want me to?"

I chewed the cuticle on my thumb.

"Why don't you want me to meet your parents?" he asked. "Am I your dirty little secret?"

"No," I said a little too quickly and forcefully. He raised his eyebrows. "I just don't have much experience bringing guys home to meet my parents." Only one experience to be exact, unless you counted my kindergarten boyfriend, Tommy, from down the street.

I stifled a yawn. Leaning my head back against the headrest, I closed my eyes, listening to the steady rhythm of the tires on the interstate. Even though I'd slept in much later than usual, I was exhausted. I had actually planned to study before leaving for the wedding, but by the time I woke up, I was pushing it to get ready on time. In fact, I'd grabbed my notebook and shoved it into my bag that was now sitting on my lap. I really should look at it.

"Cori."

"Mmm?" I murmured, my eyes still closed.

"We should go in."

My eyes flew open. We were parked in a church parking lot. I looked around wildly.

Luke's expression was amused. "You were out."

I checked the time. We should have arrived at least twenty minutes ago. "Did we hit traffic?"

He shook his head. "We were early, so I let you sleep."

I pulled down the visor to look in the mirror, hoping my

unplanned catnap hadn't screwed up my hair or makeup. I was relieved to find myself mostly intact. I rooted around in my purse for my powder.

"How late were you out last night?" he asked.

"I don't know," I said, but I did know. It was three a.m. I'd gotten rooked into helping my sisters decorate the house in preparation for a visit from another chapter, which meant I hadn't gotten to the gym for my workout until past ten. After that, I'd gone to the student center for vocal practice.

I finally understood the cliché *burning the candle at both ends*.

The powder didn't quite cover up the dark circles under my eyes, but it would have to do.

I snapped my compact shut and smiled at Luke. "Ready?"

As we waited for the ceremony to begin, I casually looked around the sanctuary. The groom was originally from Virginia Beach, a neighboring city to Chesapeake. It was unlikely I would recognize anyone, but it wasn't out of the realm of possibility.

The opening notes to "Canon in D" sounded, and in unison, hundreds of heads swiveled to watch the first bridesmaid enter. I looked appreciatively at the stylish jade-colored dress. My cousin always did have good taste. No gaudy bridesmaids' dresses here.

The doors at the back of the church swung shut, and the music shifted to the traditional "*dum-dum-da-dum.*"

When I invited Luke to the wedding, I was primarily worried about introducing him to my parents. But now that we were watching my cousin glide down the aisle in her white dress, I realized introducing him to my parents wasn't the only awkward thing about bringing a relatively new boyfriend to a wedding.

My cousin joined her groom at the altar, and after a short prayer, we were permitted to sit.

I watched Luke out of the corner of my eye. What was he thinking? More importantly, what was he thinking that *I* was thinking?

Whatever you do, Cori, don't be weird.

Sitting in front of us was the quintessential wedding guest couple. The guy was pulling at his collar where a line of sweat had beaded up on his neck. Next to him, his girlfriend leaned close to him with a smile that clearly suggested she wanted to be the one in a white dress. The guy's response? A deep swallow and loosening of the tie.

Oh, God. Did Luke think I was *that girl*? He didn't seem to notice the couple in front of us and was instead focused on the bride and groom. No visible sweat and the tie was intact. That was good, right?

I blinked and tried to focus on the ceremony.

But I couldn't stop staring at the couple in front of me. Was she… Could she actually be *blowing in his ear*?

Yup, she was. Wannabe Bride was full-on blowing in her date's ear. I would have loved to see his face, but all I could see from this angle was another tug at the collar. When she pulled away, she left a smudge of her orangey lipstick on his white shirt.

The girl caught me looking and I jerked my gaze away, feigning a fascination with the bouquet decorating the end of the pew.

Luke reached over and took one of my hands that were carefully folded in my lap. My heart warmed and I gave him a smile that I hoped he interpreted as *I'm glad you're with me* and not *I want to drag* you *down the aisle*.

Luke raised his eyebrows and leaned close to my ear. "Stop being weird," he whispered.

I started to giggle, which I ineffectively tried to cover up with a clearing of the throat.

Yup, that was me.

Number one weirdo.

• • •

Luke draped his arm casually around the back of my chair at the reception. He had to be bored out of his mind. *I* was bored, and this was my shindig.

Dinner had been served, toasts were made, and the first dance was over. I was biding my time until the bouquet was thrown and the cake was cut. Then we could make our exit without seeming rude.

My aunt and uncle stopped by our table for all of about twelve seconds. Just long enough for them to report to my parents that it was lovely to see me again, but not long enough to engage Luke in any kind of meaningful—or memorable—conversation. Just the way I wanted it.

I stole a guilty look at Luke. He wasn't my dirty little secret, but that didn't mean I was ready to announce his presence to my friends and family back home. It just seemed… wrong.

Even though Tyler and I were on the way out when he died, he had been a huge part of my life for five years. I was like an honorary widow or something.

Yeah, or something.

I didn't have anything to feel guilty about, but when I was in situations like these that reminded me of home I couldn't help but feel like I was doing something wrong. Like I was disrespecting Tyler's memory by being here with Luke.

It was like my school life existed in a vacuum. Tyler had never been a part of it, so I didn't feel bad when he still wasn't a part of it.

Luke stifled a yawn, causing me to smile. Yup, definitely bored. Yet he didn't look annoyed or suggest we leave early. He might actually be the perfect date.

But I already knew that.

I nudged him. "Thanks for coming with me."

"No problem."

"I'm sorry it's so boring."

He grinned wickedly. "It's worth it."

I arched one eyebrow. "Enlighten me."

He leaned toward me and whispered suggestively in my ear. His words caused heat to radiate through my body.

Definitely the perfect date.

"I'm thirsty," I said.

Luke started to stand, and laughing, I grabbed his arm. "That wasn't a hint. I'll get it myself. Do you want anything?"

He shook his head.

I made my way over to the bar, where I stood at the end of a very long line. I wished there was an express line. All I wanted was a diet soda.

Wannabe Bride's date was near the front of the line, sans jacket and tie, his collar undone, but she was nowhere in sight. He ordered two beers and a glass of wine. After receiving his drinks, he stood to the side of the bar and drained one of the beers. Then he walked off, beer and wine in hand, presumably to return to Wannabe Bride.

Fun times.

As the line inched forward, I glanced around the room. In the far corner was a table of guys who were about my age. I peered closer. One of them looked familiar. Very familiar.

Oh, shit.

What the hell was *he* doing here?

Eddie had lived down the street from Tyler. They'd been friends since kindergarten. But here's the thing—Eddie was an asshole. Tyler would always laugh off his asshole antics because they'd been friends for so long. But me? Not so much. Eddie and I weren't exactly friends. I couldn't get past the whole asshole part of his personality, even if he and Tyler were tight.

His gaze swung in my direction, and I ducked behind the linebacker-esque man in front of me. I counted to twenty and then peeked out.

I hadn't seen Eddie since the funeral, where he'd been a blubbering mess. Most of Tyler's guy friends had kept it together, but Eddie had broken down and sobbed like a baby. It was the one time since I'd known him that I actually felt anything other than contempt for him.

The man in front of me stepped away without warning, and I was left without cover. In that split second, Eddie's eyes met mine. His smile faded. Tightening his tie, he rose.

I had a split-second decision to make—stay and face him or run away? I only hesitated about half a second.

Then I turned on my heel and darted through the crowd.

When I arrived at my table, I was out of breath.

"Did you change your mind?" Luke asked.

"Huh?" I answered, busily scanning the room for Eddie. When I didn't see him, I sank into my chair.

Luke gave me a strange look. "Your drink?"

"Oh, yeah...that. The, uh, line was too long."

Luke shook his head slightly, the way men did when women did something they didn't understand, but they knew better than to question it.

"Do you want to get out of here?" I asked.

"I thought you wanted to wait for the bouquet and the cake." He paused, taking in the way I was anxiously toying with my silver necklace, my eyes darting around.

"Yes... No... I mean—" I stopped suddenly. Eddie was standing several tables over, and he was obviously looking for me.

I put my elbow on the table, turned toward Luke, and used my hand to shield my face.

"You're being weird," Luke said, only this time he wasn't

smiling when he said it.

"I'm just ready to go."

Luke gave me one last *you've gone off the deep end* look and scooted out his chair. As he did, the DJ called for all the single girls to join him on the dance floor for the throwing of the bouquet.

Luke settled back in his chair. Shit. We would have to wait until this was over to leave.

I peeked around my hand to see Eddie staring aimlessly around the room. He took a few steps in the direction of his table and I sighed with relief. It was going to be okay. Crisis averted.

Behind me a glass shattered loudly. In her efforts to make it to the dance floor for the bouquet throwing, Wannabe Bride had steamrolled a member of the waitstaff, causing him to drop his tray. It didn't even slow her down. She was one determined chick.

When I turned back around, I found that the incident had caught the attention of almost everyone on our side of the room.

Including Eddie.

His eyes met mine, and as he slowly took in the situation—Luke sitting with his arm around the back of my chair—his neutral expression turned dark, menacing. There was the Eddie I knew and loved. He strode in my direction.

I jumped up and headed toward him to cut him off.

"Eddie, hi," I sputtered.

He looked at me with a snarl on his face, then leaned in so he wouldn't be overheard. "You're a real bitch, you know that?"

I took a step back. How did I even reply to that?

"It didn't take you long to replace Tyler."

I shook my head. "That's not fair. I didn't replace him." Then quietly, "I loved him."

"Bullshit." He practically spat the word. A few guests around us looked up sharply. When he leaned in and quietly repeated himself, my senses were assaulted by the foul fumes of alcohol on his breath. Eddie being drunk could quickly cause the situation to escalate from bad to worse.

"You don't know what went on between us."

"I know you were the last one to talk to him before he drove himself into a tree. What did you say to him?"

"Nothing." I choked on the word.

He took a step toward me. I took another step back.

"Liar." Fury filled his face.

"You're obviously upset," I said, my voice expressing a calmness I did not feel. "Why don't you call me later when you've calmed down and we can talk?"

He clenched his fists at his sides. "You killed him, you fucking bitch."

I gasped. The room faded away, and all I could see was the darkness of his eyes, fury mixed with raw pain.

You killed him.

Oh, God. It felt like a thousand knives were piercing my heart.

Eddie's an asshole, a drunk asshole, I told myself, but his words still echoed in my mind—words I had been thinking, but had never given voice to.

I killed him.

His friends came up behind him then and pulled him away, leaving me standing there, tears starting to blur my vision.

Luke walked up seconds later.

His face was tight, his body tense. "Who was that guy?"

"No one," I whispered.

"I'm going to go talk to him."

I grabbed his arm to stop him. "No, please. It's fine."

Luke whipped around. "It's not fine for him to get in your

face like that."

"It's okay."

"It's *not* okay." Luke's voice was carefully controlled, contrasting with the cold rage in his eyes.

I wiped the tears from my face. "Let's just go."

Luke looked to where Eddie's friends were still pulling him back to their table. Eddie's eyes were concentrated on me, hatred clearly shining through.

"Don't do this at my cousin's wedding," I pleaded, putting my hand on Luke's arm again. "Let's not make more of a scene." He clenched and unclenched his jaw. "Please," I added.

He looked down at me, his expression softening a little. Then he put his hand on my lower back to lead me out.

By the time we got out to the car, I was shaking, and it wasn't from the cold. Eddie had voiced my deepest fear. Normally I didn't pay any attention to the idiocy that came out of his mouth, but I couldn't help but wonder whether he was the only one, whether others also held me responsible for Tyler's death.

In my dark moments, I certainly held myself responsible.

Luke started the Jeep but didn't put it in gear. He tapped his hand on the steering wheel. "Who was that, Cori?"

"His name is Eddie."

"Care to elaborate?"

Not really. "He's my...ex-boyfriend's friend."

Ex-boyfriend.

Was Tyler my ex-boyfriend? We never actually broke up.

How could we break up when I killed him? I bit the inside of my cheek so hard I tasted blood.

Did I kill him?

"Why would he lash out at you like that?"

He thinks I killed his friend.

"I don't know." I ran my fingers along the hemline

of my dress, smoothing out non-existent wrinkles. "The relationship...didn't end well. And Eddie and I never got along to begin with."

Luke stayed silent, the muscles in his jaw working.

"I'm sorry," I said. "I didn't know he was going to be there."

"If you had known," Luke said slowly, "would you have told me?"

I opened my mouth to answer, then hesitated. I wouldn't have told him, not if I could help it.

"That's what I'm talking about, Cori. It seems like there are always these little things you're not telling me, like about your ex-boyfriend's suicide. Or the stupid pageant."

"You didn't tell me about Lindsey," I protested.

"Yeah, I'll give you that, but that's completely over. It's not part of my life anymore. She just happened to show up at the house one day. You're obviously still having issues if you'd jump some girl at the mere mention of suicide."

I winced at the mention of *the incident*. I wouldn't mind having it stricken from the record. "It was more than the mere mention."

Luke just looked at me, disregarding my comment. "And now this."

"I had no way of knowing that my ex-boyfriend's—"

"That's not what I mean. I know you couldn't have known about him being there, but there's more to it than that. I'm not an idiot. There's more to this story than this guy being pissed because his friend's relationship didn't end well."

He waited, and I knew it was my cue to fill him in. He was asking, and I should answer. I *owed* it to him to answer. Instead, I looked out the window.

I could rationalize it all I wanted by claiming to not want to explain the Tyler situation while Luke was already agitated. But the truth? I was a coward.

"Is this the same ex-boyfriend who committed suicide?"

"Yes," I whispered.

Luke ran his hands over his hair. He was obviously frustrated, borderline pissed. I should explain. The words were there, ready to spill over, but I just couldn't. Not now, not while everything was so raw. I put my fist up to my mouth to stop myself from sobbing. There was nothing I could do about the tears streaming down my face.

Eddie's voice echoed in my mind. *"You killed him, you fucking bitch."*

"Were you…were you still seeing that guy when he died?"

When he died, or when I killed him?

I opened my mouth to answer, but choked on the words. After a few moments, Luke put the car in gear and pulled out of the parking lot. I guess my silence was answer enough.

The ride home was miserable, neither of us talking, both of us lost in our own thoughts. Though we were physically close together in the Jeep, the distance between us was great. It scared me.

Luke pulled to a stop in front of my sorority house. Had the night gone as planned, he probably would have taken me back to the Beta house. As it was, he didn't even ask me what I wanted to do, instead making the decision to bring me home. He was done with me for tonight.

"Thanks for everything," I said lamely, stalling. Even though I didn't want to talk about what had happened, I didn't want to leave things like this, either.

He nodded slightly, looking straight ahead, not wanting to look at me.

"I'm sorry," I said quietly. I didn't know what else to say.

"It's fine."

I took a chance, hoping I wouldn't make things worse. "It doesn't sound like it's fine."

"You're tired. I'm tired. Let's just call it a night."

"I don't want to leave things like this."

He finally turned to look at me. His eyes did look tired. "I wanted to pound the shit out of that guy." Luke ran his hands over his face. "Look, I'll be fine tomorrow. I just need to sleep on it."

"Promise?" I asked, my voice small.

"Promise."

I waited for a moment, wishing he would lean over and kiss me good night. When he didn't, I climbed down from the Jeep and slowly closed my door with a deafening click.

I took a step back, and he pulled away from the curb.

I just wanted to forget this night ever happened, but how could I? This could very well be the catalyst that would end us. "It'll be okay," I whispered to darkness. "He promised. It'll be fine."

A sick feeling settled in my heart as I watched him drive away. I hoped to God he was telling the truth.

Chapter Twenty-Two

Tomorrow came and went and things were not fine. Luke didn't call, and I even kept my phone on me in pageant rehearsal, risking Madame Yancy's wrath.

It was worth the risk. Luke was worth the risk.

But as it turned out, it was an unnecessary risk.

He was pissed. And justifiably so.

As I sat in traffic on interstate 81 on the way home from rehearsal, my mind went over our conversation from yesterday. Had our roles been reversed, would I have been as calm as Luke had been? I couldn't say I would be. My actions following the incident with his ex-girlfriend were a testament to this. That had not been my finest moment. I'd avoided the situation, actually tried hiding from Luke to avoid it.

Was I hiding again?

No, I'd had rehearsal. It was a legitimate excuse. *No, not excuse.* Reason. It was a reason.

But that nagging little voice in my head reminded me that there had been nothing stopping me from calling him on our break.

Instead I'd spent all morning and afternoon waiting for him to call, for him to make it better. Why was I putting it on him? There was nothing stopping me from making the first move.

I needed to try to fix this.

I swung by the dining hall on my way home and grabbed a salad, hastily scarfing it down before jumping in the shower. Now that I'd decided I was going to stop sitting around waiting for my phone to ring, I was in a hurry to get to Luke.

The Alpha pledges and the Beta pledges were doing a combined service project at a local food pantry, packing up boxes of food to get ready for the Thanksgiving distribution. Luke would be there. Come to think of it, Amber might be there as well.

I looked up the address for the food pantry online while I pulled on jeans and a hooded sweatshirt. Then I grabbed my keys and I was out the door.

When I got there, I sat in my car for a few moments in the parking lot. Luke's Jeep was there, announcing his presence.

So I was here. Now what? Did I just charge in there, declaring my love for Luke? First of all, I wasn't ready to profess the "L" word yet, even if that's where I was heading. Secondly, this wasn't some romantic movie. Grand gestures were usually pretty laughable in real life. And Luke had already established he wasn't a fan of romantic movies.

The heat in my car sputtered, alternating between cool and lukewarm air. I shivered and banged the dash, then thought better of it and pulled my key out of the ignition. It was like the car was telling me to woman up and get in there.

And really, this was kind of silly. We hadn't even had a fight. It'd just been a *misunderstanding*. The air just needed to be cleared a little. Nothing more.

So why were my hands shaking?

The front door to the building was unlocked, but the lobby

was empty. It didn't take long to find everyone though—I just followed the voices that were echoing in the empty hallway.

I found all seventeen of our pledges, the nine Beta pledges, and a handful of Alphas and Betas, including Amber, Brad, and Luke.

Luke's back was to me, so he didn't see me walk up. I slipped my hand in his and leaned my face on his shoulder. He stiffened.

He definitely wasn't *fine* yet.

"Can we talk?" I whispered.

He looked down at me, his face carefully neutral.

"Please," I said.

"Guys, I'll be back," he said to the pledges, then led me back out the door I'd just come through, my hand still in his. That was a good sign.

Once back out in the hallway, we separated. He leaned against the wall and I stood in front of him.

"I'm sorry," I said simply.

"You said that yesterday."

I lifted my chin a little. "It's true." I took a deep breath. "I have some things in my past that I'm still dealing with."

He stayed silent, crossing his arms.

"The guy who died? His name was Tyler." I paused for a moment. I'd barely gotten his name out without my voice cracking. "And yes, we were still together when he died. Things weren't...good between us, but we were still together."

"I'm sorry." His voice was softer, but his arms remained crossed. "I really am sorry that you had to go through that. I can't even imagine what that would be like."

"It's pretty horrible," I said, my eyes tearing up. What was it about people expressing sympathy that made me want to cry?

"If we're going to have any kind of future though, you're going to need to talk to me about things like this. You can't keep it from me."

"I know."

He sighed and opened his arms. I walked into them gratefully, pressing my face into his chest and inhaling.

"Here's the thing, Cori," Luke said, his face pressed up against my hair. "I care about you. A lot."

I let that sink in for a moment and felt myself sliding closer to the "L" word. If I just let myself, I could fall all the way.

"Me, too, Luke."

"But I can't do this if there's going to be secrets between us."

"I know."

Luke gently pushed me away, keeping his arms on my shoulders and looking me in the eye. "Is there anything else I should know?"

I'd already told him more than I'd ever wanted to tell him. Fear had kept me from telling him about Tyler—fear and grief. It was something I hadn't wanted to bring into our relationship. But I'd told Luke what he needed to know—I'd had a boyfriend who died, and I was pretty torn up about it.

Was torn up. It was definitely in the past. Luke was my present, and I wanted him to be my future.

I pursed my lips, then pulled them up into a small smile. "I can't whistle."

Luke grinned, chuckling a little. "Seriously?"

I put my lips together and when I blew, all that could be heard was the sound of air moving through my cheeks and out my lips.

He laughed. "That's a little pathetic. We'll have to work on that." His expression turned serious. "I get that you might not want to talk about the whole Tyler—was that his name?"

I nodded.

"The whole Tyler thing. I'm not big on rehashing the

past either, but you can't hide it from me if it comes up, you know?"

I nodded again.

"So I just need to make sure—that's over, right? I mean, if you were together when he died—"

"Luke." I grabbed his shirt and pulled him closer, going up on my toes so I could brush my lips across his. "You're it for me."

And he was. He really was.

He slipped his hand under my sweatshirt and ran his fingers along my skin, which immediately warmed at his touch.

"I wish I didn't have to hang around here," he said, putting his forehead to mine. "I can think of some better ways to spend our time."

"It's probably for the best, anyway. I was at pageant rehearsal all day, and I've got some homework to catch up on."

"And I have a pledge meeting tomorrow. You know, they keep asking about you."

"About me or the cupcakes I brought?"

"You, but the cupcakes might have come up." The edges of his mouth quirked up. "They wouldn't be opposed to you bringing some to the meeting tomorrow."

"The pledges? Or you?"

He kissed me, dragging his teeth over my lower lip. "Me. Any excuse to get you out to the house. With cupcakes."

I laughed. "I've got to go." Then my expression turned serious. "We're good now, right?"

"Yeah. We're good."

I kissed him one last time, then pulled away, only dropping his hand when I was a few steps away.

"Cori?"

I turned around.

"We'd be a lot better with cupcakes, though."

I rolled my eyes and shook my head. Luke was going to be severely disappointed when he learned cupcakes from the box were the extent of my culinary prowess, but that was a secret to be shared another time.

"Tomorrow's not good for me," I said.

"Pageant rehearsal?"

I nodded, and my heart started to race. I didn't have rehearsal tomorrow night—I was meeting Mr. Pullman for dinner.

But I couldn't tell Luke that, not after the hurdle we'd just cleared, not after I'd already told him there was nothing else to tell. Besides, the dinner didn't mean anything. It was just an obligation I felt I had to fulfill. If it meant anything I'd definitely tell him. And I *would* tell him. Eventually I'd tell him everything about Tyler, but the time wasn't right. When the time was right, I'd tell him.

Yeah, keep telling yourself that.

• • •

He was late. I'd driven almost an hour in rush-hour traffic to meet him and he was late. Plus, I'd lied to Luke. I scowled. Why did I agree to this again?

I'd already given Mr. Pullman two hours of my life. He'd given me a thousand dollars for my trouble. A fair exchange, or so I tried to convince myself. Only it felt wrong, sketchy, like I was cashing in on Tyler's death. Technically, I was. But I didn't *ask* for the money. I had agreed to meet with him the first time because it was the right thing to do.

I bit my lip. Why was I meeting with him this time? Was it because I felt I owed it to Tyler or was it the big fat addition to my scholarship fund?

There was no harm in taking the money. He was loaded.

A thousand dollars was nothing to him. So why did I feel so sleazy?

Because it *was* sleazy. I was sitting in a hotel lobby waiting for my scholarship sugar daddy.

What the hell was I doing?

Risking my relationship with Luke, that's what. This wasn't worth it.

I searched through my purse for my keys. He was fifteen minutes late. I'd take that as a sign that this meeting shouldn't be happening.

"Cori." I looked up to see Mr. Pullman striding across the lobby in a black power suit. Everything about him screamed power—expensive black suit, black leather shoes that were shined to a high sheen, and a tie that probably cost more than my entire outfit.

He held out his hand and I shook it. His lips curved in a caricature of a smile.

That was all for formalities. Once we were seated, the interrogation began.

He gazed at me over steepled fingers. "How did you two meet?"

"We had two classes together freshman year, English and Geometry." I told him about how we'd sat next to each other, how we competed academically, how Tyler had shyly asked me out after English class one day.

I didn't tell him how my heart had raced as I leaned up against a locker next to him, how his hair had curled over the edge of his collar, how his eyes had lit up when I said yes.

"He was a good student, of course," Mr. Pullman prompted. "Wasn't he salutatorian?"

I blinked, shocked that he knew that. He noticed my reaction. "I did attend graduation."

"Right," I said. "He was salutatorian."

"Did he like school?"

This was actually a very thoughtful question. I had to think about it for a moment. "He didn't dislike it," I said finally. That was the best explanation I could come up with. Tyler had been motivated. His drive to succeed paralleled mine; it was one of the major things we had in common. His good grades stemmed more from his want to be the best, though. He was like that with everything. If he couldn't be the best, then he didn't want to do it. He probably would have enjoyed things more if he didn't put so much pressure on himself.

It was like he felt he had something to prove. And the reason for that—or so I suspected—was sitting right across from me.

It was funny how an absence could be such a presence in a person's life.

God, I missed him. Tyler always knew exactly what to say when I was stressed. I could have called him after Madame Yancy laid into me at rehearsal and he'd have said—

Stark reality slapped me in the face. I didn't know what he would've said. It was like a sucker punch to the gut. He'd changed so much that last year.

He'd send me texts before and during my pageants. They didn't say anything significant. Mostly he'd just distract me with meaningless conversation about everything and nothing—the movie he'd seen last night, English homework, stupid comments people in the audience were making.

There was only one text that meant anything, the one he always sent right before I performed my talent.

I love you, and I'm proud of you, no matter what happens. Show everyone what my girl can do.

I put a hand over my eyes as my chin quivered. Raw emotion washed over me, pulling me in different directions.

I was angry at Mr. Pullman for ignoring a son who only

wanted a little bit of his time, at Tyler for selfishly ending his life, at myself for not seeing the signs. I felt guilt for speaking those final angry words, for being here with Mr. Pullman, for moving on with my life.

Tyler and I had drifted apart months before he died. But who knows what would have happened? We might have worked it out. We might have gone our separate ways. We might have remained friends. The pain came in not knowing. I had no choice anymore. My life was moving forward, while Tyler's would forever be at a standstill. He would never move beyond that last moment when we were screaming at each other.

"Miss?"

I removed my hand from my eyes. It was our waiter, ready to take our dinner orders. I quickly scanned the menu and picked the first thing that looked halfway decent.

The interruption was good timing. The last thing I wanted to do was fall apart in front of Mr. Pullman. For the rest of dinner, I stuck with safe topics, reciting facts about Tyler the way I might do for an oral exam.

As soon as the waiter cleared our dinner plates—mine still mostly full—I made my excuses to leave.

"Of course," Mr. Pullman said, reaching inside his suit.

He held out a white envelope. When I hesitated, he cleared his throat and shook it a little, his eyes commanding me to accept it. And just like I was one of his many employees, I did his bidding.

The envelope rode in the passenger seat on the drive home. Every few seconds I would glance over at it. Then I would shake my head and return my eyes to the road.

"I'm going to return it," I said aloud, as if speaking it would make it true.

I was such a liar.

Chapter Twenty-Three

"It's getting late." Luke yawned. "Do you want me to walk you out to your car?"

I shrugged. It was past eleven, which was usually when I started making noises about leaving. After a disastrous day, I'd gone straight to the Beta house.

Straight to Luke.

He'd smiled when I'd shown up unannounced, despite my ragged look. I was wearing yesterday's clothes and hadn't showered, but he was still happy to see me. We'd spent the afternoon and evening sprawled on his couch, vegetating.

He nudged me. "Come on. I'll walk you out."

I didn't move. Instead, I played with my necklace, sliding the pendant back and forth on the chain.

My fear of staying over had always been fear of it hurting my grades. Now, I'd managed to do that without staying over. I had been so tired from being out late at pageant rehearsal I slept through my alarm this morning, completely missing biology. I'd arrived to Women's Studies late, and most of the students were still scribbling away on an essay test. Even Josh had been there sporting pajama pants, disheveled hair, and sleepy eyes. I'd had fifteen minutes to do what had taken everyone else the full hour. I would be lucky to get a passing grade. It was so stupid and frustrating. I knew the material, but I'd simply run out of time.

I wouldn't think about that now. It was done.

Instead, I turned to Luke and laced my fingers through his. "I was thinking I might stay over."

His eyebrows shot up. "Are you sure?"

I nodded.

He smiled. "I'll find you something to sleep in." He rooted around in his drawer, coming up with a gray T-shirt.

I hesitated briefly. "I could stand to shower first. I woke up late this morning."

He leaned down, placing a hand on each side of me on the couch. He touched his lips to mine. "Let's go."

Once in the bathroom, Luke flipped the deadbolt.

"Does anyone have the key to that?" I asked nervously.

He shook his head. "Just me. House manager, remember?"

I nodded and pulled off my sweatshirt, leaving on my T-shirt. Luke had seen me naked before, but undressing like this in front of him was a new level of intimacy.

"Turn around," I told him.

"Seriously?"

I bit my lip and nodded. "Please."

He handed me a pair of his flip flops to wear in the shower and obediently turned around.

I stripped out of my clothes, folded them neatly, and placed them on the sink. I stepped into the shower stall and turned on the water. I stood for a moment under the scalding water, letting the steam sink into my pores.

I massaged shampoo into my scalp and stood under the spray again, letting the pressure of the water rinse out the shampoo. I imagined all of my troubles going down the drain with the suds. No more tuition bill, no more Mr. Pullman, no more bad grades.

Luke's touch made me jump. His hand snaked around my bare belly. I hesitated for a second, then placed my hands over his, pulling him closer. His lips found my neck and he slowly worked his way down. My breath caught as his tongue flicked on my collarbone.

"You're being bad," I whispered, turning my head slightly so I could see his face.

He held up a bar of soap. "You forgot this."

He ran the soap all over my body, drawing lazy circles with the suds. I spun around and kissed him, wrapping my arms around his neck.

He groaned and dug his hands into my hair. I ran my fingertips along his back, causing goose bumps to form despite the hot water. His muscles rippled under my fingertips.

I wrapped my arms around his neck again so I could nestle my body against his. He ran his hands down to grip my ass, pulling me against him.

Unfortunately, the water chose that moment to start going cold. All the heat disappeared in a matter of seconds.

I gasped and arched my back, pressing myself against him harder in an attempt to avoid the freezing water. Luke reached around me and turned the water off. He grabbed a towel and wrapped it around my shivering body.

"Does it always go cold like that with no warning?"

Grinning, he rubbed my arms through the towel to warm me up. "Most of us don't stay in here long enough to find out."

After checking the hallway to make sure it was clear, we scurried back to his room. The door was barely shut before the towels were on the floor and our hands were all over each other.

· · ·

I did the so-called "walk of shame" the next morning, but I wasn't the least embarrassed to walk in the house wearing last night's clothes. I was too absorbed in my own happiness.

After sleeping naked and wrapped around him last night, I smelled like Luke—my hair, my skin. My world was brighter this morning.

Amber put her hands on her hips when I walked into the room. "My, my, aren't you looking pleased this morning? Give me details."

I grinned and flopped down on my bed. "I never kiss and tell."

Amber just laughed. "I'm calling bullshit on that one. It's nice to see you smiling though."

"What about Brad? He makes you happy right?" In my current state of euphoria, I wanted everyone to be happy. If misery loved company, apparently so did happiness.

"The dumbass needed—and I quote—'time with the boys.' Lame," she huffed. "The trouble with him is he doesn't have any training. I'm having to break him in myself."

"Crack that whip," I said, snapping a pretend whip in the air. I closed my eyes, drifting a bit. I had a great night, but I was exhausted.

"Hey, Cori, don't you have class this morning?"

"Mm-hmm," I murmured, throwing an arm over my face.

"If you're going to shower, do it now. I've got to get in there, too."

"I already showered." I couldn't keep the smug sound of satisfaction out of my voice.

Amber jumped on my bed. "Something tells me there's a story there."

I put a finger to my lips. "Not telling." Nope, she didn't need to know about Luke's slow kisses down my throat or the feel of his hands as they slid over my skin. My belly tightened.

"You suck. By the way, the caller ID read Pullman last

night. I didn't answer it because I figured it was for you."

My eyes popped open and I sat straight up. "Fuck."

"I thought you liked Mrs. Pullman. I mean, she's your—ah—ex-boyfriend's mother and everything, but still. She's all right."

I sighed. "I do like her, but I don't think she was the one who called. It was probably *Mr.* Pullman."

"Oh," Amber said, then, "Ohhhh," with understanding. Then her expression changed to confusion. "Wait, what?"

"I've been meeting with Mr. Pullman. He's been picking my brain about Tyler."

Amber was silent for a minute. "Why now?"

"He feels guilty for being an asshole absentee father."

"And how is that your problem?"

"It's not. I just feel bad, you know? The man lost his son."

Amber snorted. "The man should have been a father."

I understood where Amber was coming from. Her dad abandoned her and her mom when she was seven. I knew she wouldn't understand why I was meeting him, so I hadn't told her. I had enough misgivings about Mr. Pullman without Amber's disapproval.

"I don't know why he would call this number. He's always called my cell before." I paused for a second. "Do me a favor though. It probably won't come up, but don't tell Luke about the Mr. Pullman thing."

Amber slammed her drawer shut. "That's messed up, Cori. I don't want to lie for you. I don't think it's good for you to see him. I mean, you're just getting back on your feet. You're finally living a little bit."

"It's the right thing to do."

"How is lying to Luke the right thing?"

I gritted my teeth. "I'm doing the best I can."

"I'm not judging you—"

"It sure sounds like you are," I snapped.

"Look," Amber said, irritated. "I don't know what it's like. I've never had a boyfriend die on me. Hell, I've never even had a grandparent die. I get that. But you don't owe Mr. Pullman anything."

"It's the right thing to do," I repeated.

"If it's the right thing, then why lie about it?"

My eyes shifted to my desk drawer where the most recent check from Mr. Pullman was tucked away.

"Drop it, Amber."

She sighed. "All I'm saying is you need—"

"I don't *need* you telling me what to do."

Shaking my head, I walked into the bathroom and slammed the door behind me. The logical part of me knew she was right. Seeing Mr. Pullman might be the right thing to do, but if it was so right, then I shouldn't feel the need to lie to Luke about it.

Or maybe I just shouldn't be doing stuff I have to lie about. Except I'd already crossed that bridge.

Luke and I were in a really good place right now. Telling him about Mr. Pullman would just fuck everything up. There was no reason he needed to know. It had absolutely nothing to do with our relationship.

I jerked my thumb away from my mouth. *Damn.* I'd been chewing on my nail without even realizing it. I examined it, hoping the damage wasn't too bad. My hands needed to be presentable for the interview portion of the pageant.

I just needed to make it through the end of the semester. With Thanksgiving right around the corner, I was almost there. By then, I'd have the tuition situation resolved, and winter break would give me some distance from Mr. Pullman.

A new semester meant a new start. No more lies.

• • •

Dr. Nantis calmly folded her hands on the desk in front of her. "I do not allow students to redo assignments without a compelling reason. Do you have a compelling reason?"

I stared at the pattern in the carpet. You might think the brown and green swirls would mask the various coffee stains, but no such luck. "I overslept."

She pursed her lips. "That's certainly not a compelling reason."

"I know." I ran my hands over my face. "I was out late the night before at a pageant rehearsal."

She scrunched her nose and pursed her lips in disgust. It was not a good look for her. It went against her whole Zen vibe she had going with the scarves. She stared down at me over her purple reading glasses that were perched precariously on the end of her nose. "I see."

I didn't think she did, but I thanked her anyway and left. It was a lost cause. No way was she giving me a break.

I'd done the math several times. Somehow I'd managed a C on the in-class essay assignment, but combined with the B- on that test, the highest final grade I could hope for was a B+.

I couldn't remember the last time I'd gotten a B. Elementary school maybe? The very thought of a B made me start to hyperventilate. My anxiety was compounded by the fact that it was my own stupidity that caused it, and I didn't mean stupidity in the academic sense. That essay test was easy. If I'd had the full time, I would have aced it with little effort.

I didn't have the luxury of dwelling on it. I had a ton of homework, including a lab report for biology. The rehearsals combined with my own personal rehearsals and workouts for the pageant had been taking up way more time than I expected. Throw in dinners with Mr. Pullman, and I barely had time to sleep.

Staying up late last night with Luke didn't help my

studying either. But I had to admit it was good for my soul.

Tingles ran up and down my body. If I thought about it hard enough, I could still feel his fingers running down my side while he lazily ran his tongue along my neck. A girl could get by for a while on those memories.

I pulled my coat tighter around me and picked up the pace. The wind was brisk, causing my eyes to water. I was regretting my decision to hoof it to the Alpha house instead of taking the shuttle.

My cheeks were chapped by the time I got home. Grabbing a blanket off my bed, I wrapped myself up in it like a burrito with arms and sat in front of my computer.

Biology lab report. Ugh.

As I read over my notes from the lab, I reached up to my neck to play with my necklace like I usually did when I studied.

My breath caught in my throat. It wasn't there.

Frantically, I grabbed at my neck, thinking it might have gotten caught up in my hair. I stripped off the blanket and felt around in my clothes, hoping it had fallen off and caught there.

No luck. I ran into the bathroom. I didn't remember taking it off in there, but nevertheless I rifled around through all the makeup and hair appliances lying on the counter. Not there.

I searched every surface in our dorm room and when I didn't find it, I crawled around the floor and looked under all the furniture. I ripped the comforter and sheets off my bed and shook them out.

My heart raced and my hands shook. That necklace was my last tangible connection to Tyler. I couldn't lose it. I just couldn't.

Except apparently I already had.

I closed my eyes and rubbed my temples. *Think. Think.*

When was the last time I remembered having it?

My eyes popped open as I remembered. The last time I had it I was wearing it and nothing else. In Luke's bed.

I didn't think twice about it. I grabbed my keys and ran out of the room. Fortunately I hit every green light on the way there. I might've run them if they had been red.

My heart pounded as I ran upstairs to Luke's room. He wasn't there, but the door was unlocked. I flung it open, my eyes frantically surveying the room, searching for the glint of silver.

I didn't see it. Hesitating only a second, I started searching his room the same way I'd searched mine. I ran my fingers along every surface and checked in the crevices between the couch cushions. The towels we'd used were neatly folded and stacked on top of the hamper.

Oh shit. What if it had been caught on the towel and went through the laundry?

I paused, the dread from my heart slowly leaching out to every part of my body.

No, I'm not doing the "what ifs." I need to know what is. When was the last time I definitely had it?

Definitely after the shower. I wasn't used to showering with it on, and my wet hair had gotten caught in it.

So it had to be in this room. It just had to be. I needed to keep looking.

"Now that's a welcome sight." Luke stood in his doorway with an appreciative expression, gazing down at me looking under his couch on all fours.

I was too frantic to be embarrassed. "I have to find it."

"What?"

"My necklace. I lost my necklace." My voice was distracted as I continued my search.

"That silver one you always wear?"

I jerked my head up and nodded, a little surprised he

noticed. I usually kept it under my shirt.

"Did you have it last night?" he asked.

"Yes."

"Are you sure?"

"*Yes!*" I was getting annoyed. "I had it last night, and now it's missing. It *has* to be here."

I climbed on his bed and felt around under the pillows. I put my arms down in the pillow cases thinking it might have gotten caught down in there.

"Maybe you lost it in your car."

I shook my head. I'd searched there already.

"Or maybe it fell off in class."

"Oh my God." I hadn't even thought of that. I'd assumed that because I remembered having it at Luke's that I'd lost it here, but just because I last remembered having it here didn't mean I'd actually lost it here. What if the unthinkable happened? What if I'd lost it in class or on campus somewhere? I would never get it back then. Tears welled up in my eyes.

I climbed off the bed. "I have to find it!"

"Calm down." He put an arm around me, but I shook him off.

"You don't understand!" I yanked the sheet off his bed and shook it. When nothing fell out of it, I threw it on the floor.

"Whoa," he said, taking a step toward me. "It's just a necklace. We can get you another one."

"No, we can't! Tyler gave it to me." It was out of my mouth before I realized what I was saying.

Luke blinked. "What did you say?"

I looked at him silently as the gravity of my mistake sank in.

"Tell me what you said." The muscles in his jaw tensed.

I shook my head. I couldn't say it. I couldn't repeat the words that were sure to drive a wedge between us.

He clenched his fists. "Tell me."

When I still didn't answer, he said, "You told me it was over for you." His voice was quiet and controlled.

Tears streamed down my face. I opened my mouth to speak—not that I knew what to say—but only a choked sob escaped.

"Yet here you are ransacking my room, tearing apart my bed where you slept last night, to look for a necklace from your old boyfriend."

"Luke—"

He wore a hard expression. "I can't compete with a ghost. I *won't* compete with a ghost."

"You're not. It's not like that."

His face was expressionless except for the fury in his eyes. "And I won't have a girlfriend who lies to me."

"Please don't," I begged. Suddenly the necklace didn't seem so important anymore. "Just let me explain."

He shook his head. "You need to go."

"No, Luke, it's not like that. Just let me explain—"

"Get out." He exited his room, not wanting to share the same space with me. That hurt.

"Wait!" I called after him shamelessly. He didn't come back.

I sat in his room for a few minutes, tears streaming, hoping he would come back. He wouldn't give up on me that easily, would he?

Except he hadn't. Giving up on me easily would have been dumping me after the incident with Josh's girl or after the wedding.

Three strikes and you're out.

He'd told me. Luke had flat out told me that he didn't want any secrets between us. The only secret I'd deliberately told since then was the one about Mr. Pullman. I wasn't lying when I told Luke he was it for me. I loved him. I didn't want anyone else.

I heard the roar of his Jeep and the spitting gravel as Luke peeled out of the parking lot. I waited. Ten minutes turned into twenty then thirty, and I was forced to accept that he was gone.

And just like Amber said I would, I'd messed it up. I'd lost him.

Chapter Twenty-Four

"You look like shit."

I picked my head up off the desk to find Josh staring down at me. I didn't have the energy to come up with a decent response, so I simply put my head back down.

Josh took a step back, holding a notebook in front of him like a shield. "Are you sick or something?"

"No."

He slid into the desk next to me. "I wasn't lying. You look terrible."

I scowled. "How do you manage to get so many girls to go out with you?"

"I'm not trying to get you to go out with me. If I were, you wouldn't be able to resist." He smiled at me in the way I'd seen him smile at countless other girls. It *was* a charming smile, but I wasn't in the mood to be charmed.

"I'm actually flattered that you don't want to go out with me. Your taste in women sucks."

He shrugged, not bothered by my critique of his love life. "Oh, I almost forgot." He reached into his pocket. "Luke told me to give this to you." He laid my silver necklace on my desk. I quickly picked it up and closed my hand around it, feeling the smooth metal that I had lost.

Then I opened my hand to look at the necklace that had cost me so much. Had this little piece of silver been worth it? Instead of putting it on, I slipped it into my pocket.

"Did he say anything?" I asked quietly.

"Nah. He just told me to give that to you."

I didn't know if that was good or bad. On one hand, Luke wasn't airing our personal business. But what did that mean? I had no idea.

I'd waited in his room after he'd left, hoping he'd come back. I had no idea where he would have gone, so I couldn't go after him. I'd remade the bed, an act of apology. If only it were that simple.

I'd stuck around almost three hours, texting and calling, pleading for him to come back. My messages went ignored.

Dr. Nantis swept into the room and promptly started class. For once, being in the front row didn't help me pay attention.

I hurt. I hurt everywhere. My hands shook and my heart throbbed.

I stuffed my notebook into my backpack and slung it over my shoulder.

"Excuse me," I said to Josh as I slipped down the aisle, doing something I'd never thought I'd ever do—I was skipping out on class. I had to talk to Luke.

Luke wouldn't take any of my calls, but maybe he'd answer if he didn't recognize the number. I'd seen a payphone somewhere on campus, but I couldn't remember where, perhaps the student center or the lobby in the dining hall. The student center was closer, so I tucked my hands in my pockets and power walked over there.

Luck was on my side for once, and I even had enough

change to make the phone call. My hands shook as I inserted the quarter into the slot, and I couldn't help but think back to the time Luke had surprised me at the vending machine. Back then, I'd been trying to avoid him. Now it was he who didn't want anything to do with me.

I dialed the number, holding my breath as it rang once, twice.

"Hello?" His voice sounded rough, distracted.

"Luke, it's me. Please don't hang up."

Silence greeted me, but at least he stayed on the line. I leaned my forehead against the wall. What could I say to him to make him understand?

"I'm sorry," I said. "I never meant to hurt you."

"Cori, my last relationship was toxic, nothing but lies and betrayal. I can't do that again."

"It's not like that. Just let me explain."

"You keep saying that, but how can you explain this? I think it's pretty obvious that guy still means something to you."

"Can I come see you?"

"That's not a good idea."

"But Luke, I care about you. I want to be with you." There it was. I'd put it out there.

"Cori...I... That's not enough. I'm sorry."

He hung up, and I stood clutching the dead phone for the next minute, not wanting to accept that he didn't even want to talk to me. He wouldn't let me explain.

But Luke was right about one thing—Tyler did still mean something to me. He always would. Was that so wrong?

I hung up the phone and started the long walk back to Greek housing. The wind had picked up since I'd walked to the student center, and I would surely have chapped skin by the time I got there, but I didn't care.

Maybe if the wind froze my heart, it wouldn't hurt so

much.

· · ·

I won.

I threw up twice, but I won the damn thing. I was Miss New River Valley and the recipient of a sizable scholarship, enough to pay my spring tuition with some left over.

I smiled until my face hurt and posed for pictures with strangers. No one I knew was there.

Amber had left town early to make it home in time to catch a flight to her grandmother's house for Thanksgiving. My parents didn't even know I was competing.

And Luke wanted nothing to do with me.

I sat alone on my bed in my rattiest pajamas, which were in juxtaposition with my elaborately done up hair and makeup. I twirled the crown around in my fingers.

God, this sucked.

I was alone in an empty sorority house. I had messages upon messages from Mr. Pullman. I'd cancelled our last meeting and hadn't returned any of his phone calls. He wasn't taking the hint. Persistence, I thought bitterly, was something I had so admired in Tyler.

Now it just pissed me off.

Where had I gone wrong? When had I let my life get so fucked up? I was normally in control of everything.

And that was just the problem. I thought I had everything under control. What an illusion.

I was so busy holding on to all the little things that the big one slipped right through my fingers.

Too late I'd learned my lesson. Sometimes you just needed to let go.

· · ·

"Honey! You should get out of bed. Grandma and Grandpa will be here soon."

I rolled over and looked at the alarm clock. 11:36. I pulled the covers over my head and closed my eyes.

Insistent knocking at my door. I looked at the clock again. 12:02.

"Honey, can I come in?"

My mom didn't bother to wait for an answer. She never did. Her asking if she could come in was basically an announcement that she *was* coming in.

She sat on the edge of my bed and rubbed my back. "Is everything okay?"

"Fine."

She pursed her lips. I knew what she wanted to ask. If you're so fine, then why have you spent most of fall break in bed? After the first two days, she wanted to take me to the doctor. Then she asked if I needed to see the therapist. I managed to convince her that it wasn't necessary, that I was just tired.

My mother wouldn't tiptoe around me all week. I was surprised it'd lasted this long.

I threw back the covers. "I'll get in the shower."

My mom nodded, placing her hands in her lap. As she looked down, I noticed tears in her eyes. My mom never cried.

"Is everything okay?" I asked her.

"I'm worried about you."

I looked at her, really looked at her. She was a mess. My mom was always polished, put together, and upbeat.

I pulled at a loose thread on my pajama T-shirt. "I'm fine."

My parents and I hadn't spoken much since I'd been home. I still hadn't forgiven them for screwing up my financial aid.

As I looked in her eyes, though, I saw concern there. And

love. I looked at her again, realization smacking me in the face. This was my mother, and I was only ever going to get one. She had her flaws, but I certainly wasn't perfect, either. It was time to kick the grudge to the curb.

"I've actually been meaning to ask you," I said, "do you want to do Black Friday shopping tomorrow? It would be nice to get my Christmas shopping done early this year."

Her face brightened immediately. "Really?" She clapped her hands together, as gleeful as a child on Christmas morning instead of a grown adult who relished the craziness of Black Friday. I went with her once. Once was enough.

I wasn't looking forward to Black Friday shopping, but I was happy I'd resolved things with my mother. It was the right thing to do. It was time to stop living in the past. I had enough problems to deal with in the present.

• • •

I took a deep breath and rang the doorbell. Once upon a time, I would have just walked right in. Those days were long gone.

The door opened and familiar friendly brown eyes greeted me. "Come in." Mrs. Pullman stepped back and waved me in.

We stood awkwardly for a second, not sure of our status. She used to be a second mother to me. A lot had changed.

She gestured to the living room where she'd set out lemonade and my favorite homemade chocolate chip cookies. I sat on the edge of the couch, my eyes drawn to the framed pictures sitting on the mantle.

She sat next to me. "How are your classes going?"

I tore my eyes away from the mantle. "Pretty good. I had some trouble in one class, but I should still pull off a B."

"Ooh, a B. Are you okay with that?"

The woman knew me well. "Not really, but there's not

much I can do about it now."

She poured a glass of lemonade and handed it to me. "Tell me about everything else. How's Amber?"

"Amber's doing well. She decided to double major in accounting and math so that if she decides she doesn't want to be an accountant she can be a math teacher."

"Aren't you two living in the sorority house now?"

I nodded. "She talked me into it. It's okay. The rooms are much bigger than in the dorms, but it's farther away from everything."

"I always wanted to join a sorority, but by the time I went through college, I had two kids at home. I wasn't exactly sorority material by that point." She laughed. "Tell me about it so I can live vicariously through you."

"There's a lot of silly social things. You know, costume parties and stuff."

She chuckled. "As serious as always. I hope you're letting loose some, too. Make sure you aren't all work and no play."

"I am," I said defensively, finding it odd that I felt the need to defend my studious nature. Shouldn't it be the other way around?

"*That's* what I want to hear about."

"I actually got roped into doing a Greek talent show thing at the beginning of the semester." I had to give her something, and that seemed safe enough. I certainly couldn't tell her some of the other things I'd been doing. Like Luke.

Don't think about that.

I grabbed a cookie and nibbled on it. "These are as good as I remembered."

"I'll bake you some whenever you want. Just let me know."

"That would be nice. Thanks."

My eyes once again gravitated toward the framed photos. There was one of me and Tyler at senior prom as well as one of my senior portraits. At the end, there was a new addition I hadn't seen before. It was the same graduation picture I had on my laptop.

Noticing me look at the pictures, she took a shaky breath. "It's still surreal, isn't it? I'm...I'm going to start going through his room. Is there anything you would like? Most of the stuff will probably go to charity."

My eyes widened. I couldn't believe she was doing that. But then I imagined how hard it must be for her to have his bedroom stay the same, as if he were still just away at college and would be coming home for breaks.

"I...I don't know. It's been a while since I've been in there."

"Do you want to go up and look?"

I didn't want to, but I also knew if I didn't I would regret it. I nodded.

Mrs. Pullman thoughtfully let me go alone. As I slowly climbed the stairs I looked with trepidation at the door that had been closed for months now. The blue Tyler Avenue sign that his sister had gotten him for his twelfth birthday was still there. Other teenage guys probably would have taken it down, but that was the kind of big brother he was.

I pushed the door open. The sun shone through the window, illuminating dust particles floating in the air. With the exception of the dust, the room was as neat and clean as always. The bed was made, dirty clothes were in the hamper, and the desk was organized. Lining a shelf were several gold trophies with soccer players performing various feats on top. I ran my finger along the name plates to wipe away the dust.

Familiar clothes hung in neat rows in the closet. I fingered a blue shirt that he'd worn to the academic awards ceremony. Or was it his cousin's rehearsal dinner? I couldn't remember. They were back-to-back nights.

Clearly labeled binders lined the bookshelf. I pulled

one out at random. Physics. Ugh. Neat handwriting lined the pages with certain sections highlighted in yellow. The highlighting was beginning to fade.

A soccer ball with the signatures of the Forrest Creek varsity team sat on the corner of the dresser. Tucked into the edges of the mirror were pictures—some of me, some of him and his soccer buddies, and some of him, his mom, and his sister. There was one of me taken after I had my wisdom teeth taken out. My cheeks were swollen, my eyes had circles under them, and I had a goofy grin on my face as a result of the meds. I *hated* that picture, but he had insisted it was cute and refused to take it down. Apparently I was entertaining when laced with heavy narcotics.

I could take it down now, but it no longer mattered.

I sat on the bed and clasped my hands together between my knees. There were so many memories in this room. How many hours had I spent lounging on this bed? Too many to count.

Now it was all going to be packed into boxes. It was all going away, like it never existed, like it never happened.

I lay back on the bed and turned my nose into the pillow. The scent of dust filled my nostrils.

And I felt...what exactly?

Sad, remorseful, nostalgic...

A knock at the door had me quickly sitting up. "Come in," I said.

Mrs. Pullman peeked around the door. "Just checking." She stood just inside the room. "Did you find anything you wanted?"

"Are you really going to give it all to charity?"

She nodded. "It's time."

"What are you going to do with the room?"

"I haven't decided. Guest room maybe?"

Chin trembling, I took a deep breath and looked around

the room for the last time. I turned my face away as the first tears fell.

Mrs. Pullman sat down next to me and wrapped her arms around me. "It's okay," she murmured as she stroked my hair.

As my tears turned to sobs, I clung to her. "Why? I just don't understand."

She pulled away from me and held me at arm's length. "You know he was sick, right?"

"Wha…what?"

"Depression."

Immediately, my mind filled with those TV commercials for antidepressants. Surely I would have known if Tyler had belonged in one of them. We shared everything.

Lie.

In the months leading up to his death, we hadn't shared much of anything. Still, something like this?

I shook my head. "He would have told me."

She sighed. "He didn't want you to know. Although you probably noticed."

How would I have noticed? I hardly saw him.

Memories of the summer before we left for college nagged at me, though. He *had* been moody. His friends and I had joked he was like a thirteen-year-old girl with PMS. He'd laughed it off. But had he really? We were all so busy, getting ready to leave home. Everything was different, so it didn't seem so weird that he was acting a little different, too.

"He used to get down sometimes," I said, "but he always snapped out of it in a day or two."

She nodded. "That was part of it."

"Why…why wouldn't he tell me?" It was silly to feel hurt, but that's what I felt. He should have come to me. He should have trusted me. He should have…*lived*.

"You know how he was. He didn't want to show a weakness. He didn't want to show that he wasn't in control."

"I would have understood." The need to be in control was something we had in common, the one reason we ever butted heads. If anyone would have understood, it was me. He *knew* that. He should have known I'd understand. Even though we'd grown apart, I would have been there for him.

"I know. He was just so sensitive about it. His sister and I are the only ones who knew he was on medication."

"What medication was he on?" I knew a bit about anti-depression medication since my parents made me talk to that therapist last summer. I had researched and learned that certain medication had strange effects on teens specifically and could actually make them more suicidal. So if Tyler's doctor put him on medication despite the risk, then he must have been really bad.

"Different ones. I don't remember the names of all of them. His doctor kept switching them to find one that worked."

"Is that why he…?"

She shook her head. "No, I don't think so." She sighed. "I should have had this conversation with you much sooner, but I've been afraid, unable to face things."

She wasn't the only one.

I took a deep breath. "I can't help but wonder…" I trailed off as my chin started to quiver and tears threatened to fall again.

"Me, too," she said quietly, squeezing my hand. "There are so many 'what ifs' running through my mind."

"What if…" Oh God, I didn't know how I was going to say it. "What if we hadn't fought?" I choked the words out. "We yelled at each other. That's what his last conversation was—me yelling at him."

Mrs. Pullman went still for a moment. Then she shook her head slowly. "It's not your fault."

I broke.

"I did it." I sobbed, nearly hyperventilating. "I killed him. I killed Tyler. I'm the reason he—"

She grabbed me by the shoulders. "Stop. I want you to stop this instant. Don't say that, don't think it. It is *not* your fault."

My shoulders sagged as the air left my lungs. She said it again softly, "It was not your fault."

"I should have known. I should have seen it."

"I'm his mother. Don't you think I've told myself the same thing? I want to tell you something, and I want you to believe me." She looked me in the eye. "It was nobody's fault.

"Here's something else I learned recently," she went on, "which is why I'm finally cleaning out this room. Life goes on. I was watching Alicia play volleyball the other day. They changed her position. She's a middle blocker now because she's gotten so tall. I thought about how proud Tyler would have been of his little sister. And it just hit me. Life goes on. And Tyler would want it to go on. No matter what his own troubles were, he wouldn't want me to lose myself like he did. And he wouldn't want you to, either."

"I started dating someone," I blurted out.

Her eyes widened in shock for a split second and then she smiled. "Good."

"I can't believe I just told you that."

"I want you to move on with your life," Mrs. Pullman said. "I hope you never forget about Tyler, but you've got to live."

I shook my head vehemently. "I could never forget about him."

She smiled. "No, I don't suppose you could. He was a great guy."

"The best," I agreed in a shaky voice.

We sat in quiet for a moment, each lost in our own thoughts. Then Mrs. Pullman cleared her throat and wiped the moisture from her eyes. "I hope this new guy is treating you well."

I looked down. "I sort of messed it up, so it's over now."

"I'm sorry to hear that, especially if he made you happy." She rose. "I'll leave you alone again. Come downstairs when you're ready." She shut the door softly behind her.

I looked around the room slowly, taking in everything that represented the boy I'd loved.

Memories flooded my mind. Tyler giving me a salute when he scored a goal. Bringing him chicken noodle soup when he had the flu. The two of us babysitting his sister. Posing for prom pictures. Adjusting his graduation cap so that the tassel lay just right.

Part of me would always love him. That was okay. I'd accepted that.

But it was time to let go.

I stood in the doorway and took one last look. "Good-bye, Tyler." I closed the door behind me.

Chapter Twenty-Five

"Jonathan, this is Cori. She'll be shadowing you this evening."

I smiled at Jonathan, a skinny redhead who looked to be several years older than me, before taking a seat next to him. The cubicle we were sitting in was empty except for a phone and some motivational posters.

"Do you need anything else?" Mrs. Young, the Student Counseling Center director, asked. She wandered off before I had the chance to answer, her mind obviously on other things.

"Have you started the training yet?" Jonathan asked.

I shook my head. "The next session starts after winter break, so Mrs. Young said I could observe for a while to make sure I really want to do this."

He nodded, tapping a pencil on the desk. "A lot of people don't make it through the mock calls."

We sat quietly for a few moments. I read the poster hanging in front of me titled *Warning Signs of Suicide*. Some of the signs were obvious, like talking about wanting to die. Not so much for some of the other signs, for instance, sleeping too much or too little and increase in alcohol consumption.

Didn't that apply to the majority of college students?

I fiddled with my watch. Only ten minutes had passed.

"So, do we just sit here?"

"Yup. The phone doesn't always ring."

My shoulders slumped. "Oh."

He laughed. "Don't be so disappointed. Think of it this way. The less calls, the less people are suicidal. It's just important that we're here if someone does need us."

"How long have you been doing this?"

"Since I was a junior, so four years now. I'm a second year grad student."

"Have you ever, you know, lost someone?"

His brow furrowed for a moment, and I thought I saw a hint of sadness in his eyes. "Not on the phones, no."

I knew what that meant.

He pulled a thick paperback, some fantasy novel, out of the backpack at his feet. "The first rule for manning the phones is to always, *always* bring something to do. There's usually a lot of sitting around."

I pulled out my criminology notes. I'd gotten custody of the front row seats in the class. I wasn't even sure Luke was still attending class until I saw him slip in to the back row at the last minute the other day. I didn't bother approaching him. He was obviously going out of his way to avoid me.

There was no news from the Luke front. Amber was still dating Brad, but Luke didn't come around when she was at the house. The one time Josh came to class and I asked him about Luke, he got an uncomfortable look on his face and went mute. I guess I should count myself lucky the boy code allowed him to associate with me at all.

A whirl of scarves flew by the cubicle, then circled back.

"Miss Elliott, is that you?" Dr. Nantis peered over the cubicle wall.

"Yes, ma'am."

"What are you doing here?"

"I just started."

"Started doing what?"

"Volunteering." I took a deep breath. "I'm going to train to work the suicide hotline."

"Interesting." She paused, her eyes inspecting me. "Did you get that"—she waved her hand to show how superfluous she thought it was—"pageant taken care of?"

"Yes, ma'am." I ducked my head a bit under her scrutiny.

No. I worked my tail off for that pageant. I wasn't going to let her make me feel ashamed of it.

Sitting up straight, I looked her in the eye. "Actually, I won."

She nodded her head slightly. "Congratulations." She paused for a moment. "Stop by my office tomorrow and I'll find some extra credit for you."

I felt something I had almost forgotten about—*hope.* I didn't know how much extra credit she'd give me, or how much it could improve my grade, but I'd gladly take whatever she was willing to give me. It couldn't hurt.

"Yes, ma'am," I said. "Thank you."

She was off before she heard my reply, a flurry of magenta and teal silk trailing in her wake. Did none of the women around here wait for responses before flitting away?

Jonathan looked up from his book to gaze at me curiously. "You won a pageant?"

I nodded. "Miss New River Valley."

"Huh," was all he said, and he was back to his book. I suppressed a smile. I guess Dr. Nantis wasn't the only one who wasn't impressed by my crown.

The phone rang and I jumped. My eyes widened and my heart pounded. I placed my palms flat on the table, my knuckles whitening. *Here we go.*

Jonathan calmly put a paperclip in his book to mark his

place and picked up the phone. "Student Counseling Center. This is Jonathan."

I watched as he listened. He rocked in his chair, making murmuring sounds every few seconds or comments like, "I understand," and "That's tough."

I gnawed at my thumbnail, only stopping when I tasted blood. God, how could he be so calm? Someone's life was on the line. I could hear the caller was female, and I pictured a scared girl clutching a phone.

After a few more minutes, he said, "Have you shared those feelings with her?" Another pause. "I definitely think you should." Then he laughed. Actually *laughed*. "Well, my name's Jonathan. I'll be happy to talk to you again. Take care."

I pounced as soon as he hung up the phone. "What happened?"

He rolled his chair back a few inches. I think I scared him.

"She had a fight with her roommate and needed someone to talk to."

"But was she…" I gulped. "Suicidal?"

He shook his head. "Probably not, but you can never be certain. The fact that she's calling a suicide hotline shows she's at least thought about it, though. So maybe if next time is serious, she'll reach out to us again."

"Oh."

"Most of the time, the people who call aren't actually suicidal. They just need someone to talk to and don't know where else to turn." He picked up his book and opened it.

"My high school boyfriend killed himself," I blurted out. "That's why I'm here. I don't want anyone else to go through that."

I felt like a burden had been unloaded. I'd avoided talking about it for so long and kept it a secret. I was still getting used to not doing that. It felt good to get it out in the open.

Jonathan looked up from his book. "My sister," he said quietly. "A lot of people who volunteer have had someone close to them commit suicide. You're not alone. And now you're doing a good thing here—you're making it so that others who feel alone don't have to."

"I'm scared," I whispered.

"Don't be. You'll go through training and learn everything you need to know. And I can tell you're going to make it through."

I looked at him questioningly.

"You already have the things that can't be taught, compassion and empathy," he explained. "Without those, you're nothing but an empty voice on the phone."

I smiled. "Thanks, Jonathan."

Pulling a twenty out of his pocket, he grinned and said, "How about you go get us something to eat? I've always wanted to have an underling."

I looked pointedly at his red plastic name tag that read *Volunteer*. "We're on the same level here."

He pressed the money into my hand. "You don't even have a name tag."

He had me there. Grumbling, I took the money and went in search of food. For the first time in weeks, I felt good. I actually had an appetite. I might have made a mess of things getting here, but I knew I was in the right place.

One way or another, everything would be okay.

• • •

I twirled the paper from my straw around my pinky finger, making it into a ring. The restaurant was empty and I was bored out of my mind. I didn't know why it was so urgent for me to work as hostess tonight, but when the manager called and told me I could have the job if I could start in an hour, I didn't question. I just put my ass in gear and made it there in fifty-four minutes. Jobs in a college town were hard to come by, and I was in desperate need of money. I'd cleaned out my bank account when I'd written a check to Mr. Pullman. I'd stuck it in the mail with no note—just *thanks, but no thanks* written on the check's subject line. I couldn't keep that money. My memories of Tyler were not for sale.

Almost everyone had left for winter break, so the only diners were a few locals—an older couple and a few professor-looking types. It was odd seeing the professors out and about. I guess when the students left town, they came out of whatever dark cave they'd been hiding in and reclaimed the town.

I was stuck in town for a few extra days helping Dr. Nantis. She had me typing up her notes for some conference she was going to. In exchange, she was allowing me to redo my essay test for a higher grade. I suspected she was going to make the new test much harder, though. If I was lucky, I could pull an A- for the class. If a miracle happened, an A.

I was never one to believe in luck. Or miracles. But I'd take it.

I leaned against the hostess podium and rotated my feet one at a time. I hoped it wasn't too late for Santa to bring me some comfortable shoes for Christmas. The only black shoes I had were heels, and after only two hours of standing my arches were screaming at me. I wondered if there was a stool somewhere I could sit on.

I crept back into the restaurant a bit to see if I could spot one. As soon as I turned a corner toward the kitchen, I heard the jingle of the bells on the door. Figures. No one had come in for the past hour, but I step away for thirty seconds and *presto!* In come the customers.

I scurried back to the hostess stand and pasted a smile on my face. I recognized the guy from somewhere. He looked on the young side, but he had the faint air of cockiness about him.

I nearly snapped my fingers. *Cocky Boy*, the Beta Chi pledge. What was his name?

"Welcome to Side Streets. Table for one?"

Before Cocky Boy could answer, the opening of the door caught my attention. I looked up.

Luke.

My breath caught. My hand flew to my throat.

He hadn't shaved. In fact, he looked downright scruffy. He pulled off his ski cap and I saw something else I hadn't noticed from the other side of the criminology classroom—his hair had grown out a bit.

It was sexy.

His eyes were as blue as ever. They locked onto mine for a brief moment before he looked away.

"Hey man," Cocky Boy said to him. Then to me, "There's two of us."

I blindly grabbed two menus and two sets of silverware. "This way."

Was he looking at me? The hairs on the back of my neck stood on alert. I wanted him to look at me. I wanted him to *see* me.

I'd shared a classroom with him twice a week for the last three weeks and there'd been nothing, no indication that he even knew I was alive. I kept watch, waiting for something, anything.

I'd gotten nothing.

I seated them at a booth in the back of the restaurant. "Is there anything I can get you until your server arrives?" My voice shook, but my gaze remained steady.

Look at me.

He finally did. His face was devoid of emotion, his eyes betraying nothing.

Nothing. I was nothing to him.

Was that better or worse than him hating me?

"We're good," Cocky Boy said, oblivious to the tension.

I nodded tightly and returned to the hostess station.

I put a hand over my eyes, my chin quivering. I couldn't do this here. I needed this job.

Tighten up, Corinne.

I'd been through worse. So my ex-boyfriend was in the same restaurant with me. So what? I'd been through death. This was nothing.

Nothing.

Except it wasn't. Not to me.

He'd walked away from me, but he didn't have the full story. I don't know if he wanted to know, but *I* needed to tell him. If I'd learned nothing else in the last few months, I'd learned the importance of closure.

I deserved closure. To hell with what Luke wanted.

I sighed. Who was I kidding? I still cared about him. He deserved to know the truth, or at least have the option to learn the truth.

I took a few steps back and peered around the corner to where he was sitting. I watched as he placed his order and handed the menu to the waitress. As the waitress walked away, his gaze scanned the room. I jumped back. A few seconds later, I peeked out again. He was talking to Cocky Boy. Why was Luke having dinner with him? He seemed like an odd choice for a dinner companion. Then again, it had been several weeks since we'd spoken. I didn't know what was going on in his life. They could be BFF's for all I knew.

He could have a new girlfriend already.

Shit. I hadn't thought about that. I squeezed my eyes shut as images of him and every other girl I'd ever seen out at the Beta house flooded my mind.

Torture.

I spent the next hour darting back and forth between the hostess station and peering around the corner, watching. No, I had no shame. Yes, I was totally being a stalker. Or as Luke once would have said, I was being weird.

I missed that.

When Luke and Cocky Boy passed by the hostess station on the way out, I bit my lip, losing my nerve. He didn't even look at me.

Maybe I should just let him go.

No. I was doing this.

"Luke."

He stopped midstride, but hesitated before turning around. Still, he said nothing, just looked at me with his hard, emotionless eyes.

"I want to talk."

He finally broke his silence. "There's nothing to talk about."

"You don't have to say anything," I said, feeling bolder, "but I have something to say. My break's in five minutes. Can you wait outside for me? Please?"

He looked at the ceiling, considering his options. "Fine," he said, his voice gruff. Then he spun on his heel and strode through the exit, the door slamming behind him.

A trickle of anger interrupted my flow of anxiety and despair. When I saw him wrapped up with his ex-girlfriend, he confronted the situation head-on, demanding that we talk about it. Where did he get off being a hypocrite?

As soon as the manager came to cover the hostess station, I went outside to see Luke. Half of me expected him not to be there, but the smarter half of me knew better. Luke was a man of his word.

He was sitting at a table on the front patio, his hands stuffed in his pockets. I sat in the seat across from him.

"Hi," I said lamely, my breath fogging out in front of me.

He nodded.

I took a deep breath. "I want to explain." I paused, collecting my thoughts. I hadn't actually planned what to say. How did one come out and say *I didn't talk to you about my old boyfriend because I was afraid I drove him to commit suicide?*

I shivered and wrapped my arms around myself.

"Where's your coat?" he asked.

"Huh?" I looked at him, confused. The thought of getting my coat hadn't even occurred to me. I was too anxious to think logically. "It's inside."

"Go get it. It's freezing."

I shook my head. "If I go back in there, I might lose my nerve, and I need to do this."

He cursed. Abruptly, he rose. "Come on." He didn't wait for me to agree. He stalked to his Jeep and opened the passenger door. "Get in."

I climbed in and he slammed the door closed. Seconds later he got into the driver's side and stuck the key in the ignition, turning the heat on full blast.

I sat for a moment, appreciating the warm air, before turning to him.

"You already know Tyler was my high school boyfriend. And that he was the one who gave me the necklace."

"You don't have to do this."

"No," I said firmly. "I do."

I shifted in my seat so that I was facing the windshield. It was going to be hard enough getting through this without looking at Luke, remembering what used to be.

Our first real, meaningful kiss had been in this Jeep. My fingers flew to my lips, and I had to force them back into my lap. Now was not the time to visit memory lane.

"Tyler and I dated all throughout high school and my freshman year of college," I explained in a monotone voice, as if I were reciting a book report instead of explaining a tragedy in my own life. "He was a great guy. You probably would have liked him if the circumstances were different. We went to colleges far away from each other, and things changed. We didn't see each other much, and it seemed that every time we talked on the phone we fought. One night last April, we had a really bad fight."

I took a second to brace myself for what I was about to say. "I said some harsh words to him and hung up. A few minutes later, he crashed his car into a tree, killing himself. At first, the police said it was an accident. It wasn't until right before school started that I learned it was suicide. I thought...I thought I'd killed him. I know now that's not true—he was sick, depressed—but it's not something you can just get over, you know? I didn't know how to deal with it, so I didn't. He was such a large part of my life, and I wasn't ready to deal with it all. That's why I still wore his necklace."

Luke had been looking out the driver's side window this whole time. Even when I stopped talking, he still didn't turn his face toward me.

"Are you going to say anything?" I asked.

"What do you want me to say?"

That you forgive me. That you still want me. That you love me.

"I don't know," I whispered. "I just felt you should know the truth. Tyler has a place in my heart that's not going away. Even if he didn't die and we just broke up, which is where we were heading, I'd always have love for him. He was a huge part of my life for five years, and I can't forget that, and I won't apologize for it. But I'm sorry for not being open about it. Look—" I reached over to grab his arm, but stopped myself before contact. "Look at me."

He looked to where I had pulled my shirt away from my neck.

"I'm not wearing it anymore."

His gaze shifted from my neck up to my face for a few seconds, but I couldn't read his expression. Then he turned to face the window again.

There was nothing left to say, so I let myself out of the Jeep back out into the cold. I wrapped my arms around myself as I walked away.

It was done.

Chapter Twenty-Six

"Is this kettle corn?" Amber asked, taking a bowl of popcorn from me.

"No. It's some low butter, low sodium, low fat stuff that my mom has." I settled onto the couch next to her.

She scrunched up her nose. "Yuck. Low taste, you mean. It's probably good, though. My mom's trying to fatten me up with Christmas cookies."

My eyes lit up, the first time they had in weeks. "Those ones with the Hershey's Kisses on top? Did you bring me some?"

She shook her head. "Sorry."

I sighed. It was just as well. "What do you want to watch? I've got *The Breakfast Club*, *Ten Things I Hate About You*, or *How to Lose a Guy in 10 Days*."

"Going vintage, I see. How about *Ten Things* first and then we'll do *10 Days*. We can have a ten marathon."

I queued up the movie and settled back on the couch, snuggling under a blanket. About ten minutes into the movie, Amber's phone rang.

"Hell-ooohh," Amber said in a sickeningly sweet voice. Fighting the urge to gag, I paused the movie.

"I'm watching a movie with Cori... No, it's okay, I can talk... I miss you, too."

I picked at a hole forming in the blanket, making it worse. Hopefully my mom wouldn't discover it until after I'd gone back to school. Amber carried on her conversation, oblivious to my looks of annoyance.

Finally she put her phone down and sighed. "I guess absence does make the heart grow fonder, at least in Brad's case. The boy calls me every day."

"That's nice." I tried to sound sincere, really I did, but I was struggling to hold down my dinner after listening to her play kiss-face for the last ten minutes.

She eyed me thoughtfully. "You know, I can call him and ask him anything you want to know about Luke. He'll tell me everything. I've got him wrapped around my finger like a pinky ring." She grinned and held up her hand, which was indeed adorned with a tiny silver ring on her pinky.

"It's over." My voice was flat. I pointed the remote at the TV and hit play.

Amber wrenched it from my grasp and paused the movie again. "If you just explained to him—"

"I did."

"You didn't tell me that. You never tell me *anything* anymore. What did he say?"

"Nothing."

"Nothing? What do you mean, nothing? How could he just say *nothing*? He had to have said *something*."

"Well, let's see, he told me to stop talking. He didn't even want to hear what I had to say."

"Why didn't you tell me?" Amber's voice conveyed her hurt.

"I didn't want to talk about it. I told him, and he didn't

care. Nothing's changed. End of story."

"He's an asshole."

I should have known I could count on Amber for a good old-fashioned ex-bashing. I'd made more than my fair share of disparaging comments about the losers she'd gone out with. Unfortunately, her comment didn't make me feel any better.

I sighed. "He's not an asshole." That was what bothered me about the whole situation. If he wasn't the asshole, then maybe that meant I was. I'd really messed up, and I hated myself for it.

Amber tossed her hair over her shoulder, diva style. "I still think it's messed up. People make mistakes, you know? It's not like you cheated on him or anything."

I smiled despite everything. "Thanks." It was nice having Amber firmly on my side, even if I wasn't in the right.

She smiled back and squeezed my hand. "Okay, let's continue with our high-school-bad-boy-Heath-Ledger drool fest. Damn, he was hot. If he can't make you forget Luke for a few hours, nothing will."

Just what I was afraid of.

• • •

My dad wiped his hands on a rag. "Oil's changed." He looked the same as he always did—dark hair that was starting to get a touch of gray, broad shoulders, capable hands. He wore jeans and a faded flannel shirt over a T-shirt, no coat despite the cold weather. I don't think he even owned one.

"Thanks." I hefted a suitcase into the trunk, then turned to pick up the other one.

"Let me do that." I let him take it from me and wrestle it into the trunk with the other one. He closed the trunk and patted it affectionately. "This car still has some years left in her."

I'd forgotten how attached he was to this old thing. He'd bought it new fifteen years ago and given it to me when I got my license, getting himself a newer model.

I put my purse and bottle of water in the passenger's seat. "I'd better get going."

He nodded. "Yeah, you want to get there before it gets dark."

We hugged awkwardly. We'd never been close.

"Listen, uh, Cori." My dad cleared his throat, his eyes not meeting mine. Geez, this better not be one of those awkward conversations like when he'd congratulated me on getting my first period. Nothing could be more mortifying to a thirteen-year-old girl than having her father talk about her newly flowing menstruation.

"About your financial aid, your mom wasn't supposed to tell you about that."

My nostrils flared. "Don't you think I needed to know? They don't let you go to school for free. Someone needed a plan to come up with the money."

He rubbed the back of his neck. "I was going to figure something out."

"I took care of it," I said stiffly.

"I didn't want you to. I was looking into loans."

This was the first I'd heard of that. But honestly? It was depending on them to handle the finances that got me into trouble in the first place, so even if he had told me, I still wouldn't have trusted him to come through.

"It's done, Dad. Don't worry about it."

He leaned against the car and crossed his arms. "I do, though. I'm your dad. I'm always going to worry about you."

"I know," I said automatically, but when I looked up and saw the disappointment and shame in his eyes—disappointment and shame for letting me down—I reached out and squeezed his hand. "I know," I quietly said again.

He stepped away from the car. "All right. Drive safely." He patted my arm in a clumsy show of affection, then stepped away from the car so I could drive off.

A mere six hours later, I put my car in park in front of the Alpha house. Home, sweet home.

The first thing I did when I walked in my room was pop the lid on a gel air freshener I had brought with me and throw away the two I'd left sitting out. I don't know what happened in these rooms while students were gone over break, but I hadn't wanted to return to the funky smell that had greeted me after Thanksgiving break.

I could tell by the mountain of bags just inside the door that Amber had beat me back. There was no sign of her as I made multiple trips back and forth to my car. No doubt she was already with Brad.

As if she'd known I was thinking about her, my phone rang. I answered it and propped it on my shoulder as I hauled my last suitcase into my room. I needed to learn to travel lighter.

"What's up?" I said

"Are you exercising or something?" Amber asked. "You're all out of breath." I could barely hear her over all the background noise.

"Um, no. I gave up the psycho exercise routine when the pageant ended. I'm carrying my suitcase."

"Oh. Well, we're all at Thirsties. You should come out."

I dropped my suitcase on my bed with a grunt. "I have to unpack."

"You-know-who isn't here," she said in a loud whisper.

"Thanks for the info, Harry Potter, but I still have to unpack."

"Cori!"

"Amber, I've got to go." I lined up my socks in the top

dresser drawer, organizing them according to color. Ah, the sight of that was pure magic.

"Don't be lame!" I heard her say right before I ended the call.

I wasn't lame. I was responsible.

And this was sounding familiar. Déjà vu even. Wasn't this how last semester began? And that didn't go so well.

"Right," I said aloud. "And last semester, I caved and went out. So that means I should stick to my original idea and stay in."

I lifted a stack of shirts out of my suitcase and refolded them to get out all the wrinkles they'd gotten from being squashed in a suitcase.

I was efficient. Everything was put away and my suitcases stowed under my bed in less than thirty minutes. The whole time my phone kept chirping, signaling incoming text messages. I'd ignored them, but now I picked up my phone.

Cori! Get your butt out here!

I mean it! I will be mad at you!

Okay, I won't get mad, just come anyway.

Why aren't you responding?

Josh has a new bimbo. You've GOT to see this one!

Another text message came in, this one a picture: a selfie of Amber with an exaggerated frown on her face. I laughed.

It's not like I had anything better to do. I'd ordered all my textbooks online and they wouldn't arrive until tomorrow, so I couldn't even start reading yet, not that I wanted to after a six-hour drive.

I could drop by Thirsties. I didn't have to stay long.

I touched up my makeup and changed my clothes before I changed my mind. Then I was off.

Amber, Brad, Josh, and Josh's bimbo were sitting at their usual table in the corner, the one that was out of view of the bartenders and the security cameras.

Amber squealed when she saw me and almost knocked me flat with her exuberant hug. Geez, it was like we hadn't seen each other almost every day over break.

Josh patted the seat next to him. "Hey, Cori. How's it going?"

I settled in the chair and placed my purse at my feet. "All right. When did you get back?"

"Yesterday."

Wow, he worked fast. I checked out his new bimbo. *Bimbo* wasn't the term I'd use to describe this chick. She was more on the goth side, complete with black hair, black eyeliner, and black fingernail polish. If I hadn't seen it for myself, I don't know if I would've believed Amber when she told me about this girl. She wasn't Josh's normal flavor. She was probably nice enough, though.

Or maybe not. Josh had flung his arm around the back of my chair and it was a good thing for me that looks couldn't kill.

Josh leaned toward me. "What classes are we taking this semester?"

I laughed. "*We?*"

"Yeah. Maybe if I take the same classes as you, I'll actually stand a chance of passing them."

I shook my head. "Don't be lazy, Josh." I plucked the side of his head. "You have brains in there for a reason."

"Yeah, but your brains are so much better than mine."

I laughed again. "That's not even true. You're smart.

You're just *lazy*."

Josh's bimbo put her hand on his arm possessively, digging her fingernails in. He looked over to her as if he just remembered she was there. "Have you met Tabitha?"

I shook my head and smiled at her. "I'm Cori." She narrowed her eyes at me, which only made me smile wider. Poor girl. Where did he find her? And perhaps more relevant at this point, at what point would he ditch her?

Amber caught my eye. She was biting her lip, trying not to laugh. When she got herself under control, she mouthed *I told you so.*

I sat back in my chair, content to watch the goings-on around me. I was happy to see that Brad seemed to be treating Amber well. He kept his arm around her chair and she hadn't even set her empty glass down before he was on his feet to get her another one. When he handed her the new one, she tilted her face up for a kiss, and I could see it in his eyes. He was gone for her.

I felt a pang of loneliness. Was this what it had been like for her watching me all those years, first with Tyler, then with Luke?

It sucked. Being the third—or in this case fifth—wheel was not fun. How did she do it all that time and keep her spirits up?

Amber laughed at something Brad said, then did a double take. She turned to me with a horrified look on her face, her eyes darting from me to something behind me.

"What?" I said.

She continued to stare at me with an alarmed expression. I turned to see what she had seen.

Luke was walking toward us.

Chapter Twenty-Seven

I whipped around and placed my palms flat on the table, forcing myself to breathe. This was bound to happen sooner or later. It was better that I got it over with sooner.

Amber scooted her chair closer to mine and grabbed my hand in a show of solidarity.

"Hey, man," Brad said. "I didn't think you were getting in town until tomorrow."

Luke circled the table and after they did some complicated guy fist-bump handshake thing, pulled up a chair next to Brad and sat. "Change of plans."

He looked across the table at me. "Hi, Cori."

I opened my mouth to speak, but I couldn't form the words, so I nodded.

"Hello, *Luke*," Amber said, her voice dripping with malice. I kicked her under the table. She looked at me and mouthed *what?*

Don't I mouthed back. She huffed, but softened her expression.

I pulled out my cell phone so I would have something

to do. What I wanted to do was scurry out of there with my tail between my legs, but that was the old Cori, the one who didn't face her problems. The new Cori was going to be an adult and face them head-on.

Right, an adult with a cell phone for a shield and a petite blonde as a guard dog.

I glanced up from my cell phone to sneak a look at Luke. He'd cut his hair since the last time I'd seen him. He was back to fuzzy mode, as I called it. He was wearing a navy blue sweater that intensified his blue eyes. He was also clean-shaven. I averted my gaze as I remembered the feel of his fuzzy hair under my fingertips and the smell of his aftershave.

Nope, I wasn't going to do this. I was new Cori, non-obsessing Cori.

Focus.

If Luke was fine sharing custody of our mutual friends, then I wasn't going to be weird about it. He was chatting with Brad and didn't seem bothered at all by me sitting across from him. It was like nothing had ever happened between us, like there had never been an *us*.

Ouch.

I needed a distraction.

I looked over to Josh and Tabitha. What was the attraction? With her spiky haircut and goth style, she had nothing in common with any of his other conquests. Come to think of it, though, most of the girls he dated didn't have much in common. His type was *female*. Unfortunately, he always seemed to choose poorly, and based on the sour look on this girl's face, he'd stayed true to his streak. *Poor Josh.*

My phone vibrated, startling me so badly I almost dropped it. It was a text message from my boss at the restaurant wondering if I could work tonight.

Hell, yes, I could.

"I just got called in to work," I said apologetically and

stood. "See you all later." I didn't look at Luke as I said this. Even Adult Cori did not want to repeat this awkwardness anytime soon. That wasn't immaturity. That was just being smart.

As I turned to leave, my eyes met Luke's before I could stop myself. His eyes were so familiar and distant at the same time. It made me sad, but I didn't feel any tears coming on.

Progress. I was going to be okay.

. . .

It was a mad scramble to get home to change and make it to the restaurant before the start of my shift. The restaurant was packed, which was surprising because a light snow was falling outside. I figured that would keep people in, but it was so busy I didn't even have time to take my break. Right before closing, though, the manager had the cook whip me up some chicken tenders and fries, so I figured I came out ahead on that deal. I even puppy-dog eyed him into a brownie pie for dessert.

While the servers finished wiping down the tables, I rolled silverware. My feet were aching. Even though I'd bought more comfortable shoes, I wasn't used to standing on concrete floors for hours at a time. I took a break from the silverware to slip off my shoes and massage my arches. Ah, heavenly. The only thing better than a foot massage was having someone else give you a foot massage. I'm just saying.

It was nearly midnight before my manager finally called it quits. I'd rolled all the silverware there was to roll half an hour before, but the rule was that everyone left together. I wasn't complaining. I was on the clock, and I didn't have anywhere to be.

My manager handed me my schedule for the next two weeks as we headed out. I was working three days this week and four days the next. Score!

"When are you working?" Christie, one of the servers, asked me. She was older than me, probably late twenties.

I showed her my schedule.

"Mondays are slow," she said, "but Tuesdays get busy for kids' night. Friday nights are also pretty busy."

"Thanks," I said. "How long have you worked here?"

"Too long." She stopped next to a rusted pick-up truck and fished around in her purse for her keys. "I took a semester off too many years ago to count and now here I am."

"You could always go back." She probably hadn't heard that gem of advice before.

"Maybe I will, someday." She unlocked her door—with the key, not a clicker—but stopped before climbing in. "Isn't that your car? Do you know that guy?"

I looked up to see Luke leaning against my car, ankles crossed and hands stuffed in pockets. There was a light dusting of snow on his shoulders. What the hell. Why was he here?

"Yeah, I...know him."

"Okay, just checking, 'cause you never know with creepers these days. Anyway, I have Monday off, so I'll see you Tuesday."

After she drove away, I slowly walked to my car.

"Hi," I said, only it came out more like a question.

"Hey," he said. That was all he said. Then we just stood there. What was his deal? It wasn't awkward enough at Thirsties, so he came to get an extra dose?

"How long have you been out here?"

"A while. I wasn't sure what time you got off."

"Okay."

"Can we talk?"

I eyed him suspiciously. His ambivalence toward me at Thirsties and his showing up now were totally throwing me for a loop.

"Sure." I wiped at a spot of snow that had fallen on my face. "We can sit in my car, I guess."

I clicked the button to unlock the doors. Luke opened the driver's side door for me and closed it after I'd gotten in, then crossed in front of the car to get in the passenger side.

We were inches apart. I could smell his deliciousness and my heart rate quickened, my palms dampened. I tried to inconspicuously breathe through my mouth.

"How have you been?" he asked.

"Okay." Not really, but I wasn't about to tell him I'd spent my entire winter break trying to get over him, that I considered not crying after I'd seen him earlier a small victory.

"Amber said something about you volunteering at the Student Counseling Center."

"That's right." I lifted my chin up a notch. "This isn't what you wanted to talk about, is it?"

I was Adult Cori now, tackling my problems head-on.

Except I wasn't entirely sure Luke coming to see me was a problem. I just didn't know what to make of it.

He looked out the passenger side window. "Are you seeing someone?"

I did a double take. "What? No."

"Good."

"You're being weird."

He sighed. "I know."

"Then cut it out."

"You don't have a monopoly on being weird."

I certainly didn't, because this was definitely weird, but it was nice being able to joke with him a little bit. Maybe I would still be able to hang out with my Beta friends after all.

The silence stretched on, and I yawned. For someone who wanted to talk, he wasn't saying much. I yawned again. "I should probably get home."

"Yeah, I guess you've had a long day."

"Yup. Driving six hours and then working a full shift just about did me in."

"I missed you," he said suddenly, slowly. "I didn't expect to, but I did. When Lindsey and I broke up, I guess I didn't miss her because breaking up with her was the right thing to do. But you—" His eyes, soft and vulnerable, searched my face. This was the first time I'd seen anything but coldness or detachment in them when he looked at me since we'd broken up. "I miss you."

"I miss you, too," I said quietly. I breathed slowly. *Now what?*

He didn't say anything. He surprised me by opening the door and getting out, tossing a small package wrapped in shiny red paper onto the passenger seat.

"Merry Christmas." He shut the door before I could say anything in return.

I quickly flipped on my windshield wipers to clear away the snow so I could watch him walk to his Jeep in the corner of the parking lot. The headlights came on, but he didn't pull away. After a minute, I realized he was waiting until I left.

He always was a gentleman.

I eyed the present as I drove home as if it were a hand grenade. It very well could be with the way he tossed it into my car and then scurried away.

Okay, he didn't scurry. He walked, but still.

Once in my room, I laid the present on my desk and stared at it from several feet away.

Then I snapped out of it and pounced on it. I ripped into the paper and tugged the box top off.

It was a silver necklace with a four-leaf clover pendant.

"Everybody needs a good luck charm," I could hear him saying.

I only hesitated about half a second. Then I grabbed the

necklace and flew out the door.

It was almost one a.m., but I didn't care. If I didn't go now I would lose my nerve.

The snow was falling harder and the temperature had dropped significantly in the last hour. I wished I had taken the time to grab a scarf, hat, and gloves. The air inside my car was freezing. There might very well be icicles hanging from my eyelashes. I cranked the heat and slapped the dash, as if that would make it work faster. Its response was to sputter and die. Typical.

I banged on the dash again. "I'll stop hitting you if you just start working," I pleaded. Its response this time? Cold air.

Fudgetastic.

I turned it off and gripped the steering wheel. At my current speed of twenty miles an hour, it would take me an hour to get there, but the snow was coming down so hard I didn't feel safe going any faster. I'd probably end up with frostbite. Toes were overrated anyway.

I was almost halfway there when I seriously started considering whether or not this was truly a good idea. I had two choices. I could press on and hope the roads were navigable, or return home on roads that I knew were somewhat passable.

Suddenly, the rear of the car swung out to the side.

Shit! Shit! It was like the car was moving in slow motion. I wished I'd paid more attention in driver's ed. What the hell was I supposed to do in this situation?

Instinct and fear took over and I slammed my foot on the brake. Wrong answer. The car started spinning. I squeezed my eyes shut and screamed, clutching the steering wheel for dear life. Not my proudest moment.

I heard a thud and felt a jolt, throwing me into my seat belt. I took a few deep breaths and opened my eyes.

The front tires were caught in a snow bank. I rolled down the window and leaned out to get a better look. My car was in a right turning lane, so I probably wasn't in danger of being hit if anyone else was crazy enough to be out in the snow. I threw it in reverse and slammed on the gas. All I managed to do was burn a layer of rubber off my tires, which wasn't good. They were nearly bald as it was.

I closed my eyes and rested my forehead against the steering wheel. "Fuck."

I fished in my purse and pulled out my wallet. Among all the random receipts and reward cards I found what I was looking for, my AAA card. My hands were shaking from the cold, but I managed to tap the number into my phone.

After being put on hold for fifteen minutes, I was told that it would take about three hours for them to get to me. Apparently I wasn't the only one stupid enough to drive in this weather.

My teeth chattered as I climbed into my backseat searching for a blanket, a spare T-shirt, anything really. I came up with a box of tissues and a frozen bottle of water. This was perhaps the only time in my life I'd wished my organization habits were more like Amber's. At any given time, a large part of her wardrobe, along with various snacks, were scattered all over her car.

Amber! Amber would rescue me. I called her, but it went straight to voicemail. I left an urgent message for her to call me back and then texted her for good measure.

Five minutes went by, then ten, then fifteen. I didn't think Amber was going to come through for me. It was probably for the best. I was actually the better driver out of the two of us.

Who else could I call that could come and get me at this hour and in these conditions? It had let up, but the roads were still covered in ice and snow.

I needed someone with a four-wheel drive. Perhaps a

Jeep with massive tires.

I pulled up Luke's number on my phone and stared at it. What other choice did I have? If AAA told me three hours, that probably meant more like four or five.

I pressed the send button.

It rang once, twice, then three times.

Please pick up.

"Yeah?" His voice was groggy.

I simultaneously breathed a sigh of relief and felt a churn in my stomach.

"Luke, it's Cori. I've been in an accident," I blurted out.

"Shit, are you okay?" He was definitely more alert now.

"Yeah, but I'm stuck." I bit my lip. "I called AAA, but they won't be here for hours."

"Where are you?"

"Main and Graft."

"I'll be there. Just don't go anywhere."

Not likely—or more accurately, not possible.

I tossed my phone onto the passenger's seat and pulled my hands up into my sleeves. I wrapped my arms around myself and rocked back and forth hoping the movement would warm me up. My breath came out in warm bursts and was the only thing above freezing in the car.

Ten minutes passed. How stupid was I to race out in this weather? We didn't get snow back home, but this wasn't my first winter here. I knew better.

And I'd paid enough attention in Women's Studies to know I had just displayed the stereotypical damsel in distress behavior. Sorry, Dr. Nantis, but I *was* a damsel in distress.

Twenty minutes. Despite the cold, I broke out in a sweat. I'd rushed out of the Alpha house figuring I'd come up with what I'd say on the drive, but I'd been so focused on keeping my little car on the road that I hadn't given it any thought. What was I going to say to him?

How did I know that the necklace meant something? He could've bought it before we split. Maybe he just gave it to me for closure.

My gut told me that wasn't the case, but I couldn't trust myself to properly evaluate the situation when Luke was concerned.

Twenty-five minutes. I poked my fingers out of my sleeve just enough for me to gnaw at my cuticles. What was taking so long? God, I hoped he hadn't gotten in an accident.

Up ahead I saw two headlights slowly moving toward me. As they drew closer, I saw the outline of Luke's Jeep.

I sighed with relief. He was safe.

And here. I gulped.

Chapter Twenty-Eight

He pulled up beside me and hopped out of the Jeep.

I started to open the door to find that it would only open about six inches. I closed it and opened it more forcefully.

Luke grabbed the edge of the door before I could do it again. "Don't," he said. "You'll just make it worse." He shut the door gently, then pulled open the rear passenger door, which opened with no problem.

I blushed, feeling like an idiot. Maybe if my brain wasn't frozen I would have figured that out.

I not-so-gracefully clambered into the backseat with my ass in the air. On the way over the center console, I grabbed the necklace box and stuffed it safely in my pocket.

Luke held out his hand, and I took it, stepping into the snow. I was still wearing my work shoes, a pair of ballet flats, and my feet sank immediately, getting soaked. I hissed from the shock of the coldness on my skin.

Luke shook his head. "Come on," he said, leading me toward his Jeep.

"Wait." I stopped. "What about my car? Can't you pull

it out?"

He looked over at it and then at me. "There's no way I can get it out now. It'll have to wait for the tow truck."

"Oh." I looked back at my car, feeling somewhat guilty abandoning it. He was right, of course. The snow was coming heavier now, and my car was getting more and more stuck by the second.

I used the door handle to pull myself up into the Jeep, and Luke kept his hands on my waist. Good thing, because my stupid wet ballet flat slipped and I would've face planted if he hadn't steadied me.

The warmth of his hands felt good and not just because I was freezing. They steadied me. *He* steadied me.

God, I hoped my gut was right and that necklace meant something.

He climbed into the driver's seat and I remained silent, thinking it would be better not to distract him from driving. He was a good driver, but then again, I had considered myself a good driver as well, and look where that got me.

He turned the heat on. I almost cried.

"Oh, thank God." I put my hands up to the vents, hoping to regain some circulation.

"How long were you stuck there?"

"Over an hour. And my heat broke on the way."

He turned the heat up to full blast. I could've kissed him.

I *wanted* to kiss him. That would warm me up.

No dirty thoughts.

He headed south on Main Street, rather than north back toward campus.

"Where are you going?"

He spared me a glance. "Beta house. I don't know how bad the roads are the other way. Besides, even if we make it back to the Alpha house, sorority house rules mean I can't stay there, and I don't want to risk driving there and back."

"But I can stay at the Beta house," I whispered. Our first impromptu sleepover hadn't gone so well. How would it measure up to this one?

"Yeah," he said. I couldn't read his expression.

His posture was relaxed as he drove, slow and steady. No white knuckles on the steering wheel for him. Earlier at the restaurant, I'd seen a side of him I'd never seen before.

Insecurity. That's what it was. I'd never seen him insecure before. But now he was back to his confident self.

What did that mean?

I had no clue, and it was driving me crazy. Logic wouldn't help me with this puzzle.

Fifteen miles an hour and twenty minutes later, we were safely in the Beta parking lot. I dreaded leaving the warmth of the Jeep for the short trek through the snow in the parking lot.

And I dreaded even more what lay beyond the parking lot.

When he got in his room, he tossed his keys onto the desk and slipped out of his snow-covered shoes. I stood paralyzed in the doorway. When he saw me standing there, he pulled me into the room, shutting the door behind me.

"I think the cold froze your brain." He rooted around in his dresser drawer, coming up with the same clothes he had loaned me the first time I stayed the night.

Déjà vu. The same, but oh-so-different.

When he pulled my old toothbrush out of a drawer and offered it to me, I lost it.

"I love you."

I hadn't planned on saying that, but now that it was out, I kept going. "I love you, and I screwed it all up." I pulled the necklace box out of my pocket. "This is just beautiful. It's perfect. And you're perfect. *We* were perfect, and I messed it all up."

He had watched me carefully through my whole speech. Now he took one step closer. "We weren't perfect." He took a deep breath. "We weren't perfect because you should have told me about your past, especially if it was still affecting you."

"I didn't want it to contaminate what we had," I whispered. "I thought you might look at me differently."

"I would have." He paused for a second to gather his thoughts. "That's not a bad thing, though. I wish you would have trusted me with it."

"I was scared of what you would think, what you would do."

He rubbed his chin. "Rightly so, I guess. But damn. How was I supposed to react when I found out you were wearing his necklace?"

"You wouldn't even let me explain. You shut me out."

"The idea of you thinking of someone else when you were with me makes me want to punch something."

"I didn't. I never did."

"I know that now. It just took me a while to figure it out." He closed the space between us and took the necklace box out of my hands, opened it. "Do you like it?"

I nodded. "It's perfect."

Perfect, perfect, perfect.

"Will you wear it?"

I nodded again.

He put the box down on his coffee table and unzipped my coat. I let him take it off me, and he tossed it onto the couch. He picked up the necklace and put it around my neck.

"It suits you," he said. "Even you could use some luck."

For the first time, I agreed. Maybe I should leave some things up to chance, to luck, rather than trying to control it all.

I reached up and touched the silver clover with my

fingertips. He took my fingers in his hand and brought them to his lips. "I love you, Corinne."

I launched myself at him, wrapping my arms around his neck, running my fingers over his fuzzy hair. God, I'd missed that. I'd missed him.

I'd come so close to losing everything, all because I couldn't let go, because I refused to lose control.

Our mouths crashed together, and there was nothing controlled about it. It was all heat and passion.

The door swung open. "Hey, awesome, you're still awake." Josh sauntered in. "We need a fourth for beer pong." A grin broke out on Josh's face as he noticed me wrapped around Luke. "What's going on here?"

Luke looked down at me. "You up for beer pong? I'll drink your cups."

I disentangled myself from Luke, and not-so-gently pushed Josh out the door.

Luke laughed. "I guess that's my answer."

"Hey!" Josh protested. He pulled his head out of the doorway just before I slammed the door in his face. "What about beer pong?" he called through the door.

"Go away!" I yelled back.

"Luke! Come on, man! Cori! We need you, girl!"

Luke grabbed my hand, pulling me to him. "Go away, Josh!" he called.

He nuzzled my neck.

"We are *so* busting into his room the next time he has a girl in there," I said. I tilted my head to give Luke better access. He did that little thing I liked with his tongue and ran his fingers along the skin at the small of my back. It was good I was holding on to him. My knees went weak.

I wasn't worried about falling though. I'd already fallen, and Luke was there to catch me. I could finally let go.

Acknowledgments

Would you believe writing this is actually more difficult than writing a book? Here goes.

Thanks first and foremost to my husband, Chris. You are my rock, my center, my happily-ever-after. Without you pestering me to get my butt in the chair and just write that bestseller already, this book (and others) would not have come to be. I can't imagine sharing this crazy life with anyone else.

To my sons, Tristan & Quentin, you inspire me every day. Watching you two convinces me that anything is possible.

To my mom, thanks for inspiring my lifelong love of books. Those trips back and forth to the library are some of my happiest childhood memories.

To the rest of my family, your excitement and enthusiasm are much appreciated, even when you don't exactly understand all the writing and publishing jargon I throw around.

It would be negligent of me not to mention the Romance Writers of America. Without that organization, I would not be a published author. Being a 2014 Golden Heart finalist changed my life.

To my GH Dreamweaver and Dauntless sisters, your friendship and support mean more to me than you realize. I'm honored to be included in a group of such talented ladies with such big hearts.

To Alycia Tornetta, my book is better because of you. Thanks for wiping the grins off my characters' faces.

To my fabulous agent extraordinaire, Sarah E. Younger, your enthusiasm and positive energy go a long way in this pessimist's world. I am also indebted to your knowledge of vending machines—a single quarter won't get you anything!

Finally, to my Moxie girls, Terri and Marnee, what can I say that hasn't already been said? In you two, I found my Pollyanna and my Twerk Twin. It doesn't get much better than that. (And by the way, Lunchables are a perfectly acceptable meal, especially in the event of a zombie apocalypse. Just sayin'.)

About the Author

Jessica Ruddick lives in Virginia and is married to her college sweetheart—their first date was a fraternity toga party (and nothing inspires love like a toga, right?). When she doesn't have her nose in a book or her hands on a keyboard, she can be found wrangling her two rambunctious sons, taming two rowdy but lovable rescue dogs, and battling the herd of dust bunnies that has taken up residence in her home.

To learn more about Jessica, please visit her website at www.jessicaruddick.com.

Don't miss the next book in the Love on Campus *series...*

WANTING MORE

Discover more New Adult titles from Entangled Embrace...

A First Time for Everything
a novel by Isabel Morin

What Hannah Bloom needs is a tutor who'll give her lessons in all the things she's missed out on, and Casey Grant is the perfect candidate. Her dorm's resident player, he's not only the hottest guy she's ever seen, he already knows her secret. The only trouble is, nothing goes according to plan. Their lessons don't feel like lessons, they feel like the real thing.

Maybe Someone Like You
a novel by Stacy Wise

Their paths never should have crossed. The bright, accomplished new attorney and the tattooed and laid-back kickboxing trainer. But when Katie opens the door to the gym instead of the yoga studio next door, everything she ever imagined was about to change. Everything.

The Heartbeat Hypothesis
a novel by Lindsey Frydman

Now that Audra Madison has a second chance at life, she's got a plan: Go to college. Get a tattoo. Date. You know, *live*. She wants to give the sexy photographer, Jake Cavanaugh, her heart, but he isn't sure it's hers to give.

www.ingramcontent.com/pod-product-compliance
Lightning Source LLC
Chambersburg PA
CBHW030932260626
47169CB00002B/444